Praise for *Running For Water and Sky*

"Sandra Kring's characters are at once unique and familiar, vulnerable and troubling, ordinary and exquisite. We fall in love with them from the beginning, and end with a new measure of mercy for ourselves and those around us."

—**Sara Gruen**, #1 *New York Times* best-selling
author of *Water For Elephants*

"Richly realized storytellin   ; paint a
vivid picture of Bless' exper

Reviews

"Kring has created a powerful story that proves while we may have a past that has shown us anything but love, it can be the same past that teaches what love really means."

—**Jessica Stevens**, author of *Within Reach*

Past Praise for Sandra Kring

For *Carry Me Home*

"Sandra Kring weaves an intricate and heartwarming tale of family, love, and forgiveness in her sensational debut novel... Kring's passionate voice is reminiscent of Faulkner, Hemingway, and Steinbeck... She will make you laugh, have you in tears, and take you back to the days of good friends, good times, millponds, and bonfires. This is a piece destined to become a classic and a must-read for devotees of the historical fiction or the literary fiction genre."

—*Midwest Book Review* (five stars)

"Touching... surprisingly poignant... builds to an emotional crescendo... The book becomes so engrossing that it's tough to see it end."

—*Washington Post*

"Sandra Kring writes with such passion and immediacy, spinning us back in time, making us feel the characters' hope, desire, laughter, sorrow, and redemption. I read this novel straight through and never wanted it to end."

—**Luanne Rice**, *New York Times* best-selling author of *Last Kiss*

For *Thank You For All Things*

"A beautiful, witty story that rings with heartbreak, hope and laughter... Kring's brilliance lies in her powerful reversals and revelations, taking readers and characters on a dramatic, emotional roller coaster."

—*Publishers Weekly*, starred review

" ... A surprising and insightful story about families, love, and the complexity of human beings. Excellent storytelling ..."

—*Feast*

For *How High The Moon*

"Kring skillfully evokes the warmth and suffocation of small-town life, as well as the heartache and resilience of children buffeted by parental failure, all delivered in Teaspoon's memorable, winsome voice."

—Booklist

"*How High the Moon* is flat out endearing. It's about love, and life, and the mess we make of both. It's about secrets, friendships, loyalty, hope, pain, betrayals, creating our own family, and the beautiful music we can hear in our hearts if we pause, for just a moment, to listen."

—**Cathy Lamb**, author of *Julia's Chocolates* and *Henry's Sisters*

RUNNING
FOR WATER
AND SKY

RUNNING
for WATER
and SKY

Sandra Kring

Published by SparkPress, a BookSparks imprint,
A division of SparkPoint Studio, LLC
Tempe, Arizona, USA, 85281
www.gosparkpress.com

Published 2016
Printed in the United States of America
ISBN: 978-1-940716-93-0 paperback
ISBN: 978-1-940716-92-3 ebook

Library of Congress Control Number: 2015959046

Cover design © Julie Metz, Ltd./metzdesign.com
Book design by Kiran Spees

They say that right before you die, your whole life
flashes before your eyes.
But what they don't say is that the same thing can happen
when your soul mate is dying.

CHAPTER 1
15TH STREET

I'm standing in Tula's Tattoo Shop on Mactaw Street, slipping three pictures across the counter to a middle-aged woman whose tanning-booth skin is wearing only one tattoo: a thick-bodied, red-tailed boa constrictor. It spirals up her right leg, creeps up under her jean skirt, and slithers out the back of her tube top to coil across her shoulder. The upper body of the snake circles her neck, the head plunging into the crinkles of her cleavage. The designer of the image—no doubt Tula herself—had taken liberty with the snake's eyes, inking them in bright yellow, with a blood-red stripe matching the snake's saddles cutting across each pupil. It's really unusual. And Tula is one tough broad, I'll give her that much.

"So you want me to give you three tats then," she says, her voice like gravel rubbed against glass.

"It's not for me. It's for my boyfriend. A graduation gift. And no, not three, just one. I was hoping you could tattoo this photo of me—my head and my torso—over the lower half of this picture." I overlap the images to show her. "And I want the bottom half in this exact shade of blue." I tap the third photo that I ran off from the Internet. "Maybe some water in the background?"

"Yeah, I can do that."

I grin. *Liam's going to love this!*

Tula sets the photos on the counter. She swivels the arm of

1

a magnifying glass and switches on a light over the picture of me, which is only wallet-size. She squints up at my eyes like she's trying to see their true color. "They're navy," I say.

She nods and makes a quick notation on paper. That's when my cell starts vibrating.

I tug my phone out of my pocket and give my head a little shake when I see that it's Maylee. Again! She's been at the beach for less than an hour now (it's Spring Up, Logan's annual celebration with live music, food, crafts, beer, kiddie games, that sort of thing), and she's called me three times already. The first time to tell me that she saw Liam—like I might not know he's there. The second time to tell me that some hot guy she was sure was European was looking her up and down as she and Aubrey, her ditsy cousin visiting from who-cares-where, passed them. (I didn't have the heart to tell her that it was probably because he was trying to figure out why someone would be wearing jeans and a long-sleeved T-shirt while at the beach on a sunny, muggy, you've-got-to-be-kid-ding-it's-only-May 84-degree day.) And the third time to tell me that she and Aubrey were heading over to the boardwalk for ice cream at Sweet Lola's, so I'd know where to find them. She'd whispered into the phone, "I don't even want to go to Lola's. Stephie and her friends are there with a couple of guys from the football team. But Aubrey wants ice cream, so that's where we'll be."

"Just a sec," I tell Tula, because I know if I don't pick up, Maylee will keep calling until I do (why she doesn't text is beyond me).

I plunk my keys and purse onto the counter and take the call. "Let me guess, Maylee. You—"

I stop when I hear how she's breathing. Hard. Moaning almost, like her soul's being torn from her chest. In the background there's the droning of music, the thumping of drums.

When Maylee's just being a drama queen, her voice gets quieter no matter how exaggerated her facial expressions become. But right now Maylee's seriously freaking out.

I stiffen. "Maylee, what is it?"

She bursts into a series of *Oh my Gods* and I picture her eyes crazed, strings of spit the only thing keeping her lower and upper jaws hinged together. I hear the rumble of a crowd in chaos. A couple deep voices shouting out orders I can't make out.

"Maylee? What's going on?"

There's rapid clicking now. Maybe the tapping of her teeth, like what happens when someone's blood goes cold. The sound makes me shiver.

I'm about to scream at her to spit it out when she cries, "It's happening, Bless. Just like she said it would!"

"What's happening? Like who said?" I ask, even though a part of me already knows.

"Verna Johnson," she cries. "The psychic. Just like she said!"

Tula is standing in front of me, her lips mouthing words I can't hear, the snake around her neck pinning me with its yellow eyes. And then, the distant scream of sirens. *In the phone? Out the smudged window?* I can't tell.

Suddenly Tula's face morphs into Verna Johnson's. Her coffee-stained teeth fall away from her gums, her colorless lips bunch. Her bleached biker hair pulls loose from her scalp until all I can see is Verna's pewter strands as she lowers her head to peer into her crystal ball.

She used a freaking crystal ball! Maylee and I agreed she was a fake. We agreed!

Another voice, probably Aubrey's, shouts into the phone. "We were inside Lola's when we heard the gunshots. Maylee ducked." *The stupid bitch laughs—she actually laughs.* "They kicked us out. Oh, the cops are coming now. Can you hear them?"

"Shut up, you idiot," Maylee hisses. "Don't say that stuff to *her*."

I scream. Maybe out loud, maybe just in my head. *This can't be happening! It can't be! He promised me!*

"Is he dead?" I shout, my hand shaking so hard that my phone is rapping against my ear. "Is he already dead?"

"I don't know. We can't see anything from here." Her voice collapses into wracking sobs.

I bolt out of the shop. I get to the curb and yank on the handle of my car door. It doesn't open. I peer down into my hands, expecting my keys to be in them. But they aren't. I glance back at the tattoo shop. I'm so crazed with fear that I don't even know why I'm looking back—all I see is that snake swaying behind a dark, glossy window.

I start running. Running, even if I'm what? Fourteen, maybe fifteen blocks from the shoreline of Lake Michigan?

My mouth is so dry I have to keep peeling my tongue from the roof of my mouth, and my stomach is convulsing as though I'm wailing, even though my eyes are dry. I'm too afraid to cry. Afraid that if I risk letting even one tear come, it will mean this is for real and I might bust apart like a storm cloud flooding the lake until the water rolls under Liam like a tongue, pulling him into the depths, swallowing him whole before I can get there to hold him and tell him I'll love him forever. To thank him for loving me. To kiss him good-bye if he's leaving me now. To breathe in the scent of his skin so I can remember it forever.

So I force my eyes to stay dry and I just run. The flapping

of my sandals matching the rapid thumping in my chest. My breaths gasping. My phone vibrating against my hip bone. And as I'm running my life begins unfolding before me as if *I'm* the one dying.

Maybe I am.

Chapter 2
159 Days Ago

I'm back in Wicks, Nebraska, getting off the school bus, the feel of packed snow hard under my feet.

George is waiting for me when I get inside, his white hair standing on end like Einstein's—though that's where the similarities between him and Al end, trust me. He scrapes his thumb against the belly of his thermal underwear shirt to scratch an itch, and his eyes pucker. "You hang the damn lights for your grandma. Right now! You hear? She says she's been askin' you to do it for over a week now."

Cactus Carol—aka, my father's mother—hears him bitching at me and comes flying out of the kitchen, her eyes as excited as an ambulance chaser's at the first sound of an impact. "All week long I told her to do it," she says. "But she won't do nothing for me."

Here we go again. I want to scream, *I don't help because it doesn't matter how hard I try, it's never, ever frickin' good enough!* But I don't scream it. What good would it do?

George lowers himself back into his chair, which time has carved to fit his nasty old ass. He picks his jackknife up from the end table and snaps it open. He glares at me, while running the tip under a yellowed fingernail. I turn away so I don't have to see the black crud curling up over the blade.

"That's not true. She asked me to do it yesterday," I say, my voice flat.

"You gettin' smart with me, Bless?" George asks. I roll my eyes.

I've been living (if you can call it that) in George's stinking house here in Wicks for almost thirteen years. And I swear, if I have to hear George speak my name one more time—chopping it into two syllables, so that it almost sounds like "Be-*Less*," the *s*'s squeezing through his clamped dentures like a hiss—I'm going to lose it for good. I hate my name, as it is. It sounds like a plea. And I don't beg anybody for anything.

I wedge my toes against the heel of one of my sopping wet shoes, and slip it off. George hates it when I ignore him.

"A seventeen-year-old kid using that tone with her grandfather," Cactus Carol says, her words like a stick to a hornet's nest. She's taunting George and I know why. When she's buzzing about me, she's letting George know that she's on his side. It makes living in this hive easier for her.

"I'm sixteen for another nine days," I remind her.

"You hear the way she mocks me, George?"

I kick off my second shoe and toss it in the corner where our boots are heaped, and George's .22 rifle is propped. I turn to head upstairs.

"Where in the hell do you think you're going?" George snaps. "The lights are on the kitchen table."

Where I'm going is none of his business. I'm bringing my backpack upstairs. And I'm going to change my pad, which is as soaking wet as my feet. Not like I have a cutesy little purse to toss a couple of tampons in. If I *had* tampons, that is. Cactus Carol thinks it's obscene for young girls to be "sticking anything in there." Wish she'd have thought that back in her day. Then my worthless old man wouldn't have been born, and I wouldn't be here. It would have been better that way. But no, she let him have at it at least seven times, since that's how many kids they ended up having. Maybe George and Cactus were going to keep trying until they got it right, then decided to give up after my old man was born. Who knows?

George leaps from his chair like a willow branch bent and snapped by the devil. "Didn't I just tell you to go string those lights?"

I don't even get to the third step when I'm yanked backward by the strap of my backpack, thrown across the mud rug (as Cactus aptly calls it), and slammed against the front door. He cuffs the side of my head for good measure and catches the corner of my mouth with the back of his hand. My bottom lip, where I'd stabbed a needle so I could wear the ring I found on the floor of the school bus yesterday, pinches. I lap my lip with my tongue to make sure the ring's still there. "Go string those lights, I told you!" He heads back to his chair. "Damn it to hell, never a minute's peace around here."

Cactus Carol shuffles back to the kitchen.

I throw my school bag at the bottom of the stairs, huff my feet back into my wet shoes, and stomp across the slanted floor to the kitchen, where Cactus is at the stove, squeezing a raw chicken into a roasting pan. She doesn't turn her head when I come in, but she stiffens, so it's obvious she knows I'm here.

Not that I expect her to turn. Cactus hasn't really looked at me since my fourteenth birthday, when she flew into a rage after I dared dipping my finger into the bowl of chocolate frosting. She grabbed a fistful of my hair, twisting it so hard I was sure she'd scalped me. That's when something in me busted apart and fell away—fear, I suppose, since it was there one second, gone the next. A rage I couldn't stop reared up from inside of me, and suddenly I didn't care if she killed me on the spot. She wasn't going to use my hair like a handle anymore.

I grabbed her wrist as I howled, and twisted her arm until she was cramped over, begging me to stop. When I finally let go I was panting hard, and spots were blotching my vision. Cactus just stood there, rubbing her welted wrist and staring at me with such horror that it scared me. Not because of how her eyes looked *to* me, but for how they looked *at* me.

I ran out of the room and to the ottoman where Cactus rests her veiny legs at night, and grabbed the scissors from the sewing box.

I raced up the stairs, taking two at a time, and locked myself in my room. And there before the oval mirror that's pocked with speckles that look like mold, I grabbed fistfuls of my long, dark-as-evil hair and started chopping. I hacked until all that was left were stubby, uneven clumps. Tufts so short that Cactus could never get her bony fingers wrapped around them again. Because I knew if I didn't, she would pull my hair again. And I knew if she did, I was likely to lose it again.

When I got back downstairs the customary five-dollar-bill birthday present Cactus had left me on the table (without a card) was gone. It never showed up again. And since that day, Cactus doesn't say anything to me unless George is in the house. And even then, her eyes always stay cocked a little to the side of my face. As for my hair, I still keep it chopped short, just in case. But I did let my bangs grow out to my cheek and wear them brushed to the side. Well, unless I need a curtain to pull down when I don't want to look at anybody. Or let anybody look at me.

Cactus is standing at the stove when I reach for the box. Her ratty gray hair is hanging halfway down her back and tied with a fat, orange rubber band she saved from a stalk of celery.

"Drape them nice, too," she warns, as she clunks the pan into the oven, then smears her salmonella hands down her scrawny sides. I yank the box off the table, and she follows behind me like the Grim Reaper.

"Put them on the blue spruce right out front. Tell her, George."

She says this as if George is her interpreter. Like what? I might not know which tree to string them on if they don't tell me? That spruce they planted eons ago, naked on its backside but for a few needles clinging to the branches as if they don't know they're already dead, is the only tree we've ever decorated.

When I get outdoors, I wipe the bottoms of my shoes over the snow-packed stoop to clean them before heading down the steps. Because while others clean their feet before they go *into* a house so they don't bring the dirt from the outside in, I wipe my feet when I get *outside*, so I don't bring the dirt from in there, out here.

It's almost dark, and the tall shadows that were stretched across the field when I got off the bus have retreated into the woods. I want to follow them, because the trees are my hiding place, too. Even in the wintertime, when the smells of the earth and the leaves of the cottonwoods are trapped under the snow, and the hum of the stream is entombed under ice.

When I was a kid, George and Cactus let me run wild. I spent most of my time in the woods, where the cottonwoods and red cedars and willows grew near the stream.

Sometimes I'd pretend that I was the granddaughter of Chief Red Cloud, a girl kidnapped from her people. I'd lug my belongings in an old pillowcase: a dented pan that Cactus threw out after the handle broke off; a scuffed plastic cup; a bent spoon; an old, naked baby doll with a bashed-in glass eye and plastic skin that smelled like the basement I'd found her in. I had plans to build myself a wigwam out of willow saplings and feed on mushrooms, wild leeks, and berries from the chokecherry and sand berry bushes. I'd keep a fire in winter, and have the cats to keep me warm. I'd make friends with the squirrels, the cottontails, the weasels, the jackrabbits, and the raccoons. And in the summertime I'd lie under the stars on a bed of buffalo grass and wildflowers and fall asleep to the yelping of coyote pups calling for their mothers. How dumb! Like what—I was going to live like freakin' Snow White? It even sounded stupid to Crystal Aims (who was stupid to begin with), my friend for the better part of fourth grade. "You can't do that, Bless. There're wild animals out there! Muskrats and coyotes. Bobcats. And what about the skunks and raccoons with rabies?" I guess Crystal just didn't know yet what I'd learned early—that animals aren't the ones you have to fear. People are.

I exhale any George- and Cactus-contaminated air I might have breathed in, then inhale deeply. When I feel clean again I look up at the sky. During the day, that vast, empty space beyond the clouds is a reminder that there's something bigger than my shitty problems. Something more powerful than the biting, stinging, nasty-tempered humans swarming around down here. And at night, when the stars open their bright eyes and wink as if to say, *We see you down there, Bless; we see you,* I can't help but feel safe and at home under the glittery ceiling they make.

I dig in the box, hoping Cactus put an extension cord in it so I don't have to go back inside to grab one. While I'm rummaging, something brushes the back of my leg. "Marbles," I whisper when I see her yellowy-orange head circle my calf. I scoop up the cat and nuzzle her to my face. I run my sore cheek down the length of her fur, and she begins to purr. But when my cheek reaches her belly, I stop.

I hold Marbles under her front legs, stretch out my arms, and let the rest of her dangle. Her body, skinny as an empty tube sock, is lumped in the middle. "Oh, Marbles," I groan, "What'd you go and do *that* again for?"

Her eyes squint with innocence, and I sigh and pull her back to me. I don't know how many litters Marbles has had in her seven years, but what I do know is that when George catches wind that she's knocked up again, he's going to start stalking the old pump house (where she always seems to have them), looking for her kittens so he can "thin down the litter." Leaving just as many as he thinks we need to keep the mice population down, but not so many he's tripping over them.

I was five years old the first time I found one of Marbles's litters—well, not *this* Marbles, the first one, her mother. The kittens were so fresh that their fur was still a wet mess, their triangle ears still folded against their heads. I ran to share the news with Cactus—I suppose because I had no one else to tell. "There're five of them," I squealed. "Three yellow, just like her, and two gray ones!"

Cactus blew out a sigh and said nothing until George got home. When she told him, he grumbled, "Well, can I at least have my damn supper in peace, first?"

I didn't know what was happening when I saw him head to the shed, come out with a mallet, and stomp to the pump house. But I got an inkling of what he'd done when he emerged a few minutes later with a gunny sack swinging from his fist, as Cactus harped behind me, "What's gotta be done, has gotta be done."

Fear beat in my ears when I saw George head out across the backyard for the strip of thorny Russian olive trees where he dumped the carcasses of the wild animals that wandered into our yard. All so he wouldn't have to put up with the stench or the bottle flies when the bodies started to rot. I threw open the door and ran across the wet grass, Cactus yelling for me to come back. George had tugged the pump house door back over the heaved cement floor, and I had to ram it with all my might to get it to open. The side of the door scraped my belly as I wriggled through and called for Marbles. She didn't come.

The kittens' crib was a crate stuffed under a tower of stubby shelves; I'd spread an oilcloth over the kittens for their blanket. I tugged the crate out and lifted the rag. There were two babies left, one gray, one yellow. Their eyes were still glued shut, and they wobbled as their front legs felt for their siblings.

I ran back to the house, sobbing. "Did he kill Marbles, too? Did he?"

Cactus, who wasn't quite as bitter back then, actually put her hand on my head, and said, "Don't worry, Bless. He ain't gonna kill that cat. She's the best mouser we got."

That night I cried for those poor kittens until I puked. But after a few winters of watching George kicking at the half-starved, freezing survivors who dared tag him up the front steps, I started thinking that maybe the ones who got "thinned" were the lucky ones. And that maybe Cactus felt the same by then, since George wouldn't let us feed them. Now, when Marbles or one of her off-spring has a new litter and George heads to the pump house, I only wrap my pillow around my head and rock until it's over.

There's a sharp rapping at the window, and Cactus Carol's face appears through the frosty glass. My cue to hurry. I set Marbles down and shoo her away. Not because I'm afraid of Cactus (I'm not scared of her anymore), but because I know that if she notices Marbles's belly, that bag of bones will rattle off to tattle to George.

I pluck a strand of lights and shake it to loosen it from the wad. By the time I have the multicolored bulbs circled around the lower portion of the tree, I'm already chilled to the bone.

When I get inside, Cactus is standing next to George's chair, flapping her gums.

George is watching the news and ranting like a TV evangelist. He uses the remote like a cattle prod to get Cactus to move out of his way. But that doesn't stop her mouth. "I told you, George, I saw it with my own eyes. That cat's as fat as that chicken roasting in the oven."

"How can you be such a dumbhead, Carol? You've been around cats for sixty-nine years. Long enough to know that they don't spit their litters in the wintertime. The thing was probably gnawin' on that raccoon I plugged out behind the house."

For the first time ever, I find myself hoping that George isn't as stupid as he looks.

Upstairs, I curl on my bed to read. Fifteen minutes later, I toss the book on the floor. I hate books like this one. Ones so sickly sweet that reading them is like drinking maple syrup straight from a jug. Ones where everybody gets what they want—as if real life is anything like that. I pull my covers to my chin and beg for sleep to come.

But it doesn't. So I reach between the mattress and the box spring until my fingers find the stiff cardboard Lincoln-cent folder I keep hidden there.

If the first mystery of my existence is why I'm here at all, the second mystery is why I have this penny folder. I found it in my bag of clothes when I got dumped off here, when I was four years old. It's one of those blue cardboard things with round holes that you press pennies into. All the dates under the round spaces are crossed out with Magic Marker. The years of the pennies that are in it—twenty-five, lined side by side—aren't in sequence.

I draw my knees up and prop the tri-fold folder on my legs. I open the front and back covers so I can look at all three boards.

I was in third grade when I learned cursive and was finally able to make out the signature inside the cover flap: Susan Marlene Harris. I cringed when I read the stranger's name, fearful that

Cactus would think I'd stolen it from this Susan. I came close to tossing it in the burning barrel while the flames were high, but ended up running back to the house, the folder still tucked under my jacket. Stupid as it seems, I've always felt sorry for pennies. Because when people hear a ping, alerting them that they've dropped a coin, they don't even bother picking it up once they see that it's just a worthless penny.

Around the first penny, on the first page, flower petals are drawn with ink, the penny the flower's center. A few rows down is an empty hole—the only empty space in the rows. A star shape encircles the empty slot, and 1972 DDO is written beneath it. The last coin in the folder is a 1997, and there's a Magic Markered heart around it.

In sixth grade, I used a computer at school to find out what the DDO after 1972 meant. I found pictures of that particular penny and the year and letters were doubled up, like how cartoon characters see after they've been clunked over the head. Just like the first penny in the book. Both were mistakes that happened when they were made, and that made them valuable. None of the other pennies were worth more than a cent each, so it wasn't like this Susan Marlene Harris had started a folder of rare coins. Yet she had to have been obsessed with finding that rare '72 DDO coin, because the cardboard edging the empty circle was worn when I got it, as if she had twirled her finger around its perimeter many times over the years. A lot of times when I loop my fingertip over the same frayed edge, I swear I can feel Susan's finger doing the same, and her longing for the space to be filled.

But not tonight. Tonight I don't feel connected to anybody, or anything.

I tuck the folder back under my mattress and drift off.

Chapter 3
150 Days Ago

It's New Year's Eve. Cactus and George are sitting in front of the TV waiting for the ball to drop in Times Square. Why they watch it every year is beyond me, since every year is the same for them. And certainly nothing to celebrate.

Cactus sees me bundled up in a hat and scarf, mittens tucked under my arm as I dig through the pile of boots looking for George's duct-taped Sorels—the boots Cactus told me I can use now that she got George a new pair for Christmas. I don't want to wear them, but they're the only option I have besides my canvas shoes. They're way too big, so I stuff two socks in the toes of each.

Cactus doesn't ask me where I'm going—she's accepted my late-night strolls. But she says, "I heard a four-wheeler out there a while ago, so don't you go on the trail. Stay out of the field, too. Tell her, George."

I tie the last boot and slam the door as I leave. I wipe my feet when I get outside, same as always.

When I'm far enough away from the yard light and half-naked Christmas tree, my eyes adjust to the darkness. Stretched before me is the long driveway that George scrapes in a jagged line only inches wider than the width of his battered plow. The hard snow is pocked with rocks and gouged with ruts. Tonight I want to walk on unspoiled snow. But the sky is clear, the moon bright, and I know Cactus will be sticking her beak to the window to make sure

I don't go into the field. So I compromise by walking on the edge of the driveway.

As I walk, the sounds of my breath and the soft crunching of snow lull me, making me wish I could walk forever.

I'm halfway down the drive when I hear mewling. I turn and see Marbles's fluffy head peeking up over an indent my footsteps left in the snow. I retrace my tracks and scoop her up. "You're sweet, but not very bright. You could have taken the driveway."

I set her down on the chiseled drive and try to shoo her back to the yard. But she just stands there, one paw raised, and mews all the louder. I cup my hand around her skinny middle and pick her up. "Did your kids and grandkids gobble up the venison before you could reach it tonight?" I hate that I resent the others when they get to the back door before she does—they need to eat, too. But I can't feed them all. George watches me like a hawk at the table, and chases me out of the kitchen the second my plate is cleaned. What I do manage to swipe, I want to go to Marbles. She's the offspring of my first Marbles, and it's as if all her mother's special ways and the love she had for me was passed down the bloodline to this Marbles.

I unzip my coat to stuff her inside it. I suck in a breath when her cold paws meet my skin, and flinch when her claws dig into my collarbone. "It's okay," I coo. In a few steps, she settles in and purrs in gratitude for the warmth.

I don't talk to Marbles as I walk; she never minds my silence. Unlike my teachers who keep pointing out that I'd have a perfect 4.0, if only I'd participate more. Whatever.

I get to County Road H and don't get far when headlights appear over the hill, invading the sky with artificial beams. I cross the road to let the car pass, rather than step into the ditch. I sigh when it slows, then starts backing up. Last summer, I was out walking one night and some greasy-looking guy tried to pick me up. I had to take off into the dark. Luckily, he was too drunk to chase after me. I'll do it again if I have to.

The car stops and the window comes down. "Hey," a man's voice calls. "Your car break down? I could give you a lift."

The muffler is rattling and Marbles's hind legs stiffen. I don't look at the creep. "Keep going, old man," I say in my toughest voice. I turn around and head back toward the driveway. When I hear his brakes squeal, his door open, my hands curl into fists inside my mittens.

"Bless? That you?"

I don't know that voice. I turn around, walking backward. The guy's about five feet eleven, his legs skinny and slightly bowed. He cocks his head to the side and his hair spills like India ink to the shoulder of his quilted vest—a light blue, or something like it. He takes a step toward me, and I scout an escape route.

"Listen," I yell, my footsteps quickening, my breath huffing. "You come after me and I'll bust your balls!"

He takes a step forward, and I bolt off the road, my legs sinking into a snowdrift.

"Hot damn, it *is* you! You sound just like your ma. Though you got a dirtier mouth than she ever had." He chuckles.

I stop and twist my trunk to look back.

"It's me. Your old man. Shaky!"

I'm too shocked to move. To speak. Even when he scurries toward me and extends his hand.

I get back on the road, and he squats and wraps his arms around my thighs. He lifts me above his head and jostles me. I feel Marbles's claws again, and wrap my arms around her so Dad doesn't crush her. "My little girl!" he shouts, his voice booming. Even with my nose a foot above his head, I can smell the stink of cigarettes and beer. But for some reason, those odors smell sweet on him.

He all but drops me, then stares down. "What's this?" he asks, tapping my coat that's puffed out from Marbles. Night or not, I can see disappointment pool in his eye sockets. And then I get why. He thinks I'm knocked up. I unzip my coat enough to reach in and coax Marbles's head out. As he laughs, it's taking everything I have in me to shove down the hope that he's *finally* come to take me home.

"Come on. Go up to the house with me. What you doin' walkin' out here this time of night, anyway?"

I follow him to the car and get in slowly, not in any hurry for the interior light to snap off. He looks different. Older, even if his face is still baby round. There are a few craggy lines around his eyes, and bags underneath to catch them should they fall. He needs a shave, too. But grubby and rough looking as he is, he's good-looking in a way I don't remember.

I shut the door, and he reaches over and pretends to pull off my nose. I jerk my head back so his fingers never reach my face. Still, he shows me my "nose" between his knuckles and chuckles. "Remember how that used to make you laugh?"

He shakes his head. "Man, I can't believe how much your voice sounds like Maura's. It's kinda creepy in a way. Well, not the sound of it—you know what I mean."

"Do I look like her, too?" I ask hopefully.

"Maybe a little around the eyes. Are yours dark blue like hers?"

I nod.

"A little around the mouth, too, best I can tell in this light—but girl, do you sound like her."

By the time we reach the house, Cactus is at the window, swishing aside the curtain. "There she is," Dad says, in a tone that could earn him a spot on a Hallmark card commercial, playing the role of a prodigal son coming home for the holiday.

Cactus cocks her head, and George appears behind her,

elbowing her out of the way. Then *wham!* The Hallmark card slams shut.

Dad gets twitchy when he sees the quick flash of George's face. "She didn't tell him I was coming, did she?" he asks.

She didn't tell me, either.

Dad yanks the keys from the ignition, and they jangle in response to his hand—three guesses why he got the nickname Shaky. And, who gave it to him.

Man, I'm not even that afraid of George.

We get out of the car and the yard light flicks on. Cactus opens the door and leans out.

"It's me, Ma!"

Cactus turns and calls into the house. "It's Donny, George. Donny!"

Dad trots up the steps and bends to lift Cactus up the same way he did me. She swats at him. "Stop that, I'm too old for that nonsense. Donny, stop it!" It's been so long since I've heard Cactus laugh—if I ever have—that I don't recognize the sound.

George mutes the TV once we get inside, but keeps his eyes fastened on the screen. "Well, well, well," he says slowly. "Look what the cat dragged in."

Dad's grin quivers.

"What you doing back here, Shaky?"

"What? Can't a guy come home to see his folks? His little girl?" Dad reaches out with one arm and tugs me to him.

Cactus shoos me away like I'm a pesky housefly, then reaches up and shimmies Dad's vest from his shoulders. Her hands are trembling like his. "Sit down, Donny. You hungry? There's venison and potatoes left from supper."

"Sounds good, Ma," he says. They share a glance that says they've kept secrets, then Cactus hurries off to the kitchen to heat up leftovers.

Dad sits on one end of the couch, me on the other. The seat feels as unfamiliar to me as he does. I watch George out of the corner of my eye. The same way he's watching Dad.

"How's it goin', Pa?"

"Same shit, different day," George says.

On TV, scenes from celebrations around the world flash under booming fireworks. "You want corn or string beans, Donny?" Cactus calls from the kitchen.

"Corn," Dad shouts.

Dad fills the empty space with small talk, delivered in quick clips: the snowdrifts he drove through along Highway 80, the semitrailer that was tipped over just outside of Hershey. When George doesn't respond, Dad turns toward me. "Can you believe how pretty my little girl turned out? I don't know about that hairdo, but the rest of her sure is pretty." Said in front of George, his comment about my hair makes me feel ashamed. (And glad that I had to remove the lip ring a couple days after George belted me, because it had gotten infected.)

George turns the sound back on the TV, saying nothing. Dad rubs his hands back and forth over his knees. "You got a beer laying around here?"

"Nope," George says. "My guts can't handle that poison anymore."

Dad doesn't say anything, but he glances at the kitchen doorway as if he's wishing Cactus would reappear.

I turn to the TV where a Barbie look-alike is shouting into a microphone. Banners are waving behind her, and excited people are reaching over the rope, hoping to get on camera. Even with all that going on, the scene has a less frenzied feel to it than the one inside this room.

Cactus reheats supper in record time and all but runs the plate to Dad. He takes it and gushes over the hunk of deer meat smothered with snotty-looking onions, boiled potatoes mashed with a fork and dotted with hunks of margarine, and corn pooled in water. Cactus glances at Dad. Then over at George. Then at Dad again. And as Dad gnaws his meat, I wonder—just like George—why he's here.

George waits until Dad's plate is cleared, then mutes the TV again. "Let's cut the crap, Shaky. You never come around here unless you want something. What is it this time? And you'd better give it to me straight."

Dad scoots his butt closer to the edge of the couch. He props his elbows on his knees and twines his hands together—probably to still them. "Well, Pa. I was hoping to get a loan from you. A grand."

I hate my stomach for sinking when my old man affirms my fear; he hadn't come back for me.

The sudden, but slight lift of George's eyebrow is his only visible reaction. Dad fumbles in his shirt pocket for his cigarettes, and Cactus hurries to get him an ashtray.

"What, you in trouble with the law? Or is some loan shark out to crack your skull?"

"Neither, Pa. I need a business loan. I'm in Wisconsin now. A nice little city called Logan. Jeanie, my girlfriend, she's got a good-sized tin shed on her property where I set up a little garage—replacing alternators, brakes . . . you know, mechanicking."

George's eyes pinch with suspicion. "And lemme guess—it ain't workin' out so good for you."

"Well, I only opened the garage in November, Pa. It takes time to build a reputation."

"Seems to me, it never took you longer than a day or two," George says.

But Dad doesn't miss a beat. "Well, most folks were just trying to get their cars to limp through Christmas. It'll pick up now, though. Still, a guy can't put all his eggs in one basket.

"Logan's got a big beach with a nice marina, right along Lake Michigan. My buddy, Oiler, he's got a charter fishing boat for sale. Not a big one, but a real beauty. I'm gonna buy it. I could take four, five guys out fishing at a time. I got a good feel for the water, you know I do."

Lake Michigan!

In second grade we watched a film about the Great Lakes. Until then, I didn't know that you didn't have to go to either coast before you could see a body of water so huge that you couldn't see across it. One you could drink from if you drifted out so far you got lost, and not have to worry about sharks. That night my bed became a raft, and I floated under a ceiling of stars, the gentle waves of Lake Michigan carrying me off. The forest will probably always symbolize safety to me. But since that film, just thinking about large bodies of water washes me with a sense of *freedom*.

"I'd be good for the loan, Pa," Dad is saying when I tune in again. "I'll be chartering big shots from Milwaukee . . . Chicago. Even Rupert Wolf—he's a big shot in Logan—says it's a good deal. The boat's an older one. Wood, not one of those tin cans they're running now. But that's all the better. People are into, uh—" He turns to me. "What do they call old stuff nowadays?"

"Vintage?"

"Yeah, vintage. But it's solid. In no time I could be makin'—"

George's face bunches, like his stomach's just gone sour.

"Thing is, Oiler won't wait any longer. Jeanie's givin' me what she can, but we're a grand short. I just don't want to miss out on this opportunity."

There's a jittery silence that Dad finally breaks by repeating, "I'd be good for the loan, Pa."

"Yeah, Shaky. We all know your word is gold." George grunts and turns back to the TV to stare at the silent screen.

Cactus bunches her apron and straightens her back. "George.

Please. We've got a bit of savings, past what we'll need for property taxes in April. Let's give Donny a hand."

George has a savings account? Could have fooled me.

I'm waiting for George to rip into her. But he doesn't. Instead, he sits staring for what feels like forever, then tells Cactus to get his checkbook.

Carol just stands there. Like she's not sure she heard him right. "You gone deaf, old woman? Get my checkbook."

Cactus looks confused, then she grins. "Oh. Yeah. We can transfer the money into the checking account, soon as the bank opens up Wednesday morning."

Cactus hurries into the kitchen and a couple seconds later a drawer slams shut.

Dad's squirming like he's jacked up on caffeine. He stands up and shuffles his feet as he rubs his palms together. "I'm gonna do this up right, Pa," he says with a nervous grin. "You'll see. I'll have you paid back in no time. Like I was tellin' Jeanie—"

"Sit down and shut up, Shaky," George says. My old man drops to the couch, like he just got sucker punched.

My chin wants to quiver. I clench my fists until I can't feel anything but my fingernails gouging my palms like little blades. *How dumb are you? Like what? After almost thirteen years, he suddenly decided he missed his kid so much he had to come back on the coldest day of the year to get her? Maybe even made a New Year's resolution to start acting like a dad?*

I'm still wearing my coat and boots, and all I want to do is get outside where I can breathe. Where the stars can see me and young willows can be bent into a haven. I get up and take a couple of steps toward the door.

"You too, Bless," George says. "Sit."

I don't sit, but I stop.

Carol comes back with George's checkbook, a pair of reading

glasses, and a pen. George bends his head to scribble and I stare down at his wiry, white hair, zigzagging out from a bald spot to make his head look like a sunrise painted by a psychopath.

Cactus is standing on the other side of George, and when I look up she's grinning at Dad, whose face has gone giddy with relief.

George rips the check out of the book and holds it between his thumb and forefinger. He props his elbow on the armrest. Dad goes to reach for the check, *thank yous* gushing from his mouth like puke. But George pulls the check back. "Not so fast there, Shaky," he says.

My old man waits.

Cactus waits.

I wait.

"Here's the deal," George says. He starts flicking the check with his f-you finger. "If you take this money, you take your kid, too. And neither one of you ever comes back."

Cactus's fingers shoot up to cover her mouth. Shaky glances at her, then looks at George, his arms stretched and pleading. "Take Bless? Pa, I can't do that. Not right now anyway. Money's too tight. And Jeanie's already got her hands full with two of her own."

George moves the check into both hands, pinching the middle and twisting until the check begins to tear, ever so slightly. Cactus gasps. "George, don't!"

"Wait, wait!" Dad shouts. He starts nodding. "I'll take her. We'll make do, won't we Bless?" He fakes a grin.

George sets the check down to rest on his knee. "Okay then," he says. "Bless, go get your things."

Tears are heating behind my eyes, and I warn them to stay put. Why I have them, I'm not sure. It's not like I want to stay in this hellhole.

"Oh, George," Cactus says. "At least let him get a good night's rest."

George ignores her, but says to me, "Go on, Bless. Get your things like you were told."

I roll a couple pairs of jeans, a few T-shirts, and a few under-things and stuff them into my backpack. I tuck the coin folder between the clothing to cushion it. I kick off George's old boots and I'm almost to the door when I spot the sickeningly sweet school library book lying on the floor next to my bed. I go back and scoop it up. I grab my pen from the nightstand. And with an angry fist, I scribble out the words, *A Novel*, and write, *A Fairy Tale*. I throw the book down, and shut the door to my room as if it's a tomb. I grab my toothbrush, shampoo, and deodorant from the bathroom and head downstairs.

George is in his chair staring at the TV. A crushed cigarette is smoldering in the ashtray beside him, the check waiting on his knee. Dad is just coming through the kitchen doorway. He's hold-ing two wrapped sandwiches with one hand, and stuffing a small roll of bills into the pocket of his black jeans with the other.

Carol follows behind Dad. I look at her and suddenly I'm four again. So small I barely come up to the waistband of her apron. Looking up in the hopes of seeing something in her eyes that says she wants me to stay. I didn't see that look then, and I know it's not likely I'm going to see it now. Not with George's glare hitting her face like a slap. I kick my shoes over and wriggle my feet into them.

Cactus touches Dad's arm, then takes a couple steps toward me. I dip my head so my bangs will cover my face. "I did the best I could," she says, her voice almost a whisper. And in some crazy way, I believe her.

She reaches out and clutches my upper arms. Then she leans in and sticks her head over my shoulder in what I think is supposed to be a hug. And wouldn't you know it? My eyes start making tears. Only this time, one slides down my cheek. Cactus must see it after she pulls back, because as she's patting my upper arm, she says (though not unkindly), "None of that now. You're too big for little-girl tears." My eyes stop leaking then, as if they remember being reprimanded with those exact words when I was four and Dad drove away.

My old man goes to stand by the door, his feet shuffling. He's waiting for George to pluck the check from his knee and hand it to him. I toss my bulky backpack over my shoulder and go to the door to wait beside Dad. Cactus stands alone in the middle of the room, her eyes glassy, her hands filled with handfuls of apron. "George?" she finally says.

George takes the check and gets up slowly. He walks it to where we're standing and glares as he holds it out. And as Dad takes the check, George says, "Shaky, you're the biggest mistake I ever made."

Dad goes out first, almost running. I pause on the landing to wipe the soles of my shoes hard against the snow-packed stoop. Inside, the TV explodes with the sounds of fireworks and a chorus singing "Auld Lang Syne."

I'm halfway to the car when I spot Marbles coming around the back of the pump house.

I call her name, my steps jostling my breaths as I run. I drop my backpack and pick her up to nuzzle her against my cheek. "Dad?" I call. "Can I bring my cat?"

Dad's walking like he can't hear anything but the rage pounding in his ears. "Dad! Can I bring my cat?"

"Leave her," he says, as if she's as worthless as a penny.

"But Dad—"

"I said, leave her."

The clouds the weatherman promised have moved in to cover

the stars and the sliver moon, so that Dad is only a dark smudge moving alongside his car. The door squeaks open, and he drops himself behind the wheel. I set Marbles down, and when Dad slams his door, she runs. Through my tears she looks like she's treading in swamp water, rather than scurrying across soft snow.

CHAPTER 4
14TH STREET

I hear the scream of tires against pavement. A honk. And suddenly there's a pickup truck so close that I can feel the heat from its radiator. "What are you trying to do, get yourself killed?" a male voice shouts.

I step back, my heel fumbling to find the curb. It's like I've been jolted awake from a dream, and I'm so disoriented I don't know where I am. Only that blood is pounding in my ears and my arms are stretched out at my sides, shaking like tree limbs in a windstorm, fingers splayed, palms facing out. I murmur Liam's name as if whispering it will make him magically appear.

The man behind the windshield of the truck that almost hit me is moving in slow motion, his raised fist wagging slowly. "Hurry! Go!" I scream at him, because all I know for sure is that I'm in a hurry.

The truck crawls forward, so slowly that I can't tell if it's moving, or not. So I dart in front of him.

"You kids," the driver shouts behind me, the sound of his words garbled like he's underwater—or like I am. "You all think the whole world revolves around you!"

I cross the road and freeze when I reach the curb. I don't know the slant of this street, nor recognize the houses. I move like a weathervane in changing wind, trying to get my bearings. And then I see it. A sign pounded into the grass beside me: Logan Realty. And down at the end of the block, the back of my Lumina parked at the corner, the paint blistered in patches, its taillights the color of eyes that have cried too long.

Yes, I remind myself. That's where I am. In Logan, Wisconsin. Hundreds of miles from Wicks, Nebraska. Months beyond those lonely, hellish days before I made friends with Maylee and fell in love with Liam Reid. Running to the shore of Lake Michigan to get to him. To Liam. The only one who really knows me—and loves me anyway.

Above me there's nothing but blue. Blue like Liam's eyes, that change shades depending on the brightness of his day. But then, everything about Liam seems to be made of water and sky. Like the streaks in his blond hair that remember the sun all winter long. Hair that, when I twirl strands of it around my finger while it's still damp, stays that way as if it's intent on remembering me, too.

An unseen hand—maybe Verna Johnson's—reaches across time and space to shred my sweet image of Liam to bits, replacing it with the image of him sprawled on the cement. Blood seeping through his hair from a bullet embedded in his skull.

Why had I let Maylee talk me into going to see Verna? I didn't want to go. Not even that first time.

But it was Mother's Day, and three days before, Maylee and I were sitting on her bed as she punched pink tissue paper into a gift bag, readying it for her mother's gift (a chunky necklace with colored plastic wedges), and she'd asked about my mom. Carefully, as if I were made of glass and the word "mom" might shatter me if she set it down on me with too much force. So I told her that Mom's name was Maura. That she died when I was four.

Maylee's shoulders folded in as if to wrap around her heart as she listened. Then, out of the blue, she bounced them back and said, "Hey! You remember my uncle Bob, the cop?"

I did, though I'd only met him once, and only for a few minutes.

Maylee dived in with this drawn-out story her uncle Bob told the family, about an old woman, Verna Johnson, who lives a few miles outside of Logan, on Treeline road. The police call on her when they need help solving a crime or finding a missing person, Maylee claimed. "She's a psychic, Bless. A real one. Uncle Bob says she can see into the past, the present, and the future."

Maylee was convinced that she needed to bring me to see Verna so I could connect with my mom. That she probably had a message for me.

I didn't know how to explain to Maylee why I didn't want to connect with my dead mom—if such a thing was even possible. She would have just thought that I was afraid of ghosts. But that wasn't it. (Okay, maybe a little.) The bigger truth was that I didn't want to communicate with Mom's spirit because you can't miss what you've never had. Or at least what you can't remember. So I told Maylee, "No."

I would have stuck to it, too, had Maylee not told me that Verna Johnson could communicate with wild animals: squirrels, birds, chipmunks, feral cats wild as tigers, butterflies, you name it. She would sit out on her porch and will them to come to her without making a sound, and before you knew it, they'd crawl up her legs to sit on her lap or perch on her shoulders. Predators side by side gathered together peacefully. And, well, I wanted to see that.

But I shouldn't have gone. Not even for Maylee's sake. I should have stuck with my first thought, that it was a stupid waste of time. Or at least my second thought: that maybe it could be dangerous to learn things you don't want to know.

I hear a loud whistle, and a lab dragging his leash along the sidewalk stops and looks back at its master. The warning stops me, too. And as the dog trots back to the boy, my thoughts hurry back to Liam.

I envision Liam's dog, fidgeting by the door, waiting for someone who's not coming. And me, rocking in the dark, curled like a kitten, my hair wet and matted with tears.

But a real psychic wouldn't use a crystal ball the way kids use ouija boards. She wouldn't!

The departing bark of the lab signals me that while he and the boy are moving, I'm not. I have no clue if I've been standing on this curb for fifteen minutes, or five nanoseconds.

I glance at the green sign above me: 14th Street. Tula's Tattoo Shop is on the corner of Mactaw Avenue and 15th Street. That means that the first sixteen years of my life have passed in only one block. One block! And not like a normal recollection, where you know you're remembering. No. I was back in Wicks as if I'd never left it. Unaware that time had rolled on and that I was now living a completely different life someplace else.

I can feel my fingertips rapping against my temples. Tapping like Maylee's teeth. *Breathe so you can think*, I tell myself. But how can I think with Maylee's words, "It's happening just like she said it would," banging in my head like bees trapped behind glass?

I turn to face east. Yes, the beach is east. The street numbers get smaller and end at 1st Street, the last one before Lakefront Drive, the street that winds parallel along the beach. So I take off again.

As I run, I do my best to focus on what's around me so I can keep the bearings I just found: oncoming traffic; two old women carrying tote bags, parting to let me through when they realize I'm not going to veer or slow down; a laugh track from an old sitcom mocking me through a screen.

I'm almost to the end of the block when a cat scuttles across the sidewalk. I have to leap over her to avoid tripping us both. It's the color of my Marbles, but tinier, with longer fur. She reminds me of the kittens Liam and I saw on our first date.

Liam was twelve minutes late—some game on TV went into double overtime—and as we pulled out of my driveway, he said we'd have to make a quick stop at the animal shelter on Loop Road, to drop off his mom's donation for their drive.

I'd never been to an animal shelter, but Crystal Aims had told me about them after she learned what George did to our newborn kittens. That spring, after Marbles's belly grew fat enough to drag on the grass, I made plans to sneak her newborn kittens to the animal shelter in Wicks before George could kill them.

I had nothing to put six kittens in, and wasn't about to carry them in a gunnysack. So I tugged the drawer out of the pump house and carried it, Marbles tagging behind me, crying for her mewling babies.

I didn't get far before my arms got so tired I had to sit down on the shoulder of the road to rest them. Marbles stretched out in the drawer, and as I watched her feed her babies, I realized that I wasn't going to make it. Town was miles away (how many, I wasn't sure). And even though it felt as though I'd walked forever already, I could still see our house in the distance, ugly as a scab. Besides, even if I could make it that far, could I really be the one to take Marbles's babies away from her? Or their mother away from them? So I turned back.

I slid out of the SUV to help Liam carry the dog food into the shelter, but he grabbed both twenty-pound bags in one jerk and hurried to the door. I tagged him inside, and while he turned over the donation, the echo of dog barks drew me to the metal door across the lobby. I felt sad for the animals locked inside. Dropped off here and forgotten, doomed to lie on cement until someone deemed them worthy of picking up.

I peered through the narrow, oblong window, but saw nothing but a short hall, doors off to the sides.

"You can go in, if you'd like," said the woman who'd taken the bags.

Liam asked me if I wanted to, and I reminded him that we'd be late for the movie. He said, "Yeah," and headed toward the exterior door like I'd said "No," when really, I was only trying to find out if he'd mind being late. He looked back once he reached it; I hadn't budged. The woman at the desk gave me that guys-can-be-so-clueless look, then said to Liam, "I think she wants to go in."

Liam's eyebrows bunched. "Oh, I thought—"

He checked later movie times on his phone, then decided he could get me back home, and still get himself to work on time, if we went to the next showing. We could get something to eat first. Maybe go down by the water. "Well, if that's what you want to do," he said.

"I want to see the cats," I told him.

My eyes welled up when I knelt beside a cage housing two yellow-orange orphans, the same size as the one now ditching under a white porch.

And then I just said it. Told Liam point-blank what George did to our newborn kittens.

"Are you kidding me?"

He crouched down beside me. My bottom lashes were damp. I tried to turn away before Liam noticed, but it was too late. So I told him how George did it. As if adding that grisly detail would somehow better justify the fact that I was crying.

"Oh wow," he said, his voice a deep murmur. "That's mean."

I tripped all over myself apologizing. Desperate for him to know that I wasn't one of those bawl-baby types that get on guys' nerves. But he just draped his arm across my shoulder as if we'd known each other forever. He poked a finger into the cage to scratch the fur of the one huddled near the door. "I don't care if you cry," he said. Then he cringed. "Well, I don't mean that I don't care. I do. I just meant that it's okay if you cry. I'd think you were weird if you didn't, over something like that."

He was right beside me. So close I could smell his soap. And before I could catch myself, my head lolled over to lean against his shoulder. He reached up and touched my hair. And in that single moment, the only thing I knew besides that I missed Marbles was that I already loved Liam Reid.

Chapter 5
150 Days Ago

Dad's car is cold, the windows frosted over. But that doesn't stop him from jamming the car into reverse while my right leg is still on the ground. I draw it in and tug the door shut, which isn't easy with the wind shoving against it.

The tires spin when Dad stomps on the gas pedal, and he's forced to let up on the accelerator to let the tires get a grip on the snow. He swipes at the frost coating the windshield, and cusses when it steams right back over.

"I can't believe he'd say something like that to me," he rants, as we bounce over icy ruts. And I swear he's crying.

"I should have popped him right then and there. Like what, he's something special because he spent his life punching a time clock, plucking parts off a paint line like a trained monkey? Yeah, maybe he made a decent wage, but you'd never know it. Look at that dump Ma has to live in. No wonder my brothers and sister never looked back after they left. At least I kept in touch with Ma, and called her from time to time."

I look over at him. "You called the house?"

Dad shifts himself in his seat. He grabs another cigarette and fumbles for his lighter. He glances over, forcing a grin. "What? I had to know how my little girl was doin', didn't I?"

I turn away, and his sigh fills the front seat. "I probably should have asked to talk to you, Bless. I know that. But it would've killed me to have you keep askin' when I was comin' for you, and me havin' to tell you each time that I couldn't take you just yet. It broke your heart the first time I had to tell you that. I didn't want to have to keep breakin' it."

I turn my face toward the side window and clear my throat.

Dad slams his fist against the steering wheel. "Damn it. I shouldn't have let Ma talk me into coming and asking Pa for the loan. Ma thought it would help end the cold war between me and the old man, if we saw each other face-to-face. Then maybe I could come around now and then to see her. See you. But I knew he'd be an asshole. "

Dad jacks the blower up to high and cold air slaps my face.

"But, to hell with him. I've got my check and a chance at a fresh start. The old man can go to hell. I'm done with him."

But he isn't done with George. A mile later, he starts ranting all over again. "Do you know what he did to us boys when we were kids? Bought us two pairs of boxing gloves so we could learn to fight like men. He took us out to the yard. I wasn't more than five or six years old. I didn't know how to lace up boxing gloves; I could barely tie my own shoes. He laced his gloves up, and while I was trying to wiggle my hand into the second one, he hauled off and boxed me in the face. And I mean hard! I skidded back a good four, five feet before I thumped to the ground. Then he laughed while I laid there bleedin' out of my nose like a stuck pig. 'Lesson number one,' he said, 'keep your gloves up to protect your face at all times.' My brothers and sister left home soon as they were old enough to stick their thumbs out. I wouldn't have looked back after I left, either, if it hadn't been for Ma."

I stare out the window, blinking against the cigarette smoke that's stinging my eyes.

"Hand me a beer, will you? On the floor back there."

Dad pops the top and takes a couple quick swigs. Then he proceeds to tell me more stories of George's meanness. He doesn't pause, either. Well, except when we meet another car. He thinks every one of them has their brights on and are trying to run us off the road. So he flashes them his, and flips them off, even if it's pitch-dark and they can't see his finger.

I stop listening and curl my arm around my head. Lean against the glass and try not to think of Marbles. How tomorrow she'll be waiting outside the back door for me to bring her her supper, and I won't be there.

Dad settles down some after he finishes his first beer, and we turn down Highway 83. But he's still talking. Not so much about George now, but about himself. About the jobs that went bad and the women who broke his heart. "Job or woman, though, I gave my best to both. Nobody can say I didn't. But now I got Jeanie, and two businesses. Nobody's ever gonna bring me down again."

We've been on the road over a half an hour, and Dad hasn't asked a single question about me. The fact that I even notice makes me hate myself. How dumb could I have been, thinking that when he lifted me in the air like he was happy to see me, I believed him?

Dad starts telling me happier stories of when he was a kid. Things he and his brothers did. The pranks he pulled on Cactus. I laugh on cue, but I'm not really listening. I'm watching the patches of ice my old man's weaving around, and thinking about what I might say if he ever gets around to asking about me.

Maybe I'll tell him that I don't have any pictures of Mom, but that I wish I had. Because in every memory I have of her she's wearing a scarf tied tight around her head. So that now when I think of her, I don't see hair and a face with eyes, nose, and mouth. Only bright flowers and neon pinks. Hearts floating against clouds and bold zigzags and pastel plaids. Scarves that—I figured out when I was around thirteen—she wore to cover her scalp that had been plucked bare from chemo.

Maybe I'll tell him that the last time I saw her she was in a hospice (I suppose that's what it was), lying in a bed with metal rails like a crib, in the middle of what pretended to be a living room. And that I don't remember who brought me there, only that they made me color her a picture, and that Mom cried when she saw the stick figures that were supposed to be the two of us standing side by side on a beach, holding hands under a waxy, yellow sun. I might even tell him that she always cried when she saw me, and that her tears made me feel sad and scared enough to want to crawl under her bed. All because I knew what was coming when it was time to leave. Her holding the sides of my face with hands so dry that they felt like they could crumble, whispering my name over and over again. "Bless . . . Bless . . . Bless . . . ," as if it were a prayer she was begging somebody to hear.

If I were brave enough, I'd tell him how I don't remember who took care of me until he came to get me— only that it still pains me that he never took me to his house, as I was told he would. And how I remember that we drove for what seemed like forever, stopping only when we had to pee or were thirsty, and once when he ran out of cigarettes. That it was fun laughing over his silly jokes, even if I didn't get half of them.

It could be I'd remind him that he'd said, "Well, here we are" when we pulled down Cactus Carol and George's long driveway the next morning, and ask him if he'd noticed that I'd scooted closer to the dash to look at the yard I believed to be his. All because I was hoping to spot a swing set. But instead, what I saw was a dead deer hanging upside down from a tree, rocking in the wind, its fat tongue dangling, its stomach split open and emptied.

Maybe I'd tell him that I remember him saying, "Congratulations, Grandma, it's a girl!" with a laugh that sounded more like a cough, and point out that when he told me to hug my grandma, I *did* take baby steps forward to give her one so he wouldn't think I was a bad girl, but it was Cactus who stopped me by turning to him and snapping, "Donny, what kind of a joke is this?"

Possibly, I'd remind him that he told me to go play with the kitten that was tiptoeing across the grass, so the two of them could talk. Tell him that I remember the kitten vividly. Her eyes were green and looked like shiny, new marbles. She had short, orange fur, the same shade as the leaves she was walking across. She ducked when I brought my hand down to pet her, but soon was cupping my bent knees with her whole being, and purring. I'd ask Dad if he realized that the cat he forced me to leave behind was the daughter of that kitten.

And for sure, I'd tell him that I remember how, when he asked Cactus and George if they could keep me because my mom had just died and he didn't have a place fit for a kid yet, Cactus said, "I, I don't know, Donny. I thought I was done raising kids."

And when George asked him for how long, he'd answered, "A month . . . maybe two," like he meant it.

I feel a soft punch against my arm. "Hey, kid. You fall asleep on your old man?"

I sit up straighter. "I'm awake."

Dad sighs. "Sorry if I was boring you, but a person can't help but remember stuff when they go back home."

Or, when they leave it.

"Whoa!" Dad shouts, as he yanks the steering wheel to the right to make an exit ramp. The car rocks to the left, and I brace myself, certain we're going to roll over. "Whew!" Dad whoops. "Almost missed our turn."

We go down the ramp and we're on a divided highway. Down the road a ways there's a sign that says West 80.

Dad jerks the wheel hard, and the empty beer cans on the back-seat floor clank. "You're going the wrong way," I tell him.

"Nope," he says. "This is right."

"But to get to Wisconsin, we have to go east."

Dad doesn't respond.

And then it hits me. And in a voice that's almost a whisper, I say, "You're not taking me home with you this time, either. Are you?"

Dad gives me a nervous glance. "Much as I wish I could bring you home with me, Bless, I can't." He takes a quick swig, then brings the beer can down and props it between his legs. "Jeanie's got two kids of her own. Both of them heading straight for the juvie home. I can't bring you there. I wouldn't do that to you, Bless. Or, to Jeanie."

"Then where are you taking me?"

"Well," he says. He lifts his hips and reaches into his pants pocket. He pulls out a roll of bills and brings the wad to the steering wheel to unroll it. Even with the dash lights burnt out, I can see the white smudge of the scrap paper he plucks from the center. He holds it out for me to see, as if I'm wearing night-vision goggles. "This is your grandma Gloria's phone number. Ma doesn't know if it's still good since she's never called it. But we're gonna give it a try."

"My grandma Gloria?" I ask in disbelief.

"Yeah. You remember Grandma Gloria, don't you? Man, you screamed until you broke blood vessels in your cheeks when I pulled you off her leg to take you. Remember that? Course, you didn't know who I was—I'm sorry about that—so who could blame you?"

I'm blinking hard because I don't know what he's talking about.

"I don't remember another grandma," I say as I shift in my seat.

Dad laughs. "You're kiddin' me? You weren't *that* little. What, five, six? Hell, I was that age when we got those boxing gloves and I remember it like it was yesterday."

"I was four," I remind him.

"Still, you gotta remember her. Your ma and you moved in with Gloria after she left me. Gloria took care of you until she had a little stroke. She could still talk okay, just slow, but her mind and hands weren't working well enough to take care of a kid your age. So she called me, even if she didn't want to. I'm your daddy, after all."

"I don't remember her," I say again, in a voice that doesn't sound like mine.

"Well, she sure as hell remembers you. She sends you five bucks on your birthday every year, doesn't she?"

I blink in disbelief. *Why hadn't Cactus told me?*

"Where does she live?"

Dad nods at the road ahead. "Not far," he says. "Over in Paxton." He hands me the scrap of paper. "Here, hang on to this."

I had another grandma living forty, maybe fifty miles from me, this whole time? God.

"Gloria's a good woman. She never cared for me, but then, I *was* pretty wild back then. Probably wouldn't have mattered if I wasn't, though. Gloria's a man-hater. She's got her reasons, though. She was married to a real slimewad. He wanted a wife and a kid until he got them, then took off, leaving Gloria holding a squalling baby and an empty purse."

My mind is muddled, my insides quivering. "What's her name again?"

"Gloria. Grandma Gloria. And just for the record, I don't care what she or your ma might have said about me—I wasn't *all* that bad. Just young and trying to find my way."

My stomach starts churning.

"Thing is, I wasn't any more equipped to take care of a little kid at the time than Gloria was. Still, I knew I had to do right by you, and took you to Ma." He reaches over and squeeze-shakes my knee. "I still plan to do right by you, Bless. That's why we're gonna call Gloria in a bit. Because for right now I can't do best by you, by taking you home with me. Not until I get these businesses off the ground and Jeanie gets her punks in line. Ma said she heard a couple years ago, that Gloria's doing good—not like you're little anymore, anyway, and need somebody cooking for you and givin' you baths."

He rolls his window down and tosses out the empty can. Cold wind blows into the backseat, then curls around me. I breathe deeply, trying to get my stomach to settle down. It doesn't help though, and bile rises up my throat. I shout at Dad to stop the car, and while it's still rolling I shove the door open, lean out, and empty my stomach.

"You okay there, kid?" he asks as I'm closing the door. "You got a little stomach bug or somethin'?"

"No. I just throw up sometimes. Not on purpose. I just do."

He digs in a crushed McDonald's bag for a napkin so I can wipe my mouth. "Poor kid. You ain't had it so easy, have you, losing your ma so young." My stomach—or maybe my heart—clenches when he says it.

When we get close to North Platte, Dad gets out his phone. "It's twelve forty-five," I remind him. "She's probably in bed."

"Won't matter. Trust me, with the news I've got for her, she won't mind getting woken up."

Dad asks me to read him Gloria's number, and flicks his lighter so I can see.

"I'll put this thing on speaker so you can hear how excited she is. She's gonna go nuts."

I picture this other grandma bitter like Cactus. Scrawny, wrinkled, and worn, her heart as dehydrated as beef jerky.

"Don't do that," I plead. But he hits *speaker* anyway, and the rings chime out.

She sounds scared when she answers.

"Gloria? It's me, Shaky. Don't hang up, okay? I've got somebody here who wants to talk to you." He holds the phone out. I push it away. "Come on, Bless. She won't bite."

I hear her gasp. "Shaky, you have Bless there? Oh my goodness. Bless?"

Dad is holding the phone out between our seats, and he leans over and shouts, "That's right, Gloria. I've got her right here. And guess where we are!"

Gloria starts crying. "Bless? Sweetheart, is that you?"

Her voice drips over me slowly, like honey slipping from a spoon. Sweetening my hope that maybe this move will be different.

Dad shoves the phone at me, and I take it. My hand is shaking. I dip my head. "Hello?"

"Oh, Bless . . . Bless . . ." My hands feel tingly. "Grandma thinks about you every day. Every single day. How are you, sweetie?"

"I'm okay," I tell her.

She starts crying harder, but now she's laughing, too. "I can't believe it. You sound just like my Maura."

Suddenly, I feel cotton fabric pressed against my face, and someone's thigh—Grandma Gloria's?—warm and soft beneath it. The cloth is damp from the spit and tears and snot I'm leaking, and it sucks into my mouth between sobs. The memory feels so real that I put my hand to my mouth to remind myself that the fabric isn't still there. That I *can* breathe.

"We were making a Thanksgiving turkey out of construction paper when your dad showed up—remember that?" Grandma Gloria asks. "We had one red and one yellow handprint cut out when he got there. I still have it. And oh, your stuffed skunk. I was heartsick when I found Stinky tangled in your blankets and realized I hadn't packed him. You wouldn't go to sleep without him. But I was just so upset I couldn't think straight. I was trying to make sure I'd remember to give you Maura's penny collection. She wanted you to have it. Still, every night since your Dad took you, right before I drift off, I picture you crying for that toy. Who cries for their old stuffed animal at *seventeen*?"

The penny folder—Mom had Susan's penny book?

I don't remember Gloria, and I don't remember a stuffed skunk. But I don't want to hear her cry, so I say, "No, Glor—Grandma Gloria. I didn't." She sounds so crushed, that I add, "I got a new stuffed toy after I left." It's a lie, of course. That doll with the bashed-in eye and a checker game were the only toys I remember owning. Cactus always got me practical things for Christmas. Like spiral notebooks and socks.

I want to ask her more about the penny folder—how Mom ended up with Susan Marlene Harris's penny collection, and why Mom wanted me to have it—but I can't talk to her anymore. My stomach is swirling again and my throat is stuffed tight with tears.

I shove the cell back at Dad. "Gloria?" Dad hollers. "Guess where we are. We just left North Platte, and are heading in your direction. So get out the cookies and hot chocolate. Your grand-baby's coming for a midnight snack!"

"You're bringing Bless here to see me?" she asks. Her voice wobbles. "You'd do that, Shaky? You'd bring her to see me for her birthday?"

Dad glances at me, a *huh?* look on his face.

I'm coming close to crying again—good tears this time, if there is such a thing.

"I ain't just bringing her to *see* you, Gloria. I'm bringing her to *stay* with you. Just for a few months, until I get on my feet."

The phone goes silent. And my old man, like me, suspects that we've lost our signal. He shouts into the phone, "Gloria? You still there? Gloria?" Then, "*Shit!*"

Dad's about to end the call when she says in a frail voice, "I'm here."

"Did you hear what I said?" My old man cocks his head and waits. I do the same.

"Shaky," she says, "you know how much I love that girl. But I can't take her in. I'm sorry—*so, so* sorry, Bless—but I can't." She starts whimpering. "I'm on disability because of my strokes. It's not enough, so I took in a friend who wasn't making ends meet, either. This place is a one-bedroom, and so small that I can hardly get my walker between our twin beds. We don't even have a full-sized couch you could sleep on, honey. We don't even have that."

She's blubbering by now, to the point where she can't finish (as if there's a need to).

The phone lights Dad's face and shows his shock. Followed by an *I'm-sorry-you-heard-that* look.

But I'm not surprised. Really, I'm not.

"Look," Dad says into the phone, his voice hard now. "We did our part with Bless the last ten, eleven years. What are you saying? That you aren't going to do your part now? Jesus, Gloria—to say that to your own grandkid after you haven't talked to her in years."

The knot in my throat thumps down to my stomach, and I stuff my fists into my coat pockets. How dumb could I have been, thinking even for a split second that this woman might be my saving grace? I should have known she'd be nothing but a sweeter-talking Cactus Carol.

"Shaky," Gloria says quickly. "It's not that I . . . just let me see my granddaughter. Please. Iris made pie. We'll have some and Bless can tell me about her life. Do it for her. For me."

Dad steers with his knee and rolls his window down as Gloria pleads, and frigid air whomps its way into the car. He flicks his cigarette out. "You ain't my old man, Gloria, so don't go tryin' to boss me around. You don't want her, we'll leave it at that." He snaps the phone shut and rolls up the window.

I'm watching the flame from his cigarette through the side mirror. It shoots like a star, then bursts into tiny sparks that skip across the pavement and die.

"What a poor excuse for a grandma," he says. "Look at Ma. She's not exactly rolling in dough, either, but when I needed her help, she took you in like any decent grandma would do. All that blubbering—what kind of show was that? Sorry you had to hear that, Bless."

Shaky looks for a place to turn around. "Looks like I'm gonna have to bring you home with me after all."

I tuck my lips into my mouth and turn my face to the window.

Shaky.

Yeah. That's what I'll call him from now on. Because a "Dad" would want his daughter in his life, wouldn't he?

Chapter 6
149 Days Ago

Sixteen hours and one cheesy hotel later, we pass through Logan under muddy skies. I ask Shaky where Lake Michigan is, and he points east without saying how far away it is. A few miles farther, we approach a ranch-style house and Shaky says, "Well, here we are."

I smirk at the irony of it all when I see at the edge of the lawn, a swing set, its candy cane–striped poles bowed out to the sides like the legs of a fat man. Only one seat is left, dangling by a single chain. Nearby, there's a basketball hoop with no net and a bent rim.

The house could use new paint, and one window is cracked. The handle of a lawn mower is poking up out of the snow, and there's a bike tipped on its back under the bay window, pillows of snow asleep on its pedals, one wheel missing. The lawn is littered with Mountain Dew bottles, quivering in the wind.

"There's my shop," Shaky says, proudly.

I turn my attention to where Dad's pointing. Rusted car parts, old tires, and plastic jugs skirt the Christmas-green colored building like gifts from the Island of Misfit Toys. A white car hood hangs from a frame made of pipes, and on it, *SHAKY'S FIX-IT SHACK* is spray-painted in blue letters bunched at the right margin.

"Those damn kids didn't even shovel," Dad harps, as we spin up the driveway.

As we walk to the house, my old man is as nervous as when he brought me to stay with Cactus and George.

Jeanie's about my height, five feet three, but towers above me in four-inch, cork-bottomed platforms. Her hair is the color of a cherry Popsicle, her roots are not. A spandex shirt hugs her muskmelon-sized boobs, her back fat, and the doughy bulges above the waistband of her jeans.

She looks crazed when we come through the door. I assume it's because Shaky brought me home. But when she rushes to grab the cigarette from his mouth and sucks on it like it's her air, I think it might be a nicotine fit that has her looking so wild-eyed.

Am I ever going to live in a house that isn't choking with smoke?

"If that kid doesn't stop stealing my smokes, I'm going to thump him good," she says, smoke curling from her nostrils. "I can't afford this." She glances at me, her expression saying, *I can't afford you, either.*

Dad leans down to give Jeanie a quick kiss, then plucks George's check from his vest pocket. He waves it like it's his report card and he scored all aces. "Told you he'd give it to me," he says. "Now we're gonna be cookin', baby."

Jeanie rolls her butt onto a bar stool. "Isn't that what you said when I handed over the bucks for that diagnostic thingy you just had to have?" Jeanie shoves cereal bowls of jelling milk aside with her arm and drags an ashtray closer.

"Jeanie, I told you. Everything on vehicles is digital now. I had to get one."

Jeanie grunts. "Alls it's gotten you is bar buddies coming over to get a free diagnosis, before they take their cars to a *real* garage."

I wonder if either of them remembers I'm standing here.

Back at George and Cactus's, I could escape to my room when the two of them started ragging on each other. But here, I don't even know where my room is.

"Well, it's like Rupert said. You can't put all your eggs in one basket. And he should know. That guy's got more money than the Catholic Church."

Jeanie grunts, then glances up at the clock. "Well, you don't get that check over to Oiler, and Rupert's gonna be putting his eggs in *your* basket. Oiler said you've got 'til four o'clock, then he's selling the boat to him."

Shaky gets excited. "See? See? Rupert knows it's a moneymaker!" Shaky does a little happy dance, then stops. "Oiler wouldn't sell it without waitin' on me," he says, sounding more hopeful than certain. He glances at the clock. "I'd better get over there. You got a check written out for the rest of it?"

"I told you I was giving it in cash so Oiler can put less on the bill of sale, and keep the sales tax down," Jeanie snaps.

Shaky turns to me. "Jeanie's a smart one, I'll tell you that much."

Jeanie thrusts her chin in the air. "Yeah, well, we'll see how smart I am after I give you my very last red cent."

I stand forgotten, holding my backpack and waiting as Jeanie digs in her fat purse for a roll of bills. She grabs a wad of junk and drops it on the counter. A lipstick tube and a few coins roll away from the mound and drop to the floor. I pick them up and try to look inconspicuous as I check the date on the pennies.

Shaky chuckles. "Your ma used to do that, too," he says. "Check pennies."

I put the pennies and lipstick in the nest of junk Jeanie's making on the counter, and I wait. I'm not sure exactly what I'm waiting for. For someone to tell me where my room is, I suppose. But Shaky and Jeanie are busy bickering about if he should run back to town to deposit George's check, or just sign it over to Oiler.

They exchange a quick (even warm) kiss, like they hadn't just been pecking at each other with the same mouths, and out the door Shaky goes to turn over the check to Oiler.

Jeanie leans over to pour more coffee into her cup, then asks if I want some. I shake my head, and she lights another cigarette.

Two seconds later, Trevor, who's pimple-faced, ugly, and fourteen, comes rushing into the kitchen. The whites of his eyes are the color of hot dogs, probably from staring at a computer game for hours. He goes to open the fridge and says, "Move it," and bumps me out of the way. Jeanie, wrapped up in her own world, snaps at him to leave her smokes alone. He ignores her, grabs a soda, and leaves the room.

Twelve-year-old Jud, who's my height and has purple bruises on his arm (probably from Trevor), pops into the kitchen. "You could have gotten me one, jerk," he shouts down the hall. He grabs a soda, then races out of the room because Trevor's shouting, "You're getting killed, fuzznuts!"

Jeanie sighs after they're gone. "Good luck with those two," she says to me, like we're unarmed comrades in a war zone.

I wander into the living room, my backpack cradled in my arms. The TV's on, but no one's watching it. My stomach feels hollow. I wish I was back in Wicks. At least there, I had a room to escape to. And Marbles.

I go the window and look across the snow-packed road where the forest is thick with balsam and silver maples. I turn back to the kitchen and wonder if I need to tell Jeanie I'm going out. I laugh at the thought. Her kid doesn't ask permission before he takes her cigarettes, so um, probably not.

Bitter wind stings my face, and oppressive gray clouds hang low.

There's a logging road almost directly across from the house. The Wisconsin woods are thick with trees everywhere, not merely in clumps here and there, like back home. I feel like an intruder as

I head down the road. It's dusk. Too dark to see far into the trees, but maybe if I come here in the daylight, I'll find a stream like I had back in Nebraska that I can sit beside and listen to the water run when the ice melts. I come across two felled trees lying like Lincoln Logs in the road. My toes are already numb, so I turn back.

I'm crossing the road in front of the house when I spot a bluff across the field on the other side of Shaky's garage. Atop the hill is a grove of tall red pines, standing like majestic angels. Their lowest branches are wavering over the snowdrifts, making them look like they're walking in swishing skirts. I want to go to them now, but the snow's too deep, the wind too bitter. So I go back inside, feeling better, because I know where my hiding place will be.

Jeanie's staring at the TV, her thick thighs pressed together as she sits on one pinched butt cheek. She has an ashtray balanced on the armrest of the chair, a can of diet soda against her hip. She's mesmerized by two reality stars with ruddy complexions and witchy black hair, who are threatening to knife each other.

"You watch this one?" she asks.

I shake my head.

"Oooo, it's so good. Just shove that laundry aside," she says, nodding to the couch.

I sit down, my backpack on my lap. And as Jeanie fills me in on the racy past of the women who are screaming, her eyes not leaving the screen, I take in the room. There are enough dirty dishes and garbage lying on the coffee table alone to fill two sinks and a trash bag.

Shaky gets home after midnight, startling me so that my cheek falls off my hand. Jeanie's still in her chair, her head back, her mouth open, and snoring. "Cripes, Shaky," she sputters, even before she opens her eyes. "What you trying to do, wake the dead?" She doesn't seem to notice that the volume on the TV alone could do the same, say nothing of the computers down the hall.

"You're drunk," she says after she blinks herself awake.

Shaky weaves himself to a chair and fumbles to unlace his boots. "Nice to see you girls watching TV together, all cozy. I knew you two would hit it off."

Really?

He squints at the TV, where the same two hags are having the same argument, even though it is a different episode. "What you watchin'?" he asks. He squints, then looks at me. "I don't care for the programs Jeanie watches—all that screamin'. I like that one on Animal Planet. What's that one I like, Jeanie? The one with those two crazy bastards who catch alligators with their bare hands? I like that one."

So, this is my new home. I sigh, and mentally count the months, days, and hours until I graduate and can live on my own.

The two loudmouths come down the hall and slip into the kitchen, blaming and shoving each other for the game they lost as they dig through the cupboards. Shaky tells them to come into the living room. They don't, but they peek in from the kitchen doorway. "From now on, you boys can call me Captain."

"Captain Loser, maybe," Trevor says. Jud snickers.

From what I've seen, Shaky *is* a loser. But still, when the boys say it, it bugs me.

"You'll be eatin' those words come spring," Shaky shouts.

Trevor has disappeared back into the kitchen. "At least then, there'd be something to eat in this dump!" This sparks Jeanie, who shouts back a list of what frozen dinners are in the freezer, and what snacks are in the cupboard.

Home sweet home.

Shaky turns to me. "Cripes, we have to figure out where you're gonna sleep." He turns to Jeanie. "Hey, why can't Jud move in with Trevor, and Bless have his room?"

Trevor returns to the doorway. He's tugging hard on a bag

of Doritos. The bag busts open and triangles fly like throwing stars cast by a schizophrenic ninja. "That little creep isn't going to stay in my room!" He dips his hand into the bag, the triangles on the floor crunching under his shoes as he stomps back into the kitchen.

Shaky wags his head. Jeanie sighs. And that settles that.

While the boys go back to their rooms like boxers to their corners, I follow Jeanie and Shaky through the house—twice—until it's decided I'll stay in the little room off the living room where the washer and dryer are. I don't know what the room was originally meant to be, since it's too small to be a bedroom, yet too big to be a real laundry room.

Dad brings a rollaway bed down from the attic, and a little nightstand, and we scoop dirty clothes from the floor and heap them on three already-filled baskets. "Look at this, Bless. You got a washer and dryer right in your room. That'll be nice, huh?"

An hour later, I'm lying in the dark on a stained mattress, the penny folder tucked under my cot, and a rod cutting across my back, listening to metal snaps cracking against the dryer drum. Well, until Jeanie asks Shaky for the title Oiler signed over, so she can get the transfer registration sent to the Department of Natural Resources. I don't hear Shaky's answer, but I sure do hear Jeanie when she shrieks, "You mean you handed him my grand and your old man's check and you didn't get the title?"

They're standing right outside my room, but might as well be standing in it.

"The title's there somewhere," Shaky says. "I'll get it soon as Oiler gets back."

I pull the covers up over my head.

It's insane to me that I should be crying inside because I want to go back to Wicks, but I am. At least there I had a real bedroom that nobody but me had a reason to enter. It won't be the same here. I curl on my side, my knees butted against the wall, my pillow rolled in my arms.

The next day, while Shaky's off to admire his boat, and Jeanie's at work, I'm at the island making myself a peanut butter and jelly sandwich with a steak knife because all the butter knives are dirty, when Jud shoves me. "Get out of the way, bitch."

I catch him off guard when I grab his wrist. And just like I once did to Cactus, I twist with all my might until he's hunched over. Then I lean in close, even if his breath smells like an unflushed toilet, and hiss through my teeth, "Listen, you little asswipe. You lay a hand on me again and I'll smash your balls." Trevor snickers. I glare up at him, my fingers still digging into Jud's arm. "The same goes for you."

"Yeah, right," he says.

Quickly, before my rage dissipates, I say in the deepest voice possible, "You doubt me? I've held my own with dirtbags a lot bigger and meaner than the two of you." I shove Jud's arm away and just for effect, I let them see me pick the knife back up. I go back to my sandwich-making, my back to them to prove that I'm not scared. The boys go silent. The fridge opens and shuts. A cupboard slams. And then, as they're walking out, I hear one of them (I think Jud) say, "Man, that bitch is crazy."

Maybe I am.

Monday morning comes, and the boys go off to school. But I don't. Dad has to take me to get enrolled, but he's not any more concerned with getting me registered than he is the boat he's decided to christen *The Carol. Seriously?*

I know I can't spend the day in my windowless cubbyhole with nothing to read, so after everyone is gone I pick up the living room and do the dishes. There is a dishwasher, but I have to soak them first. Then I start in on the mounds of dirty clothes in my makeshift room. I don't really know how to clean, but I find myself enjoying putting things back where they belong.

When Jeanie gets home, she blinks, her head moving like an oscillating fan. She turns to me, her mouth hanging open. "*You did this?*"

"Yeah."

Her shoulders go soft. "I don't think anybody in this house has ever even brought a dirty glass to the sink. I used to keep everything clean, but I finally gave up. Wow, I can't believe how nice it looks in here. Thank you, Bless."

And I can't believe I'm being thanked for something I did.

Two hours later, Jeanie's taking me to the mall to pick out some new clothes for school. And when we get back home, she tells Shaky he's taking me to school in the morning to get me enrolled.

I don't intend to make friends at my new school. I haven't really had one since Crystal Aims, and I don't want any, either. So on my first day, I find a table in the lunchroom that's empty but for one girl, sitting at the corner. She's tall, kind of homely, and wearing an oversized sweatshirt in bubblegum pink. A bracelet she probably beaded herself flops on her bony wrist. She's a misfit. But not one by choice, like me. She doesn't look up when I take a seat at the opposite corner.

Lunch is pizza. Cactus never made pizza, but that's pretty much all I've eaten at Dad and Jeanie's. Not that I'm complaining.

I ignore the kids at the surrounding tables who are sizing me up. The boys, no doubt trying to figure out if I put out so they know if they should put any effort into *liking* me. And the girls trying to figure out if I put out so they know if they should put any effort into *hating* me. Little do they know, I don't care what any of them think of me.

The girls at the table directly across the aisle from me (the kind who can't get through lunch without reapplying lip gloss between bites) gawk and whisper about me. That is, until one of them brings up last night's episode of some reality show I'm sure Jeanie watches, too. Then they start debating the name of "the blond slut" who took off her bikini top when the guys got into the pool. "Uh-uh, Stephie. It was Nicole," one of them spouts. Stephie, the one who looks most like she could make the cover of *Seventeen*, with her perfectly symmetrical features and silky blond hair hanging halfway down her back, gets out her phone to prove that it was Bridget who "showed her tits." I sigh at their meaningless banter and shift in my chair to get them out of my peripheral vision.

Across the room, a couple of jocks are taking little jabs—literally—at a boy who looks to be South Asian. The teacher on lunch duty strolls past, her arms crossed, and tells the jocks to move on—but she's wearing a faint smile as she says it.

And I wonder why I hate people, for the most part?

The misfit at my table, whose complexion is pasty as a potato, is using her fork and knife to cut her pizza into one-inch squares. She lines three of them on her tray, then begins snapping her carrot sticks into one-inch lengths. She uses her butter knife to whittle a carrot that she's snapped a fraction too long. *What a wacko.*

Once she's satisfied that her three carrot sticks are uniform lengths, she lines them alongside the pizza bites. She must feel me watching her because she tucks her ashy-brown hair behind her ears and looks up. What I see in her hazel eyes instantly thaws me. It's the same fear I used to see in the eyes of the older cats who knew to run when they felt the vibration caused by George's foot stomps. The same vulnerability I saw in the kittens who huddled against the door for warmth, too innocent to know to scatter when they felt the same tremor.

The girl's shoulders rise up to meet her ears, and she giggles. "I have a small stomach so can't eat much at a time." She says this as if it explains why she's cutting her lunch into one-inch portions and lining the bites in a row.

I turn away, like I had to turn away from the cats I couldn't save or feed. I look down at my half-empty plate, ignoring her so she'll ignore me back. But I can't keep it up for long. A few years ago Marbles had a kitten who didn't thrive, even though Marbles fed her. I couldn't ignore that cat, either. She was too weak to run when George strode across the yard one afternoon and his kick killed her.

"I throw up sometimes," I tell her. "Not on purpose. I just do."

The girl grins awkwardly when I say this. She tells me that her name is Maylee Bradley and that she's a junior. I tell her I'm Bless Adler, and that I'm a junior, too. She likes the name Bless. I don't tell her that I don't. We don't say any more than that, but she flashes me a shy smile when we reach the tray drop-off area at the same time.

Chapter 7
120 Days Ago

Within a week, Maylee and I were eating our lunches across the table from each other and taking side-by-side seats in World History (the only class we share). And now, a month later, I guess we are what those who believe in forever call BFFs. I like Maylee. Even if she's insecure, mousy, and not the brightest crayon in the box. But she's nice and says what she thinks—at least to me. And she needs somebody to watch her back.

For the most part, kids are ignoring me now. Well, except for the new boy from Maine, who started at Logan High two weeks before I did. He's a senior, and eighteen. Every time I pass him in the hall, he slows down like he wishes I would, too. I don't though. I keep walking, my eyes straight ahead.

"You don't think Liam Reid is cute?" Maylee asks me as she carves meat from a chicken nugget, then tries mashing it with her fingers into a square. "Every other girl thinks he's hot."

Maylee's right. At least about the other girls. They can't seem to take their eyes off him. Not because he's perfect-looking—he's not. His nose is a little too big, and the rest of his facial features, kind of ordinary. But that's not what they're looking at. The preppy ones think he's hot because his blond hair is cool, his skin dark enough to look tanned, and because he has a grin that says he's not a bad boy yet, but that for the right girl he could become one.

The girls who put out have their reasons for thinking Liam Reid is hot, too. He's not all *that* tall—five feet ten, maybe—but as Miss

Seventeen Stephie pointed out to her friends, "He's got great abs and a nice ass." She thinks his toned body comes from pumping iron—and likes that idea. But his rough palms and the silvery scar on the back of his right hand tell me that his great body comes from hard work. And I like *that* idea; I despise guys who are so into their looks that they pump iron in front of mirrors to impress girls and intimidate other boys. So yeah, I think he's hot like everybody else does. But mainly because his eyes have depth to them.

"I didn't say he wasn't hot," I tell Maylee.

"Well, you don't act like you think he is."

"Why? Because I don't toss my hair and giggle like a chimp when I see him, like every other girl in this school?"

"You don't have hair long enough to toss," Maylee says. I think she's serious. "You run to the other side of the hall when you see him coming."

I don't bother pointing out to her that I not only cross the hall when I *see* him coming, but when I *feel* him coming. And I do feel him. Right through the bricks before he even clears the corner. I don't know how that can be, any more than I know why I hurry to avoid him. Except that his eyes get intense when he looks at me as if he's *really* seeing me. And although I've waited a lifetime for someone to really see me, now that somebody does, I feel uneasy.

"I just can't believe you don't like him. If I were you—"

"I didn't say I didn't like him. I just don't have any interest in guys, that's all."

Maylee's eyes spring open their widest, and her already-pale skin goes as white as the string cheese she's chopping into chunks. "Wait. You're not a *lesbian*, are you?"

I roll my eyes and mock her tone as I say, "You're not an *anorexic*, are you?"

Maylee's neck stretches like a Slinky. "What? I eat."

"Never mind," I say. "None of my business."

"Well it isn't any of my business if you're a lesbian, either. Except, well, if you are one, I don't know if I'd be comfortable going to your house for a sleepover. Just sayin'."

"Geez, Maylee. I'm not gay. It's just that I'm not interested in falling for some guy who's going to love me only until he gets what he wants, then cut out on me."

"Not all guys are like that," she says. "Look at Edward. He wasn't having sex with Bella, and he didn't cut out on her."

I lean over my plate. "Are you freakin' kidding me?"

Maylee's eyebrows vault halfway up her hairline. "No. He *couldn't* have sex with her, or he would have killed her!"

I drop my fork. "It's a novel, Maylee. Fiction! It's not *real*."

"Well, Mrs. Hampton says that all fiction is based on truth."

"Hmmm," I say, as if I just had an epiphany. "No wonder all people with pointy cyeteeth fear sex."

Maylee runs her tongue over her canine teeth.

I roll my eyes. *Just once, I wish I had someone I could really talk to.*

"You're making fun of me," Maylee says.

"No, I'm not," I reply, even if I was. But geez.

So I distract her. "Is there somebody here you like?"

She dips her neck into her shoulders, cranks her head around to check out the lunchroom, then quickly snaps it back. "Don't look now," she says, her cheeks blotchy, "but the boy at the table kitty-corner from us? The one with the real curly brown hair?

"Bless!" she hisses. "Don't look *now*, I told you!"

The boys at that table are the kind to spend their whole lunch hour debating the pH levels of brand-name sodas.

"You mean the one who looks like Napoleon Dynamite?" I ask.

Maylee slaps her hands together and whoops. "Aha, got you! Napoleon Dynamite isn't real, either. He's a movie character. Played by Jon Heder."

"Yep. You've got me there," I say, like I'm shocked at my own stupidity. Because she's gloating, and it's probably the only thing she's had to gloat about in years. Maybe ever.

"Do you talk to him?" I ask. "And I'm not talking about Jon Heder, either."

"Are you kidding? Kenneth Dubble is one of the smartest boys in the school. I wouldn't even know what to say to him. He gets straight As in *Statistics.*" Maylee dips her head and goes back to her food detail.

"So what? You talk with Abby all the time, and he's brilliant." I'm referring to Abby, short for Abhaya, the boy the jocks were jabbing on my first day at Logan High (and at least fifteen other days since). Abby is her only friend besides me. Which means she has one friend more than I've got, which is all right by me.

"That's different," she says. She glances around to make sure no one's eavesdropping, then mouths, *"Abby's gay."*

I roll my eyes. "What does that have to do with it? He's still brilliant, and you talk to him. Yet you're afraid of talking to Dubble? And hey, you can have Abby for a friend, even though he's gay, but you couldn't have me for one if I were gay?"

Maylee looks confused. Like her reasoning on both counts is somehow a mystery to her.

"Never mind," I say. I pick up a nugget and dip it in BBQ sauce. The second lunch period starts in five, and soon the lunch hall monitors are going to start nagging at us to get moving.

"Hey."

I don't need to look up to know who's standing at our table.

Maylee busts out in nervous giggles and clamps her hand over her mouth. The girls at the next table stop talking midsentence to stare, and someone at the cheerleader's table—I think, Stephie—calls out, "Hi, Liam!"

He must acknowledge her with a nod, or maybe a wave, because the girls at her table giggle like Maylee, only they don't hide their teeth as they're doing it.

"I was wondering if I could have your cell number?" Liam asks me.

I keep my head level. "I don't have a cell," I say, my voice (hopefully) sounding disinterested. It's embarrassing to admit that I don't have a phone, considering that even the majority of grade-schoolers have at least a prepaid one.

The cheerleaders crank up the volume of their chatter and giggle to show Liam how fun and cool they are.

"You have a landline? We could at least talk, if we can't text."

I don't want him calling while Jeanie and Shaky are arguing. And I certainly don't want him calling while the boys are under-foot. They might be leaving me alone now for the most part, but if they knew I was talking with a boy, I know it would turn into a free-for-all.

"I'll call you," I say.

I can't believe I'm agreeing to this!

Maylee's got a notebook under her accounting book, so Liam asks her for a scrap of paper. Her ears scald red as she fumbles to separate the lined pages, and she giggles nervously. I don't have a pen on me, and neither does Liam, so he asks to borrow one of those, too. I don't look at him while Maylee paws through her purse, but I can feel him watching me.

Maylee hands him a pen and a half sheet of paper. "Is that too big? That's probably too big."

"It's fine," Liam says. "Thanks."

While Liam's jotting his phone number, Michael Jenkins comes up from behind and bumps him, shoulder on shoulder. "Does your mama know you're giving your phone number out to girls?" Michael taunts.

Liam gives Jenkins a shove. "Least I can give my number out

without having to make the girl wait while I go to settings to find it."

"What? I was drunk. I'm lucky I could remember my name."

I look at Maylee and roll my eyes.

Jenkins' face flushes, and he swaggers off like he's cool or something.

Liam folds the paper into a little wedge. He holds it in front of me, but doesn't let go once I grasp it. I glance up expecting to see a tease in his eyes, a flirt in his grin. But his eyes are serious, his smile sincere. "I really do want to get to know you," he says.

I can't tell if what I'm feeling is fear or excitement. All I know is that I long to talk to someone who doesn't believe that Edward and Bella are real. Someone who doesn't call me Bitch like it's my name. Someone who might even want me in his life.

Liam lets go of the note, and I stand up. "I have to get to class," I say. I shove his number into my jeans pocket, and Liam moves toward the lunch line. The popular girls are watching as he looks back and smiles at me, *what-the-hell?* looks on their faces.

Chapter 8
12th Street

A few seconds ago, I could smell the lunchroom and feel the triangle of paper with Liam's number on it in my hands. Reliving that moment as though I was still living it, with no awareness that it was only a memory. And that's messed up.

My heart is hammering with fear. Fear not only for what's happening to Liam at the moment, but fear for what's happening to me. My stomach is so sick that I have no choice but to stop.

"Gross!" a kid on a bike shouts when he sees me leaned over and gagging. He veers farther into the street to avoid being splattered. But all that comes is dry heaves.

As I straighten up, there, across the street, is an old Victorian house painted the color of Pepto-Bismol. Glass globes line the walkway, and a wind chime with tin cutouts of stars and sliver moons dangles from the eave. Stenciled letters on the front window advertise tarot card readings.

It's the kind of house Maylee expected Verna Johnson to live in. Instead, Verna's house was cramped and Moses-old, slumped and ugly, the siding the kind that looks as rough as a cat's tongue. The yard was empty but for a bird feeder with white globs of bird shit dotting the overgrown grass beneath it. A plastic clothesline sagged between two trees. And the inside didn't smell of incense and oils, as no doubt Maylee expected it to. Instead, it smelled musty. Like an attic with windows that had been painted shut decades ago.

My breaths are coming in pants, and I will my stomach to settle, my mind to stop thinking of Verna Johnson. Because I know if I think of our first visit to her house, I'll cry. And I know if I think of our second visit, I'll scream. And I can't afford to let myself do either. So I tell myself to keep running. Just keep running. And as I run, I grope for a strand of hope that this is all a mistake.

Sure, I'd heard Maylee's voice, her words. But would someone who talked about Bella and Edward as if they were real know the difference between a tangible threat and one created by someone's imagination—either Verna's, mine, or maybe even Aubrey's? Probably not.

Aubrey!

I've never met her (and don't want to, after learning what she did to Maylee), but I've seen her picture: fake, brittle, blond hair, a crooked smile. We had a few Aubreys in school back in Wicks, all of them just like Maylee's cousin. Dumb as a broken motherboard in some ways, yet smart enough to dream up a prank too cruel to be funny, but just mean enough for her to go through with it. No doubt Maylee had told her about Verna's premonition (even though I'd forbidden her from talking about it to anyone, including me). It's possible that somehow Aubrey has Maylee convinced that the premonition is unfolding. Aubrey would be just the type to find someone's gut-clenching fear hysterically funny. I suspect that when I reach the beach, she'll be waiting, Maylee shaking beside her because she's still clueless. And that when Aubrey sees my face and my perspiration-soaked shirt, she's going to start snickering over how easy Maylee and I were to fool.

Maylee will giggle when Aubrey says it, too. Not because

she thinks Aubrey's prank was funny, but because that's what she does when she gets nervous. But I won't laugh. I'll pull every strand of that bitch's straw hair out of her head and shove it at her, telling her to stuff it back up the ass of the scarecrow she stole it from.

I catch the call right before it goes to voice mail. "Maylee?"

"Maylee?" I shout again, my mind already fast-forwarding to the scene I imagine when Liam learns of my overreaction to Aubrey's prank. Him shaking his head, then kissing the top of my head and whispering into my hair his favorite reminder: "Bless, you've got to learn how to just let life be good."

"Bless, where are you? Are you almost here?" Maylee's voice, still choked from shock and sobs, knocks the denial I was clinging to out of my grasp to shatter on the sidewalk. A reminder that hope is an heirloom that nobody left to me.

"I'm coming—what's happening now?" My question is punctuated with laborious huffs.

"I don't know anything more. We're standing out back. I can't find Uncle Joe. If I could only find Uncle Joe."

"Out back of where? Lola's? The Landing?"

I wait. She doesn't answer. "Maylee? Maylee!"

I hold my phone out. The screen is black.

I charged it this morning—didn't I?

I hold the End key down, and the words "Rethink Possible" light the screen. I give a quick glance at the sidewalk, then look back at my phone when my home screen reappears. Then in a blink, "Rethink Possible" taunts me again, and the phone powers down.

Chapter 9
118 Days Ago

I'm in the kitchen staring at the phone, trying to decide if I actually have the guts to call Liam. We've been exchanging a few words in the hall; I promised him I would call this weekend. And I guess there's no better time than now. Jeanie's off playing darts with her all-girls league, and Shaky's snoozing on the couch. Trevor never showed up after school, and Jud is on his laptop. I size up the length of the cord to determine if the receiver will stretch to the back porch. It will. Then quickly, before I lose my nerve, I dial Liam's number and ditch out the door.

He answers on the second ring. "Hey, Bless." I can tell by his voice that he's grinning. He's also munching on something. Maybe Cheetos. Last week while we were talking in the hall after lunch, Richard Peters rammed into him from behind and pushed him into me. Liam had to grab me to keep me from toppling into the lockers. He didn't pull away immediately. Instead, he dipped his head and turned slightly, his breath warm and smelling like Cheetos as it brushed my cheek. "Sorry," he said, though it was obvious he wasn't any sorrier than I was.

I'm not good at making small talk with boys. With anybody, for that matter. And I'm nervous because I know he's going to ask me stuff. Maylee and I have been friends for weeks now, and even though she's told me her whole life's story, I still haven't told her much of mine.

Sure enough, Liam's first sentence is a question. "So, is Bless your real name?"

I roll my eyes. "If I made up a name for myself, you think it would be this one?"

"I think it's cool," he says.

"I hate it."

"Why don't you like it?"

"Just don't. That's all."

I hear some shuffling and picture Liam reaching down between the couch cushions for something. "Would you stop it, already?" he says, with mild-to-moderate irritation.

The hairs on my arms bristle. "Stop what?"

Liam laughs. "Not you. My dog, Peg. He's begging for more popcorn."

"*He?* You have a male dog named Peg?"

"Yeah. He only has three legs. You know, Peg, for peg leg. He gets around pretty good, though. You guys have a dog?"

"No. And I didn't have one back at Wicks, either. Good thing, too."

"Why, don't you like them?"

I don't plan to spill my guts about anything, yet before I know it, I am.

"It's not that," I say. "I love dogs. I love all animals. But George— my grandpa, or so my DNA would say—would have made a dog try to fill his belly on field mice, like the cats, and he would have starved to death. George wouldn't let me or my grandma, Cactus Carol, even throw the cats table scraps."

"Wow," Liam says. "You call your grandma *Cactus Carol*?"

"Yeah. Not only for the obvious reason—because she's about as cuddly as a cactus—but because she doesn't shave her legs. The hairs on them jut straight out from her skin like the spines on a cactus. Like even they are trying to get away from her."

"Gross," Liam says, even as he's laughing.

"Speaking of legs," he says. "When I was ten, I tried making Peg a prosthetic limb. I found this wooden coffee table in the garage and sawed off one of the legs with my dad's hacksaw. Mom was so pissed. I guess she'd picked it up at a thrift shop because it was just like the one they had when she was a kid. She was going to refinish it. Peg wasn't much happier about the leg when I duct-taped it to his stump, either."

I'm bouncing. Not only because I'm laughing harder than I ever thought I could, but because it's early March and so cold I can see my breath.

When my laughter settles down, Liam blurts out with the same ease with which he told the story of Peg's leg, "I tried to hang myself once."

I stop laughing. "You serious? What happened?"

"The shoelace broke."

I kind of laugh. "No. I meant, what happened that you tried it?"

"I don't know," he says. "I'd read this book of essays by this guy who went by the name of Train Wreck. In one of them, he wrote about watching an old movie when he was twelve; it was *Jesus Christ Superstar.* In it, Judas hung himself. So he tried to emulate him, but the shoelace broke and he thumped to the ground. With a name like Train Wreck, I figured he had to be a mess who couldn't do anything right, so I set out to see if I could succeed where he had failed—I know, dumb. So I took a shoelace from my dad's work boot and tried it. I thumped to the ground, too."

Liam laughs, but I don't. I get quiet.

"You still there?" Liam asks.

"Yeah."

"You're not laughing."

"Why would I laugh? That's a sad story."

Liam chuckles. "No it's not. Had I succeeded, *then* it would have been a sad story."

I bite my lip. I'm really getting into him, and now I'm second-guessing if I should.

"You aren't bipolar, or something, are you?"

When Liam speaks again, he sounds as defensive as I feel.

"What? You think I'm a nutjob now, because I did a stupid-assed thing as a kid? All kids think about offing themselves, at least once, don't they?"

"Maybe. But they don't try it just because they read someone else tried it."

Gee, why don't you just call him stupid while you're at it?

"I suppose I was upset about something. I don't know. Let's just drop it, though, okay? Because this subject is getting depressing."

I hold the phone away from my ear so Liam doesn't hear me take a deep breath. *Stop being so tense. So defensive. You're making him defensive. If you're going to talk to him, talk to him!*

"Okay, your turn," Liam says. "I just told you something not everybody knows. What do you have to offer?"

"Not sex, if that's what you're wondering." I cringe, but I keep going. "I don't do that. I'm not about to risk getting an STD, or bringing a kid into this stinking world."

"That's what condoms are for," Liam says, matter-of-factly.

"Yeah, so I've heard. But just so you know, I don't put out. And I don't blow boys in the locker room, either, as I've heard some girls around here do." It's a little embarrassing to be this blunt, but I know that if, down the road, I found out that Liam was only pretending to like me so I'd have sex with them, and I fell for it, I'd be far more embarrassed.

"Okay," he says. "But not like that's a secret. If you put out, everybody and his cousin would know it. What else you got?"

And before I can think of the ramifications, I'm saying, "What do you want to know?"

"Something you wouldn't post online," he says. "Something that tells me who you really are, past a wicked cunnin' girl."

"*Wicked, cunnin'?*"

"Oh, it's how we Mainers talk. Wicked, as in good. And cunnin' means cute."

I almost giggle. Almost. But I'm not about to let myself sound like one of those girls who are tuned to the dumb channel, their minds filled with nothing but white noise. Still, his comment makes me feel warm. So warm that I can only faintly feel the cold seeping through my hoodie anymore.

"Well?" he asks.

"Well, what?"

He laughs. "You're supposed to tell me something about yourself that means something."

I hear Peg whine for more popcorn, and without thought, I blurt out, "I had to leave my cat, Marbles, behind in Nebraska. I swiped food for her when I could. Some nights I can't sleep because I picture her waiting at the back door for me to bring her something." I clear my throat. "I'm afraid she'll keep meowing when I don't come, and George will shut her up with his .22."

"Oh, man," Liam says, the last word dragged out and dipping.

"Yeah, well, that's all I've got. Not very exciting. Certainly not funny. Not really anything." I sound snippy, even though I don't mean to.

"Bless, I didn't say *oh, man* because I thought you told me something stupid. Those words were supposed to say, *Oh, man, that sucks. I'm sorry.*"

"I'd known Marbles longer than I knew the guy who brought me here."

"Your dad?"

"Yeah."

"You didn't want to come to Logan, either, did you?"

"It's not that. It's that my dad didn't want to bring me here. But so what? They didn't want me back in Wicks, either, so it's not like I'm out anything. Besides, Wisconsin, Nebraska, what's the difference? One place is the same as the other."

"You really think so?" Liam asks. "I don't. I think everybody has a place where they belong. A place that will always be home to them. Only some aren't born in that place, so they have to go find it."

His words make my throat constrict, and I swallow to loosen it. "Were you born in the place where you belong?"

"On the shore of it, anyway," he says.

"You talking about Maine?"

"Yeah. Stonington, Maine. A little town on the southern side of Deer Isle."

"You lived on an island?"

"Yeah. I wanted to stay there with my dad, but, well—it's kind of complicated. My folks are 'having problems.' That's how they put it to me. Like I'm five. Mom has always refused to fight in front of me, and my dad doesn't argue, period. He just says what he thinks—or doesn't—and goes about his business. So who knows what's going on there. Mom moved back here where she grew up. How'd she put it? Oh, 'Until things cool down.' Even though if things got any cooler between the two of them, they'd both die of hypothermia."

I think of George and Cactus. Mom and Shaky. Shaky and Jeanie. And I wonder if any couples stay happy, if they ever were to begin with.

"Anyway," Liam says. "Mom was having some issues with her back, and Dad was worried about her being alone—not like she has family here anymore. I didn't want to come, but when my old man says you're doing something, you're doing it. He said I can go back after graduation, whether Mom is ready to go home then or not. At least I got to fish during the peak season and bring Peg to Wisconsin with me. Everything else I love, I had to leave behind."

"Like what?" I ask, hoping he doesn't say a girl.

"I don't know . . . like the smell of saltwater in the wind. The sound of water lapping the boat, gulls squawking overhead. The mist hovering above the water on cold mornings. That sort of thing. Oh, and the lobster."

"The lobster?" *Did he really say that?*

"Yeah. My old man and I are lobster fishermen. It's in my family's blood, and all I've ever wanted to be.

"When I was three, I got a plastic lobster in my Easter basket. The first thing I did was dump out the candy and have Mom tie a piece of ribbon to the basket handle and fill the tub, so I could play lobster fishing. I made the bathroom such a sopping mess from hanging over the tub to bring in my lobster pot that she started making me climb into the tub, rather than kneeling beside it."

I'm smiling. Not only from the image, but because of the way he says some of his words. He doesn't have a really strong accent, yet lobster sounds more like *lob-stah,* and water, like *wa-tah.*

"I was the cleanest little creep in town," he says.

We laugh.

"Dad has a boat, *The Meredith.* And a little lobster company. We weigh the lobster we bring in, and pack and ship them out to restaurants and stores. We buy from a few other fishermen, too. Mom used to work the front desk, selling to the locals and taking orders. She dragged me to work with her when I was little, and every afternoon, I'd go wait on the dock for *The Meredith* to come in. It was like waiting for Christmas."

"That's sweet."

"My old man was forty-six when I was born—he's thirteen years older than my mom—so he's an old geezer now. But you'd never know it. Still fishes every day, year 'round. He rarely docks with his live tank carrying less than the limit. He's one of the best, most well-respected fishermen on Deer Isle. Everybody knows him as 'Captain Frank.'

"One day when I was about six, maybe seven, I was tagging him across the deck, asking him the same questions I asked him every day. How many pounds he'd brought in, how many were hens, how many rags—I had to know everything. My old man stopped, rubbed the top of my head—and I'll clue you in, he's *not* the affectionate kind—and he said, 'You sure do love this business, don't you boy?' I nodded, and he said, 'Good. Because one day, when your old man loses his sea legs, *The Meredith* and the lobster company will be yours.'

"Dad turns sixty-four in July. His back is bad, and his knees and wrists are shot. Plus, the lobster business is struggling. The ocean's warming, and well, I won't get into all that, but there's so many softshelled lobster coming in that the price has plummeted. Old Jib, who runs the hauler on Dad's boat—he's like a grandpa to me—gives me a call from time to time, and he thinks the old man will stack his last lobster pot this year. I called bull. Dad's been saying that for the last five years. When he does retire, though, I'm going to feel bad for him, because the sea is his home. But when that day comes, I'm going to do everything in my power to make him proud. To keep his legacy alive."

Liam is speaking with a passion I know nothing about, and I'm so awestruck I can't speak.

"I'm probably boring you," he says.

"No," I tell him. "I'm mesmerized. I can't imagine how it would feel to know your purpose. To know where home is. To have pride in your father, and know the freedom of being on the ocean."

"It's awesome. And, well, I'm glad I didn't bore you. Most girls wouldn't take the time to listen to stuff like this."

"I'm not most girls," I say. "I'm not bragging. It's just a fact."

There's a short pause that I'm hoping he'll fill soon.

"My first time out, we brought in a blue lobster. Jib said it was a good omen. It meant I was born for the sea."

"A *blue* lobster? Literally, blue?"

"Yeah. Like the color of a blueberry before it fully ripens."

"Seriously?"

"Yeah. The coloration variant is caused by some sort of mutation. I kept a chunk of its shell. I'll show you some time. Anyway, you remind me of a blue lobster."

"So you're calling me a mutant? A defect?"

Liam laughs. "No, no. I just meant that you're like the blue lobster in that you're rare. Rare in that valuable sort of way."

"As rare as a 1972 doubled died obverse penny?" I ask.

"I don't know. How rare are they?" he asks, playfully.

"Rare enough that I've never found one."

Liam laughs. "Well, only about one in every two million lobsters are blue. Girls like you are just as uncommon."

Wow.

Peg starts barking, quick, distressed yips, just as the porch door opens. Shaky's fingers are bobbing the phone cord. "I was wondering why the cord was in the door," he says. His hair is standing on end, his feet bare. He shivers when the night air hits him, and he gives me an I-don't-get-it look.

"I'll let you go and take your dog out," I say to Liam. Because suddenly I'm done talking to him. *He tried to hang himself when he was twelve. He's leaving in the spring. He's not going to stay in my life any more than my mother did. Than Shaky did.*

"I suppose I'd better," he says. "Want to hang out tomorrow? It would have to be during the day, because I've got to work tomorrow night."

"We'll see. I'll call you." I say bye and hang up.

Dad's still standing there. He holds the door open for me, and I slip inside. "A boyfriend?" he asks.

"A friend," I say.

Shaky closes the door, and I kick off my shoes. I head to my room (if you can call it that) and by the time I get there the heat is stinging my toes. I curl on my cot and tuck my feet under the covers. I feel like crying. I don't know why, really, since I should feel happy. But then I think, *maybe hearts are like toes, in that you can't feel them stinging when they're frozen, only when they begin to thaw.*

Nineteen hours later, Liam and I are sitting at a place called Angelo's, where we're going to hang out for an hour and a half while we wait for the next round of movies. I've sipped so much caffeine that I feel like I might jump out of my skin—or maybe it's happiness that keeps my heels popping off the floor. Happiness that came while we were crouched down by the cat pens at the animal shelter, and Liam *got it.*

"So what did you do with your time back in Nebraska?" Liam asks.

"Read, mostly. And I spent a lot of time in the woods."

"I thought Nebraska was all prairie?"

"No. Not all of it. We weren't far from the North Platte River. There are trees there. Not as many as here, but they're there. Pretty boring, huh?"

Liam shrugs. "No. I like trees. And I read. Not a lot, but I do."

"Really? You're a reader?"

He grins. "Well, I read the Harry Potter books anyway."

"All of them?"

His cheeks flush. "No. I watched the movies."

I shake my head, then laugh.

"So what did you do in the woods?" Liam asks, no doubt to get the heat off of himself.

"Just walk, just be," I tell him, because I don't want to say *hide*.

"We all need a place to just be," he says.

Liam takes another slice of pizza and dips his head back to devour the floppy point. He studies me as he chews, and after he swallows, says, "You write poetry?"

"No. Why do you ask? Do I look like one of those moody types who sit around writing bad, sad poetry all day?"

Liam laughs. "No. You just strike me as someone who reflects a lot. Short stories and stuff, then?"

"No. I tried to write a story when I was in fifth grade. I used up most of my math notebook, and Cactus found it and figured out that it wasn't an assignment. She threw a fit because I was wasting paper and refused to buy me any new tablets for the rest of the school year. I had to borrow paper from a kid too timid to say no for a whole semester."

"You didn't have a laptop to write on?"

"Are you kidding me?" I think of Cactus and George bringing me home a laptop, and the thought is so absurd I laugh. "No, I'm right out of the dark ages. No laptop. No tablet. No iPhone, no iPad, no iNothing."

"What about at your dad's?"

"My dad's girlfriend's kids have it all. But they'd beat the crap out of me if I touched their stuff."

Liam gives me one of those I-don't-get-it looks, then says, "Hey, if you love books, I know what you'd love to see. Authors Ridge."

"What's that?"

"This place in Concord, Massachusetts, about five hours from

Stonington, where Hawthorne, Thoreau, Emerson, and Louisa May Alcott are buried."

"You're kidding."

"Nope. In Sleepy Hollow Cemetery."

I start laughing. "That's a real place?"

"Yep. Writers and readers come from all over to visit it. They leave things on the graves. Pens and pencils, notes weighted down with rocks. Things like that."

"I'd love to see that someday."

"And the ocean," he adds. "You've got to see the ocean. You like whales?"

"I wanted one when I was a kid."

Liam laughs.

"Have you seen whales?"

"Of course," he says.

I feel stupid for asking. Because, duh, he fishes on the Atlantic.

Liam looks off and up to the side, his eyes going soft. "Every time I see their massive tails slicing the surface, or their snouts rising up out of the water when they're feeding, I'm always reminded that there's something bigger than all the stupid shit we idiotic humans preoccupy ourselves with. Seeing one always makes me feel . . . makes me feel—"

"Small?" I ask, my voice quiet, thoughtful. "Insignificant. Yet at the same time, a part of something so big. So majestic, that all you can feel is awe?"

Liam's eyes open wide. "Yeah! Yeah, that's it—

"Wait. You've seen a whale in the wild?"

"No. But I've seen the sky."

Our eyes stay locked. And for the first time ever, I wonder if maybe there *is* such a thing as soul mates.

Chapter 10
11th Street

I'm nearing the end of 12th Street when I hear the rise and fall of sirens. The sound saws at my already-frayed nerves. I jerk my head toward the wails. Down a couple tree-lined streets— on Erie, maybe?—an ambulance parts traffic, and a rescue truck follows, the red lettering on its side smearing like blood. In the distance are more sirens coming from the south.

Both Maylee and Liam take Erie when we go to the lake, and when we reach Lakefront Drive, we're always on the widest section of the beach where people spread their blankets, kids make sandcastles, and the bulk of the swimmers and waders go in. I scan my brain, looking for a map of the beach so I can figure out exactly where I'll come out when I get to the end of Mactaw Avenue.

On the north end, but hopefully not so far north that I'll come out where there's nothing but a thin strip of shoreline. Because even if I come out farther south, where the kiddies' playground and restrooms are, I'll still need to run between a quarter to a half of a mile to reach the far southern end where the concrete pier is located, just a stone's throw away from the marina, where a couple of gift shops, an art gallery, Sweet Lola's, and The Landing Supper Club are lined up along the boardwalk.

Maybe I should cut over and follow the rescue vehicles down Erie? But I can't think. Can't reason. Can't decide. The beach is ahead, and that's all I know. So I just keep running straight.

A small rock kicks up and wedges between my toes. But I don't break my rhythm to kick it out of my sandal. The fading sirens tell me that the ambulance is about to reach Liam, and they can't take him before I get there.

And then I hear them. See them. Four, maybe five shiny pennies, tinging the sidewalk from God knows where, three steps-on-a-crack-or-you'll-break-your-mother's-back   ahead of me, even though there's nothing above the sidewalk, but ripples of sweltering air. Pennies! Just as they'd dropped seemingly out of nowhere when we were leaving Verna's that first time.

Maylee had just stepped out the door behind me, when a series of sharp whacks sounded against the rotting floorboards. We looked down to see a scattering of pennies at our feet. Maylee checked her purse, thinking it was open and the pennies had fallen from it. Then she eyed my pockets. But I knew they hadn't come from either place. Pennies that fall on a hard surface scatter and roll and spin before they come to rest on their sides. These hadn't. I reached down and picked one up. It was so warm I almost dropped it. What had sent them careening to the porch floor with such speed that we hadn't seen them falling, then landing flat, was beyond me. I glanced at Verna, who was standing in the doorway, waiting for an explanation.

I don't break my stride, but when I reach the pennies gleaming on the sidewalk, I sweep my arm down and scoop one up. It's not just warm, it's hot. I gawk around frantically— as if what? I'll spot Verna standing erect behind a streetlight pole or crouched behind a parked car? Yet that's what I half expect to see. I can feel her in the air.

I don't have time to check the penny, nor to pick up the rest. But I tuck the one I grabbed into my pocket holding my dead phone, and keep running.

In the distance I can hear the low thumping of drums and the buzzy drone of voices echoing in mics; the festivities are still going on as if nothing awful has just happened. So for a second, I'm tempted to dart back to my hope that this is a prank. But logic kicks me away from that thought. The fact is, the booths and music tents are set up on the widest expanse of beach, a distance from the lighthouse, marina, and board-walk. With a band going, and so much activity, people on the beach would be oblivious to what happened until word spread, mouth by mouth. And no doubt the cops want it that way. Abby said that ten to fifteen thousand people show up for Spring Up. The last thing they'd want is for a crowd that size to panic.

Yet, obviously, some of them know what happened. Somebody had to have heard the gunshot, or seen the gun go off, because I see panic in the faces of a few of the people in vehicles that are fleeing Spring Up.

I'm crossing the road to reach 10th Street when the signal of one such car warns me that they're about to turn right. The driver doesn't seem to notice that I'm in the middle of the street. The woman beside him doesn't seem to, either. Her mouth is yapping, her dark eyebrows are bunched.

As the car turns in front of me, I get a glimpse into the backseat where a little girl propped on a booster seat holds a pinwheel; Sweet Lola's gives away free pinwheels to kids on Spring Up day. The girl is crying, the blades of her pinwheel motionless. As the car finishes its turn, I look through the rear window and see the mother's arm coming over the seat to comfort the girl. The sight makes a dry sob erupt from my throat; I know that if Liam should die, my mother won't be here to comfort me.

Then, in an instant, a breeze kicks up, and I'm smelling lilacs.

My gaze crisscrosses the street, looking for bushes plump with lavender blossoms, petals scattered on the grass. But there are no lilac trees here.

Lilacs!

Verna Johnson talked about lilacs!

I was so convinced beforehand that I knew exactly how that visit would go. Verna would say some general crap about how my mom loved me and was proud of me. Stuff any carnival psychic with half a heart would say to a girl with a dead mom. It would be a joke, of that I was sure. But I'd chosen to go anyway, because, well, how could I not? Maylee believed she was about to give me a Mother's Day miracle. And I couldn't rain on her parade, just because life had pissed on mine.

Maylee and I stood at the hood of the car when we finally got to the end of Verna's long driveway. She grabbed my arm, her fingernails biting into my skin. "What if your mom, you know, comes right into the room and we can see her? I know she's your mom and all, so she shouldn't be scary, but she's . . . well, dead."

She looked so scared that I almost laughed. Instead, I reassured her that we wouldn't see a ghost. So Maylee tried a different tactic—reminding me that her dad made Mother's Day dinner reservations for seven o'clock, and she still had to shower and change. I reminded her that that was five hours away, and assured her she'd make it home with plenty of time to spare.

But I was wrong about that, too.

I could tell Maylee was ready to turn around and dash to the car, so I moved to block her if she tried. Because as much as I didn't want to admit it to myself, much less to her, when I'd seen the simplicity of Verna's house, I felt a spark of hope that maybe she wasn't a fake after all.

As it turned out, I didn't need to block Maylee's path. Not after she glanced down and spotted a garter snake slicing through the shaggy lawn, just inches from our feet. Maylee bolted for the porch, screaming and shaking her hands as if there were snake scales stuck under her fingernails.

I'd just reached the porch when Verna opened the door. Maylee's face lit up like a kid seeing Snow White at Disney World, and she blinked at me with a can-you-believe-it? look. It hadn't dawned on her that maybe it was her scream, louder than a howler monkey's, that tipped Verna off that we'd arrived.

Bent over like a question mark, Verna was still a good four inches taller than I. Pewter strands clung to her scalp like cat hair on a pink couch. And when she said hello, her colorless lips pulled back to show baby-bare gums.

Maylee smiled back at Verna, her whole body sighing with relief. That's how Maylee is about people. If they smile, they're good (which explains why she gets pranked and poked fun of so often).

There's a honk to remind me that although my thoughts are racing, I'm not. I'm still standing in the middle of the street.

I realize how I must look, my arms flailing, my eyes no doubt showing that faraway look that says I don't quite know where

I am. And the last thing I need is someone calling the cops because they think I'm in trouble. I raise my hand in a quick apology.

More sirens. God.

I hurry to the curb, my breaths heavy, sweat beading along my hairline.

Okay, maybe I didn't exactly take Verna to be some evil witch capable of casting spells on any innocent Gretels who happened to wander into her yard, but I wasn't convinced Verna was harmless, either. I didn't like the way she pinched her watery gray eyes half closed when she looked at me, that first time.

Verna introduced herself, using only her first name. She asked which of us was Maylee, which was Bless, in a voice that seemed to believe that it had all the time in the world. But she didn't take her eyes off me the whole time Maylee answered. "Have you been here before, dear?" she finally asked me.

I shook my head.

"Hmmm. You look familiar."

She watched me for a while longer, then asked where her manners were and invited us in.

She led us through a tiny kitchen and into a living room cramped with an ancient piano and other old junk. Grandma Moses–style portraits on cardboard that had buckled with time were propped on shelves, small tables, and affixed to the walls with thumbtacks. Blotches of white, green, or red paint were intentionally smeared over the temples, foreheads, or throats of the subjects. The whole house smelled like my old doll with the bashed-in eye.

Verna took a chair, grass green, and pointed at the two old chairs facing hers. I sat down first, then looked up to see what was taking Maylee so long. She was fumbling to untangle her purse strap from her hoodie, which she'd peeled off, no doubt, because the house was about one hundred degrees.

Once Maylee was settled, Verna made small talk. She asked who our families were, talked about how much Logan has changed over the years, and mentioned that her hair used to be as thick and dark as mine.

Finally, she asked, "So what can I help you girls with today?"

Maylee cleared her throat, then blah, blah, blahed about my mom dying . . . Mother's Day . . . any messages. And the whole time she was blathering, Verna was watching me with pinched eyes that had gone foggy again.

Verna leaned toward me, cutting Maylee off. "I can't force the spirits to talk, you know. I can invite them to, and if they have something to say and are able to get through, they will. But I have to warn you, these aren't parlor games. I see whatever the spirits want me to see. Sometimes it's comforting, sometimes it's not. The question is, do you want to know everything the spirits show me?"

Maylee flinched. Like maybe she was suddenly wishing she'd gotten me a candle, or made me a bracelet for a sorry-your-mom's-dead-on-Mother's-Day gift instead.

"Whatever you see," I answered, though I squirmed when I said it.

I was buying into the whole thing at that point. Well, until Verna pulled a lopsided TV tray on wobbly wheels in front of her, and yanked a faded dish towel up to reveal a crystal ball. A crystal ball? REALLY?

Who knows? Maybe Verna read my mind as I scoffed in my head, because she chuckled slightly and told me that the crystal was only something to focus on, while her third eye looked at what the spirits wanted her to see, hear what the spirits wanted her to hear.

She peered closer to the orb, and Maylee leaned over, too, as if she half expected to see Auntie Em and flying monkeys in it. Verna shot her a frown, and Maylee leaned back in her chair and crossed her hands on her lap like she'd been scolded for looking at her neighbor's paper.

The room went silent, but for the soft ticking of an old clock on the end table next to Verna's chair, the hands reading six minutes after one.

It seemed we sat like that forever, waiting for something to happen. Yet according to the clock, not even a minute had passed. Then the room went cold. So cold that I half expected our breaths to appear. I glanced over at Maylee to see if she'd noticed, and she held out her arm to show me that it was nubbed with goose bumps.

Verna didn't look up when she explained, "Rooms always go cold when spirits enter them. If we were outside, the wind would kick up, too."

Maylee's eyes started darting. She reached over and grabbed my hand.

The first image Verna saw was a young woman with auburn hair (my mother, she claimed), holding a dark-haired baby (me) next to a lilac bush. She was bending a blossom to my baby nose and showing me how to sniff because she loved the scent of lilacs.

Verna saw more images of the two of us—or so she claimed. Every scene so generic that they could have belonged to any mom and her kid. I forced myself to look entranced every time I felt Maylee glance at me, but what I was thinking was that I hoped she wasn't paying Verna for this.

I doubt I would've believed one thing Verna said, had she

not looked up then and told me that mom smiles at how I wipe my feet when I step outside. And that when I go for walks, she watches over me like the stars. The second she said it, a tingling started in my feet and rippled like northern lights all the way up to the top of my head. Verna couldn't have known those things. Maylee didn't even know them.

Verna peered in closer, her head cocking just slightly, as if she were listening to whispers. She saw my mother sitting up in bed. Mom had a black stuffed toy—a skunk, Verna concluded once she saw the white stripe—and Mom was holding it to her face as she cried. "The poor thing is so afraid," Verna said.

I fidgeted on my chair, wrestling with tears I wasn't about to cry. Why would Mom want me to see something like this?

Mom had something on her lap, Verna said, but she couldn't see what it was from that angle. A book maybe? No, a calendar, Verna speculated, because Mom was telling her that it was used for marking time. Verna could see Mom's thin wrist rotating slowly, even as she cried.

The minute Verna said that, I knew what Mom was holding. The penny folder! And that it was her finger that had worn down the sides of that hole!

Verna cocked her head again, then said slowly, "She's showing me this so you'll understand that she knows the heartache that comes from having a mother born in the year of the doubled die."

Maylee gasped, and my head hurt as my scattered thoughts scrambled to connect with each other.

My thigh muscles tightened and I wanted to run. But Verna told me to stay put. Maylee reached over for my hand again. Hers was clammy. Mine probably was, too.

The picture was fading, Verna claimed, but another was forming.

Verna saw Mom lying in a different bed, a scarf tied around her head. She said Mom looked frail and sickly, but that there was a gentle peace about her. A halo of pure light.

Verna could see her handing a plastic store bag wrapped around something book-shaped, to a woman with curly hair who stood beside the bed. Verna didn't know what was in the bag, or who the woman was, but the woman stepped back and was shaking her head because she didn't want to take it. But my mother insisted.

The penny folder. It had to be what was in the bag. And the woman—Grandma Gloria? She was the one who packed it in my bags.

Verna looked up then. "She wants you to find it. Do you understand what that means?"

I nodded.

Verna's eyes went intense, and she tilted her head slightly and listened again. "She is warning you to not forget what she is about to say."

I waited, not bothering to try to breathe.

"She says the doubled die will come to you unexpectedly. Someone will place it in your hand. And when a penny drops, you'll understand the nature of fear."

Verna said that Mom was gone then, and the exhausted mystic sagged back against her chair.

Maylee stayed sitting erect, her face pale with shock, her eyes glassy. "What does that mean—the double die stuff?"

"That is for Bless to say," Verna told Maylee. "I am the conduit. Nothing more."

Maylee looked at me with cold dread. I knew the word "die" was enough to have her seeing me in a casket, my hands folded, my eyes sewn shut.

As Verna dropped the dishcloth over the crystal ball and

pulled the TV tray back beside her chair, Maylee started bab-
bling. But I was too stunned, too confused to hear what she
was asking. I only zoned back in when Verna was answering,
"Oh, dear girl, where the dead reside, time does not exist."

Just like it didn't exist in her house? Like it doesn't appear
to be existing on this sidewalk? For a fleeting second, I crazily
wonder if maybe that truck on 15th Street did hit me, and I'm
dead, too, but don't know it yet.

I shake the insane thought away and divert my mind to
the scent of lilacs, hanging so heavily in the air now that I can
taste it on my tongue. Yes, that's what I'll remember. Not the
sad image of my mom crying into a stuffed toy. Not the eerie
riddle I still haven't figured out, nor the reason those pennies
dropped as we were leaving. I'd picked one up while Maylee
was busy checking the zipper on her purse. I looked at Verna,
standing in the doorway. She was grinning with glossy gums,
like we were sharing a private joke, and I already knew the
punch line. Though I didn't.

Maylee and I picked up the rest of the pennies after Verna
went inside. All of them were warm, but not one was the penny
Mom wanted me to find. "These aren't parlor games," Verna
had said. But the peculiar smirk on her face right before she'd
closed the door said that maybe they were.

The breeze gets stronger then, picking up a few stray leaves
and skipping them across the pavement. I relish the cooling
wind against my hot skin, and the way the lilac scent makes
me feel. Like my mom is with me. Watching over me. I plead
with her to pick me up and fly me with her angel wings down
to the water. But then, shocked that I'd asked such a childish
favor, I ask her instead to watch over Liam until I get there. To
remind him that he has so much to live for.

The scent, the feeling, the brush of cooling breeze, it lasts for a block, and then, just like that, the scent whooshes away.

Chapter 11
117 Days Ago

I must still be smiling when I get in the house after Liam drops me off, because Shaky, who wasn't home when I left, notices. "That a boy who dropped you off?" he asks.

"Yeah."

"Who is he?"

"Liam Reid. He's not from here. He's from Maine." Shaky looks suspicious, like I'd just said he was from Mars. So I add, "His dad is a lobster fisherman. Liam is, too."

That reels Shaky in, as I knew it would. "That right? Did you tell him about my boat?"

Shaky doesn't wait for my answer. "Man, Bless. You should see The Carol. Like Oiler says, she's got character. She needs a little work, but she's going to be a beaut when I'm done fixin' her up."

I glance around but don't see Jeanie. The shower's going. It has to be her. And hopefully she can't hear this conversation, or when she gets out all hell will break loose again. Oiler's still not back from Florida, which means Shaky still doesn't have the title. Jeanie's been bitching about that fact for two weeks now, and Shaky still hasn't called Oiler's son to find out what's going on. She's livid that Shaky's putting time and money into a boat that's not legally his yet.

It's not like me to beg, but when Dad finally stops yammering about The Carol (gag), I ask him, "Do you think I could get a cell phone? Jeanie's the one who brought it up. Last week. She said it wouldn't cost much to add another line. But I think she forgot about it."

Shaky blinks, like he can't figure out why a seventeen-year-old girl who just got home from a date might want her own phone. Then he shrugs. "Well, I suppose. I'll talk to Jeanie about it. If she's willing to pay for it, why not? The boys have one."

The boys are in the living room watching a movie when Trevor shouts out, "Hey, Gilligan. Somebody's coming up the drive."

I follow Shaky into the living room, hoping it's Maylee, since I already warned her that even though I'd be home early because Liam had to be at Taco Bell by six o'clock for his shift, I wouldn't be calling her until everyone turned in for the night. A dumb thought, really, since coming to my place once was probably enough for Maylee. Shaky and Jeanie were cussing at Trevor, and Jud called Jeanie ugly right to her face. After meeting her family, I knew why she'd practically run out. Maylee's house and family are what you'd see in a Disney movie. The first time I was there, her dad was watching the Packers and drinking beer in his recliner— *root* beer. "Gosh dang it," he said, when a receiver dropped a pass. And Maylee's mom, who was baking Toll House cookies from scratch, actually scolded him for *cursing* in front of us. So I'm not surprised to see that it's a guy in a beat-up pickup pulling into the drive, steam rolling out from under the hood, rather than Maylee.

Shaky hurries to the door and slips his bare feet into his boots. As he's going out the door, I hear him shout, "You came to the right place, buddy!" He opens the door a crack after he closed it, to free his dangling shoelace.

Shaky is pathetic. I know it, and obviously Jeanie's brats do, too. But *Gilligan*? I glare at Trevor. "The next time you call Shaky *Gilligan*, I'm going to pound the crap out of you." Trevor flips me off without taking his eyes off the TV.

After dinner, the boys wander off to play World of Warcraft III, and I go into the kitchen to clean. Dad and Jeanie are cuddling on the couch, watching TV. Shaky's all happy because he made a few bucks putting a used radiator into the desperate guy's car. Jeanie seems happy, too. Maybe because Shaky isn't drunk for a change.

Nobody goes to sleep around this place before eleven on weeknights, and whenever they please on weekends. But I want to call Maylee to tell her about Liam taking me to the animal shelter, and how he took my hand when we were leaving the Marcus and pouted because he was sorry he didn't buy Twizzlers (which has me wondering how I can get my hands on a bag before school on Monday). I glance at the clock; it's 11:06. I'm afraid Maylee will be asleep before they all turn in.

I'm so energized that I get the dishwasher loaded in record time. Then, while I'm wiping off the counters, I see Trevor's phone sitting by the toaster. I glance down the hall, where I can hear him belittling Jud for failing to kill somebody. I bite my lip, then snatch the phone. I'll just delete the call from his log (can't be hard to figure out), then sneak it back on the counter when I'm done.

His phone is gross with fingerprints, so I swipe it down with an antibacterial wipe and slip off to my room. The TV's on so loud, no one will hear me.

As I dial Maylee's number, I decide I'll stay cool about my date. I don't want to sound desperate. Even to Maylee.

Maylee listens, but she doesn't swoon, like I expect her to. And she doesn't interrupt to ask if he kissed me, either. So I stop before I even get to the part where we're leaving the theater and he took my hand, and I ask her, "What's up with you tonight?"

"Nothing," she claims.

She's lying.

I press her, and finally she blurts out, "Mom says it's not a good idea to interfere with somebody else's relationship. But, oh, I feel so awful, you being my BFF."

"What are you talking about?"

She groans like she's got a toothache.

"May-lee. Tell me."

"Okay . . . okay. I ran to the store for Mom tonight—it was around five thirty, maybe five forty—"

"And?"

"Bless, on my way there, I saw Liam's car parked in front of Stephie Dillon's house." I can feel her cringing. "Stephie lives just two blocks over from me, in the rich neighborhood. I go right past her place on my way to the IGA."

I roll my eyes. "Geez, Maylee. It's not like Liam's the only one who drives a black Yukon."

"He was coming out of her house, Bless," she says, her voice rising like a stringed instrument being tuned to crazy.

"It had to be pitch-dark by that time. It was probably someone who looks like him."

"The yard light was on, Bless. And Stephie came out with him. They were both laughing."

I freeze.

Liam had to get to work. That's what he told me.

"Boy, I wouldn't have taken Liam for a cheater," Maylee says. "He seems so nice."

Maybe he only likes me as a friend. He didn't try to kiss me when he dropped me off, even if I wanted him to. Or maybe he IS a cheater, only I'M the one he's cheating with.

"I checked out Stephie's tweets," Maylee says. "She mentioned them stopping for Twizzlers tonight. I'm sorry, Bless. I didn't want to tell you. But I didn't want to *not* tell you, either."

My heart flips over to expose its rough side. And when I speak again, my voice is hoarse. "It's okay. I mean, it's not like we're going out because we hung out for one day. No big deal. We had fun. End of story. Like I said, I'm not interested in getting involved."

I pretend Jeanie's calling me from the living room and tell Maylee I have to go.

"Maybe I should have kept my big mouth shut," she says.

"No, I'm glad you told me." And I mean it. Then I slip into the part I don't mean: "Like I said, no big deal."

The second I get back to the kitchen, Trevor is on me, struggling to get his phone out of my hand. "Thieving bitch!" he shouts as he grabs it. Then he starts pummeling me.

I can't help yelping when he socks me hard on the back. "Touch my phone again, and I'll kill you!" He grabs a handful of my hair. That's when I go nuts, slapping and scratching at him until he's the one yelling *Ow! Ow!*

Jeanie screams from the other room, "Damn it, you kids stop that fighting!"

I stomp off, almost glad for my throbbing back. At least now, I have an excuse if I should start crying.

At George and Cactus's, I went to school even when I had fevers high enough to make my teeth chatter, just to get out of the house. But on Monday, with Jeanie working, Shaky off messing with his boat, and the boys in school, staying home seems like a better option than spending the day pretending I don't care if Liam Reid and I are done before we started.

By noon, I'm wishing that I could skip school every day. I've done four loads of laundry (clothes that everybody just flings into my room, not caring if they land on my bed or on the floor) and polished the living room furniture and vacuumed. Then I try to read. But it's useless.

I can't stop thinking about how Liam said he had to get to work, then instead, went straight to Stephie's. *Stephie, of all people!*

The phone rings, and I glance at the clock. Maylee would be

finished cubing her lunch by now, and has six minutes until World History class starts. So I pick up.

"You sick?" she asks.

I hoist myself up to sit on the counter. "Yeah."

"Bad?"

"No."

"Man, Bless. I can't believe that Liam had the guts to ask me where you were this morning. I couldn't even look him in the eye."

"You can never look him in the eye," I remind her.

"You know what I mean.

"It made me wish that I was more like you. If I was, I would have called him a dirty rotten cheater boy whore."

Miserable or not, I laugh out loud. *Maylee will probably wash her own mouth out with soap when she gets home.*

"I would have called him that," she insists. "And Stephie something even worse, when I saw her chasing him down in the hall."

My stomach clenches. "I've got to go, Maylee. My stomach's sick."

I flop on the couch and cover myself with a throw. I click the TV on, then off, and lie in the quiet, my hands clasped behind my head. I watch water from icicles drip from the eaves for a time, then decide to go outside.

We've had a few warmer days now, and one glance at the glossy crust sitting over the snow in the field tells me that I won't break through on my way to the ridge of pines. I watch the sky as I walk, and try to remember that there's something bigger than my crummy problems. But thinking that only makes me think of Liam. So I watch my feet instead.

I climb up the hill and find a stump to sit on. I close my eyes. The trees are singing as the breeze blows through them, the sound working on me like a lullaby. Yes, this will be my refuge. My hiding place. As for Liam, forget him. I don't need a boyfriend.

And I certainly don't care if anyone at school thinks I'm a loser because I don't have one. I'm not scared of being alone. I've been alone all my life, and I've done just fine.

I sit until I'm breathing without effort, and my fingers and toes are stinging, then I head back to the house. And as I walk over the packed snow, I vow to go back to being like I was before I met Liam. Like snow after it's been warmed just enough to start melting, then becomes frozen hard again. Compressed. Impenetrable.

CHAPTER 12
114 DAYS AGO

I've refused to talk to Liam for three and a half days now. Even tossed the note he passed through Maylee in the trash without reading it. But now I'm coming out of Phys Ed, and he's standing there with his hands stuffed in his pockets, leaning against the wall, obviously waiting for me. "Bless," he calls when he spots me.

The hall is short and narrow, and so cramped with girls leaving the locker room that there's no escape route when Liam steps in front of me. "I don't get it, Bless," he says. "I had the best time on Saturday. I thought you did, too. Why are you avoiding me?"

I dart around him.

"Move it!" I snap at the cluster of girls blocking my escape, flipping their damp hair and tugging at their clothes in an effort to put themselves back together before we spill into the main hall. I'm stalled just inches ahead of Liam, aching to turn and both hug him *and* slap him, when, wouldn't you know it, Stephie Dillon turns. "Hi, Liam!" she squeals. She bumps me aside to get to him, and Misty Brown and Melissa Smith snub me as they pass. "Thanks a million for helping me with my algebra last night. I got a B on the quiz. I would have done better, but I forgot—"

My jaws are clamped tight enough to splinter my molars. I squeeze between the chubby girls who always take a table next to the cheerleader's table (either to listen in on their gossip, or to pretend they're a part of them, I'm not sure which). I hug the wall as I push forward.

"I gotta run, Stephie," I hear Liam say. I slip into the main hall that's crowded with kids moving like cattle. I don't get far before Liam catches up. He takes my arm. "Bless, come on. Tell me why you're doing this."

I'm so steamed it feels like my eyes are going to pop right out of my head. And to make it worse, Stephie, Misty, and Melissa pass, yucking it up like The Three Stooges. They don't stop, but Stephie calls out, "See you tonight, Liam." Liam doesn't take his eyes off me, when he answers her with, "Yeah."

I skirt around him and start walking again. "Bless, come on! Why are you brushing me off?"

I spin around. "Seriously?" I hiss. "You have to *ask*?"

He gives me a boy blink—that vacant *What?* look they get when they just don't get it.

I move in closer, my whole body a trembling mess.

Don't cry. Don't cry. Don't cry.

"Look," I say, my finger in his face. "I don't know what kind of a game you're playing with me, but if a girl who calls it a great day if her hair doesn't frizz after blowing half the football team in a steamy locker room is your type, then fine. Go for it. But leave me alone!"

(Abby filled me in about Stephie and her sidekicks. Maylee didn't know if was true or not, but it seemed like something they'd do to keep their popularity.)

Liam scratches his head and squints his eyes like he's trying to figure out what I'm talking about. Then his mouth morphs into a circle. He jabs his thumb in the direction Stephie headed and says, "You mean, her? Stephie Dillon?"

"Uh, duh—you think? You left what I assumed was a date on Saturday and went straight to her house. Even though you told me you had to work. And obviously, you were with her again last night."

Liam looks relieved. *Relieved!*

"Bless, her mom and mine were friends in high school, and they've reconnected now that Mom's back. Stephie's car was in the garage on Saturday, and her mom had a meeting and couldn't drive her to dance class. She called our house to see if I could drop her off on my way to work. And last night, her mom had my mom and me over for dinner. Stephie's struggling in algebra and had a quiz coming up, so I helped her after we ate. There wasn't anything else to do."

"And tonight?"

"I'm going over there to snow blow their driveway. Mr. Dillon is in China on business, and the kid who usually does it didn't show up yesterday."

"How convenient," I say.

Liam makes a half turn and runs his hand through his hair. He shakes his head and turns back to me, looking puzzled. "You know, I wouldn't have taken you for somebody like this."

I don't even know what he means, but still the statement cuts me like a razor. "Like what?"

"Well, someone who jumps to conclusions. Who doesn't just ask outright if she's questioning something."

All around us, the pace is picking up, kids hurrying to get to their classrooms before the second bell. I blink rapidly. "What right did I have to ask you anything? It's your life. We hung out for a few hours—big deal."

"It was a big deal to me," he says. He actually looks like he means it.

I look away, suddenly so embarrassed that I want the floor to crack open and swallow me. But Liam sighs and puts his hand under my chin, forcing me to look up at him. "I guess I probably would have thought the same thing, if the tables had been turned.

"As far as Stephie goes—" But he doesn't get to finish because

Michael Jenkins butts him with his shoulder and says, "Hey, Reid, you ready to pummel Spats and Pinky Dick Peters again with a little two-on-two after lunch?"

I wait, as Richard Peters starts trash-talking Liam and Michael from down the hall, making those still in it laugh—including Liam.

I wait, fuming that Liam should be laughing about anything right now. Waiting, hoping he'll tell me that he was pissed that he had to drive Stephie. Annoyed when he got roped into going to her house for dinner and tutoring her. And furious that he's been suckered into snow blowing their driveway tonight. I'm waiting for him to say that he knows that Stephie is a stupid slut, who really just wants to blow him, and that she doesn't have a chance with him. But instead, when he's done horsing around with the guys, he says, "Look. Stephie's okay. But we're just friends. Got it? It's you I'm interested in."

I've got a textbook and a notebook cradled in front of me, but Liam moves in as close as he can get. He takes his index finger and runs it softly along the side of my hand and up my sleeve. "I haven't been able to think about anything but you since Saturday," he whispers.

After that, all I want to do is get on my tiptoes and kiss him. But the warning bell is ringing and all the kids have ditched into their classrooms to make the last bell. "Can I drive you home after school?" Liam asks quickly.

I nod.

Behind us, women's heels are cracking the hall like a whip. "Get to class, you two," Mrs. Pell, the English teacher, snaps as she passes, her face pinched with disapproval. Either because she's never been in love, or was, but fell out of it and landed on her head. Just like I'm afraid I'm going to do.

After school, Liam and I are heading to his car, as Stephie,

Misty, and Melissa are heading to theirs. Stephie sees us and starts yakking at her friends, her hand waving as if she's saying, "He probably got roped into driving her." She's acting all cool about things, until she sees Drake Collin's car parked next to hers. Then she looks annoyed. Drake was once Stephie's boyfriend—which I found impossible to believe when Maylee told me. He hardly seemed like Stephie's type, with his twisted back, and one leg dragging funny when he walks. And that hair, long and so dirty you can't tell what color it is. But I guess in his sophomore year, he was All State in football—and popular. Abby pointed him out to me in the State Championship photo tucked in the trophy case by the principal's office, and admitted that Drake was so hot back then that even *he* was interested in him, even though jocks typically aren't his type. Drake crashed his motorcycle last summer, though, and almost died. Now he walks the halls like a ghost nobody sees. And according to Stephie, he won't leave her alone.

The second Liam and I slip into his Yukon, I forget about Stephie and her diva dramas. About everything but Liam.

He asks if I want to slip over to the beach and walk out to the lighthouse. The ice might still be edging the shoreline, but Liam says he stops there every night when he doesn't have to race to work.

Lake Michigan. I've only seen it twice since I moved here. Once during the day, and once at night. But both times, only from Lakefront Drive when it was snowing so heavily that I couldn't even see the lake.

"Wow," I say, when we get there. "It's huge!"

"Three hundred and ten miles long," Liam says, "and a hundred and ten miles wide."

I turn to Liam, my eyes stretched so crazy-wide that the corners hurt. "I thought it would look like a lake—but look at this!" I point across the water, where the lake meets the sky. "It looks like an ocean!"

Liam laughs, "Pretty much."

"But with smaller waves, I suppose," in case the comparison was stupid.

"Yeah. But somebody told me that when the winds blow from the northeast, or the west, southwest, the open water swells can reach twenty-four feet or more."

Liam wants to walk out to the lighthouse. There's an inch of snow packed over the concrete, and no guardrails. But I don't want Liam to know I'm scared. I've already disappointed him once. So I just nod and smile like I think it's a great idea.

We walk with our backs against the whipping wind. Water is beating against the boulders propped against the pier, but I feel safe because Liam has his arm around me.

When we reach the lighthouse, Liam leans his back against it and stares out over the water with such longing that it's almost painful to see. Then he slips his hands inside my coat and pulls me to him. We kiss until our winter-cold lips soften and our bodies are warm.

CHAPTER 13
81 DAYS AGO

On Saturday, I go home with Maylee, where I'll wait for Liam, who has to work until eight.

Maylee's mom is at the stove, stirring a pot of chili. Pats of butter are melting over a pan of cornbread on the counter. And I'm not kidding, there's an apple pie in the oven. I'm curious to see how Maylee plans to cube her chili.

Maylee and I go up to her room, which looks like it belongs to a ten-year-old girl. The walls are lavender, the ceiling pale pink and dotted with glow-in-the-dark stars. Her bedspread and pillows are splotched with the same multicolored polka dots as the ruffled curtains. The first time I came here, I looked around, expecting the walls to be plastered with boy-band posters. Instead, what I saw were big butterflies, their wings made out of pastel netting and sprinkled with glitter. Maylee had made them from a craft kit. She loves craft kits.

The house is warm, but Maylee is still wearing a sweatshirt over at least two other layers, even when it's warm enough that I'm only wearing a T-shirt with my jeans. I flop on her bed while she feeds her goldfish and tell her that Mr. Wilks paired me with Kenneth Dubble for next week's science lab. Her eyes get huge. "I'm glad it isn't me!"

"Why? You're the one who likes him."

"Because, he's so smart! Before the first class was even over, he'd know just how dumb I am."

"You get Bs and Cs in science," I remind her. "What's wrong with that?"

"But I'm in environmental science. You guys are in physics."

Maylee spots one of her bras peeking out from under her purple bed skirt, and almost lands on her head trying to fetch it before I see it. "Geez, Maylee. Kenneth isn't peeking out from my backpack, you know."

I grab one end of the white mom-bra, and it stretches like a slinky. "Wow, look at the cup size on this baby. Who would have guessed that you have boobs *this* size hiding under those layers?"

I let go of it and the bra pings back to her. She looks ready to cry as she rolls it and stuffs it in her drawer.

"Geez, Maylee. I'm a girl. What's the big deal about me seeing your bra?"

She shrugs, her head down.

"Let me guess—back in junior high, while other girls were buying padded push-up bras to look like they had more, or any at all, you were binding your nubs with ACE Bandages."

She doesn't laugh, so I nudge her, trying to get her to.

She doesn't.

"Hey, when Kenneth and I are working together, do you want me to put in a good word for you?"

Her cheeks flush. "Don't you dare!"

I shrug. "Your choice."

Maylee's got a heap of teen movie magazines on her nightstand. I pull one off the stack and start paging through it. The boys in them look like they're twelve! Maylee points out the ones she thinks are hot and gives me their bios.

"If you and Liam were famous, you'd be on the cover of these magazines."

"Yeah, I suppose we would be. That's usually where famous teens end up, isn't it?"

Maylee actually gets my jest. "Come on, you know what I meant. But really. You guys make such a cool couple. And your story is so romantic."

"Yeah, well, until Liam graduates and goes back to Maine."

"Oh, Bless," Maylee says, her voice sticky with sympathy.

I flip the magazine page and point to the first toothy smile I see. "Who's this?" I ask, just to change the subject, or I'm going to get really sad.

But Maylee doesn't bite. Instead, she looks down at her hands, which are limp on her lap, and says, "Bless? Can I ask you something personal?"

"Sure. Doesn't mean I'll answer, though."

She squirms and her face pinkens. "Have you and Liam, you know, done it?"

I can't believe she just asked me this!

"Where would we have done it? At the animal shelter? In the theater? In my locker?"

"I suppose. But—are you going to when you get the chance?"

I shrug, even though I know the answer. Yes. Not any time soon, I hope, but I know it's coming. I knew it the second he slipped his hands inside my coat to pull me against him at the lighthouse. And again, when he brought me home at two this morning, and gave me what was supposed to be a good-bye kiss. I didn't get as far as the steps, when I looked back. I could barely see him leaning against his car since the yard light wasn't on, but I could feel him watching me. Pulling me back to him. So I went back and pressed myself against him, licking his bottom lip before sticking my tongue in his mouth. Our kisses got harder and hotter, and I could feel him, swollen and throbbing against my belly. We were both panting when I pulled away, a little embarrassed. And that's when I knew that Liam would be my first. The thought both excited and scared me. Excited me for the obvious reasons. Yet scared me, because when it happens, it will probably be the beginning of the end.

Maylee looks down to where her fingers are twisting on her lap. "I've only been kissed by one boy. And, well . . . I hated it."

I think of my crazy-wild physical reaction to Liam's kisses, and his hands when they're running over me, even though it's over my clothes. "Then you must have not liked the boy very much," I say.

Her face pinches with distress. "I didn't like him at all!"

"Then why did you kiss him?"

"It wasn't my idea," she protests.

Then she spills her guts. Maylee's family had gone to Illinois to spend Christmas with her dad's family. They stayed with her aunt, and Maylee hung out with her cousin, Aubrey. Aubrey dragged her to a party, where everybody was drinking beer and smoking pot.

"I didn't even want to be there when I saw what kind of a party it was."

"Considering what Aubrey's like, what did you think they were going to do? Play Twister and eat Rice Krispies treats?"

Maylee shrugs. *Jesus, that is what she thought!*

"Well, I didn't know she was *that* wild. She and her boyfriend were going to slip off into a bedroom. I think to have"—she gives the door a quick glance, then mouths the word—*"sex."*

"There was a couple on the couch and he was sucking on her . . ." Maylee uses her eyes to point to where her boobs are hiding. "Well, you know."

I mimic a TV censor; *"Bleep. Bleep."* Maylee stops and looks confused. "Never mind," I tell her. "Go on."

"Well, I didn't have anyone to talk to. Everybody was paired up. But right before Aubrey slipped off with her boyfriend, she stopped and whispered something to this guy named Todd. She took something out of her pocket and gave it to him. I don't know what it was. Maybe a five dollar bill—or maybe some pot. At the time, I thought maybe it was to help pay for the beer she was guzzling, but now I'm wondering. Because he kept looking at me after she walked away."

I roll to my side and prop my head on my hand. "You think she paid him off to spend some time with you? You serious?"

Maylee shrugs.

"He seemed nice, even though he was ugly—like I should talk. He came over and handed me a beer. I didn't want one, but I took it. He talked to me a little, then the next thing I knew, he had me pinned against the wall and was sticking his tongue down my throat.

"His tongue was fat and bumpy and sour tasting—like a pickle."

Don't let me laugh. Please, don't let me laugh!

"He wouldn't stop, even though I was trying to turn my head away and squeeze my hands between us to push him away. And then he started digging at my crotch, his fingers pushing so hard that it hurt."

There's no chance of me laughing now. I sit up.

"His tongue was still in my mouth, dripping with that sour spit, and I could feel his thing all hard against my hip." Maylee quickly clamps her hand over her mouth, her head pitching forward because she's gagging.

"He was trying to get my zipper down," she says, once she composes herself. "Like he was going to stick it in, right there, in front of everybody." Maylee starts gagging again, her eyes watering.

Oh, God. Don't let her say he raped her. Please don't let her say that!

"I hope you scratched his eyes out," I say.

She gulps. Hard. "No. I did something worse. I puked. While his tongue was still in my mouth."

"Good! That fucker had it coming!"

"No, it wasn't good," Maylee says, her eyes filling with tears. "He pushed his hands against my boobs—hard—to shove himself away from me. Then he started spitting on the floor. And right in front of everybody, right over the music, he yelled, 'What in the hell kind of'—well, you know—'*f'in'* freak are you?'"

I scoot next to Maylee and squeeze my arm between the wall and her shoulders. "Good for you for puking in his mouth, Maylee. He had it coming."

"Good for me? I humiliated myself, Bless. Everybody in the room heard, and they were laughing. And Todd just kept it up, shouting stuff like, 'What kind of a psycho bitch pukes when she's getting kissed?'"

"One who's being kissed by some creep with a tongue that tastes like a sour pickle, who's grabbing her crotch, that's who!" I say.

Maylee tugs at her sweatshirt like it's so tight she can't breathe, even if it's as big as a pup tent. She looks up at the clump of butterflies and tears start spilling down her face. "Everybody made fun of me, Bless. Even Aubrey, when she heard. And last time she called, she brought it up all over again."

"Wait a minute—you're not afraid that if someone kisses you now, you'll puke again, are you?"

Maylee smears tears across her cheeks. She looks at me, pleading. "I might. Because when I even think of a guy's tongue in my mouth, it makes me gag."

"No, Maylee. When you think of *Todd's* tongue in your mouth, it makes you gag. What about Kenneth? What happens when you think of kissing him?"

Her eyes widen with horror. "I wouldn't dare think of that!"

There's a knock at Maylee's door, and she panics because she's crying. I give her a nudge and point to the bathroom. She ditches inside, and I call out, "Come in."

It's her dad. "Hey, pumpkin," he calls as he's turning the knob.

"She's in the bathroom," I tell him when he pops his head inside. I force a smile.

"Oh," he says. "Hi, Bless." Mr. Bradley looks like one of the chubby teddy bears lining the shelf above Maylee's bed. And suddenly, I feel just as sorry for him and Mrs. Bradley as I do for Maylee. All three of them are like helpless kittens in a world where the mean people all wear steel-toed boots.

"Well, I'm supposed to tell you girls that supper's ready."

"Okay. Thanks," I say. He nods and leaves.

The bathroom door is partially open, and I peek inside. Maylee's standing at the sink, swabbing her cheeks with her hands.

I go in and close the toilet lid. I sit Maylee down, then wet a washcloth with cold water and hand it to her. "Put this over your eyes."

I squat down beside her, my hands on her knees. "Maylee. Not all guys are like Todd," I tell her, hoping that I'm telling the truth. "And when you really care about one of them enough, trust me, his kisses won't gag you."

Ten minutes later, Maylee is picking the kidney beans out of her bowl of chili and decorating miniature squares of cornbread with them. Mrs. Bradley shakes her head. And with a gentle smile, she says, "Maylee? Honey, stop playing with your food."

She looks at me and shakes her head sweetly. "I don't know why she does that."

But I do.

It's almost midnight when Liam brings me home. Lights are on in every room, so he asks if he can come inside to meet my "family." He knows all about Shaky, Jeanie, and the boys—even George and Cactus. And he knows they aren't me. I want to show him my coin folder, so I take his hand and lead him to the house. The boys will be shitheads—but probably only after Liam leaves. Jeanie will no doubt think he's cute. And Shaky will talk to him like they're seafaring twins, separated at birth.

Or so I think.

Instead, I find Jeanie curled on the couch, staring at the TV with teary eyes. She doesn't look when I close the front door.

Shaky is at the kitchen table, engulfed in a cloud of cigarette smoke. His head is turned toward the window above the sink, even though it's pitch-dark so there's nothing to look at. I call to him, and he gets up fast, a cigarette pinched between his thumb and finger. He goes out to the back porch without saying a word. I turn to Liam, confused.

Trevor comes into the kitchen then to grab a soda. "What's going on?" I ask him.

"Gilligan lost his boat," he says. He cocks his head and then says with a smirk, "Wait—can you lose something that was never yours to begin with?"

Liam leans over and whispers into my hair. "I think I'd better go. Next time, okay?"

Jeanie isn't on the couch when I walk Liam to the front door. I give him a quick kiss and say good-bye. Then I grab Shaky's quilted vest from the closet and head back to the porch.

"What happened?" I ask as I hand him his vest. He slips it on, not bothering to zip it. He braces his hand on the ledge and stares down.

"He stuck it to me good this time, Bless."

"Who? Oiler?"

"No. The old man."

"George?"

"Yeah."

"What do you mean?"

"Well, Jeanie was raggin' on me to get that title, so I called Oiler's son like Jeanie told me to, to ask him why his old man wasn't back yet. He told me that Oiler got rooked into staying longer to help his son-in-law do some remodeling, and that he'd be back on Friday. So I told him that was good, because I needed the title for my boat. That's when the kid told me that my old man's check didn't clear the bank. Pa must've put a stop payment on it the minute the bank opened. So the boat's gone. And so is my chance of making something of myself. 'Cause I ain't got a grand to cover that check."

I feel bad for Shaky. Maybe he wasn't going to do jack with that boat, but he believes he would have.

He takes a drag off his cigarette, and the smoke threads through the screen.

"You've still got your garage," I remind him.

"That garage isn't bringing in enough to pay the electricity it costs to turn on the lights. And it ain't gonna."

"It might, if you'd do a little advertising. We could put an ad in the paper. Offer a discount to new customers—maybe a free tire rotation with an oil change, something like that. I could make you up some posters on the computers at school. You could hang them around town. You know, until word of mouth spreads. All you'd need is—"

"Alls I need," he spits, "is a dad who believes in me."

He chokes up and turns away, his head down. Geez, I don't know what to say to a grown man who thinks he needs the support of his father. Even I don't need that.

"You don't find good boats like that around anymore," he says, wagging his head. "It was vintage. And I put another couple hundred in it already. Christened it, even. Now Jeanie's all worked up, thinking I ain't gonna get her grand back from Oiler." He straightens up and bends his head back. "I can't believe it. I drove all the way out to Nebraska and back, for nothin'."

For nothing? Your daughter is nothing?

He takes a jagged breath. "Bless, would you grab your old man a beer? I can't go in there and face Jeanie right now. She believed in me."

Without a word, I go inside and grab a beer. I toss it to him from the doorway, then go to my room and sit on my cot. The house is unusually quiet. So quiet that I can hear Jeanie blowing her nose in the bathroom. I grab the five dirty towels at my feet and toss them in the washer just for the noise.

CHAPTER 14
60 DAYS AGO

It's the day before Easter, and Liam insists we go to his place so his mom can meet me. Up until now, I've managed to avoid it. Not because I think I might not like her, but because I'm afraid she'd rather see her son with a *Seventeen*-pretty blond, whose dad has a prestigious job—or a job, period.

Peg greets us at the door and wobbles on his three legs until Liam gives him attention. I crouch down, cup his fat head in my hands, and ruffle his fur. His tail wags so hard he's swaying. "Awww," I say.

The house is small and cute. Clean, but with a lived-in look.

Liam's mom comes out from the kitchen, wiping her hands on a dish towel. Her brown hair is frizzy, like it's still carrying moisture from the sea. She has half of it clipped back, and she's wearing jeans and a flannel shirt tossed over a T-shirt. Her smile is just like Liam's.

I like that she doesn't apologize for the magazines and decorative pillows strewn on the floor in front of the TV. But mostly, I like that she knew who I was before the introduction, even though this is a surprise visit.

"Nice to meet you, Mrs. Reid," I say, and she tells me to call her Cheryl.

Cheryl bounces my hair a little. "Cute cut," she says. I run my fingers through the back of my hair. It's growing out, so that it drops to my neckline in back; the sides are longer. I think I'll let it grow long.

Peg starts whining to go outside, so Liam grabs his leash. I stand there, not knowing if I should follow him or stay with his mom. Cheryl answers that for me when she takes my hand and says, "Come. I was just making myself some tea. You like tea?"

I've never even tasted tea before, but I don't want her to know that. "Sure."

I'm nervous. I wish I was better at making conversation with strangers. I may not care what most people think of me, but I want Liam's mother to like me.

In the kitchen, dishes are draining on a wooden rack and a kettle is sitting over a blue flame. "Earl Grey? Cinnamon and spice? Well, here, you can look." She hands me a tin and I select a packet at random. Cheryl grabs two mismatched cups from the cupboard. "I've heard so much about you, that I feel like I already know you."

She sets the cups on the counter and takes the little bag I'm holding. "He's madly in love with you, you know."

I can't believe she just said that! Liam hasn't even said that to me!

"I can tell you're madly in love with him, too," she says, and my ears drone. Either from the teakettle's whistle, or her words. Cheryl's eyes look almost sad when she says this, even though she's smiling.

She sets spoons into our cups and gets out some honey. "I was your age when I met Liam's father, though he was much older. I remember how it feels to be a girl in love. That's why I'm going to say to you what I wish someone had said to me back then—not that it would have mattered."

Um, okay.

"Liam's a wonderful person. I'd say that even if he wasn't my son. He's kind. Ambitious. Handsome. But he's a lot like his father, too. And he can get moody and distant at times. He's good-natured and positive—but when he's not? And, like his dad, he'll always be more comfortable on the water than in a house. Just so you know. Take your time, Bless. Life is long."

I hear the front door open and turn just as Liam and Peg are coming in. Liam is all happy because he's just decided that we should color Easter eggs.

His mom laughs, as if she hadn't just said what she had. "We don't have a coloring kit, you know. You'll have to run to the store."

"We'll use markers," Liam says.

"We're going to color whole eggs in with markers?"

"Nope. Ours are going to be white, with just features drawn with black Magic Markers. You know, like cartoon people. We're not even going to cook them first."

Cheryl picks up her teacup. Mine is still steaming on the counter. "I'll leave you two to your masterpieces," she says with a smile.

Liam goes to the fridge for eggs, and I sit down at the table. Peg sits next to me. Already he knows I'm a pushover when it comes to animals and will pause to pet him every time he butts his nose under my wrist.

Liam takes an oversized cookbook and props it up so I can't see what he's doing, while I stare down at my egg, making it look like I'm contemplating what to do with it, when in reality I'm contemplating what to do with what Liam's mother just told me. I look up when Liam goes to the cupboard for a plate. He clinks it on the table behind the cookbook, and I hear an egg crack. I try to peek, and Liam scolds me.

A few seconds later—while I'm still pretending to contemplate my white, bald egg—he yanks the book from the table and shouts, "Ta-da!"

He has three eggs propped along one edge of the plate, stuck in place with dabs of peanut butter. The face of one egg is showing shock, the other two are wailing. All because in the center of the plate, a raw egg is smashed, the insides of the little egg guy pooled like yellow blood across the plate. There's a gasping face on one piece of broken shell.

I clamp my hand over my mouth and roar. Our laughter lures Cheryl back into the kitchen, and she has to hold on to the counter to stay standing, her legs pressed together so she won't pee as she laughs.

None of us hears the doorbell until Peg starts barking. Cheryl goes to answer it.

"Sorry, we didn't hear the bell," Cheryl says, still giggling.

I hear a woman's voice, and Liam stops laughing. "Great," he grumbles under his breath. And when their guest comes into the kitchen, I see why. It's an older version of Stephie. She's gobbed with makeup and has big eighties hair. Her lips are so fat that they look like two night crawlers with compulsive eating disorders. Her yap stops when she sees me.

"Hi there, Liam." She verbally ignores me, though she's staring right at me with a glare that hints that she's probably pushed more than one little girl off a stage, to ensure that her dear little Stephie got the center spot in a dance recital.

Liam glances up at the clock, then at me. "Hey, didn't you say you had to be home by six?" I never said that, but I nod.

Liam takes my hand, obviously determined to get me out of there fast. Cheryl says good-bye and tells me to come back soon. Peg follows us to the door with wonky steps.

"Sorry," Liam whispers when we get to the front closet. "But I knew you'd want to get out of here." He opens the front door and stretches his leg in front of Peg to keep him from escaping when I slip out.

"Liam?" Stephie's mother calls. "When you come back, Stephie could really use some more tutoring on her algebra."

"Sure," Liam says. "But I don't know when that'll be."

Don't say a word when we get outside. Not a word!

Regina Dillon eyes me, her ridiculously long fake lashes pointing at me like black daggers. "Who's your little friend?" she asks.

I can't even hear Liam's reply. Not with the roaring in my ears, because of her condescending tone.

Cheryl steps in to explain, while waving us out the door.

"I'm not really taking you home," Liam says once we're in his Yukon. "It's too early."

"What about Stephie?" I ask, working hard to keep my sarcasm tempered.

"She can wait."

We go through a drive-through for sodas, then head down by the lake. It's half raining, half snowing, and the wind is whipping, so we stay in the car. I watch Liam as he watches the water, his eyelids heavy with homesickness. And for those few seconds, I miss him, even though he's right beside me. Graduation is only six weeks away. He hasn't brought up his leaving, and I'm afraid to.

We sit quietly for a time, the fan of the heater the only sound in the car, then he looks over at me. I must look sad or something, because he asks, "What? You're not upset at the thought of me helping Stephie, are you? Because if you are—"

I stretch my arm out and put my fingertips over his mouth. "No." Then I scoot up on my knees and stretch over the center console. I let my kiss say what my voice can't. That he's the best thing that's ever happened to me, and I don't ever want to lose him. Not to another girl, or to the sea. Liam lifts me over until I'm sitting on his lap, his hand running up my thigh, my hip, as we kiss. We make out until the windows are steamed and we're sweating inside our coats.

When I get home, Jeanie hands me a cell phone box. The phone's cheap, and there's nothing *smart* about it, but I'm grateful to have it. I call Liam as soon as I think he's home to give him my number, and we lie in our beds talking until we're so sleepy I doze off. I wake as he's asking, "A penny for your thoughts?" I laugh then, and so does he. "Sorry, my mom always uses those stupid, old expressions."

He tells me to have sweet dreams, and we hang up.

Chapter 15
49 Days Ago

I'm barely awake, when I hear Trevor and Jud whooping it up in the living room. "Yes! Yes!"

Jeanie's lucky to get the boys out of bed by seven fifteen on school mornings (even if the bus comes at seven thirty), so I grab my cell in a panic, thinking I set the alarm wrong. That's when Jud shoves my door open and shouts, "Ice storm! No school today!"

Ice storm? It's April 10th!

Trevor and Jud might be carrying on like excited hyenas, but I'm sighing. The last thing I want is to be stuck here with them all day, missing Liam. My phone vibrates, and I open a text from him. *"Ugh. Will miss u."*

I shuffle into the bathroom and peek out the window. Everything, and I mean everything, is encased in a thick coating of ice. And with the sun brilliant in a cloudless sky, the whole landscape looks magical.

I pee, brush my teeth, and hurry to dress. I grab my sunglasses (seriously, it's that bright out there) and step outside. The wind stands still, as if it, too, is frozen in place, but the sounds of branches groaning, snapping, and ice popping are everywhere! I've never heard anything like it, so I open the door and shout in, "Hey, you guys, you've got to hear this!" Nobody comes.

The steps are so slippery that I have to hang on to the icy railing to keep myself from face-planting when I wipe my feet. Then I shuffle along as though I'm skating down the walkway and across the crusted snow. I laugh, even at the littered Mountain Dew bottles, sparkling like emeralds dropped by the giant from the top of the beanstalk. I may feel sad for the animals huddled on frozen beds, and even for the trees, with ice coating their naked limbs, but still I think of how I've never seen a day more beautiful than this one.

I slip and slide my way to the red pines and have to bash notches with my boots into the side of the knoll to scale it. I slip backward four times, and fall once.

The hems of the green angels' dresses, laden with ice gems, are sagged to the ground. I tuck myself into one tree, and lift two heavy limbs to drape down over my shoulders. I prop my sunglasses on top of my head and let one clump of ice-encased needles drape over my forehead like bangs. Then I get out my phone, and snap a picture of myself. I laugh when I see it. My eyes are rolled up and off to the side, my mouth making a can-you-believe-this circle. I send it to Liam, and he texts back: *"Sweet!"* A few minutes later, he sends me one of him standing outside in a T-shirt, two skinny icicles sticking out of his ears. I laugh all the way back to the house.

When I get inside, my old man is on the couch, a breakfast beer in his hand. Jeanie is jabbing him with orders to get over to Oiler's and get her money back. I ignore them and get busy vacuuming up the potato chip crumbs in the hallway, before giving my essay for World History class another edit. I'm determined to have a good day no matter what mood everyone else is in. Around noon, Liam texts me a picture of Peg sitting on the futon in his bedroom. He's wearing a stocking hat and holding his front paw up, a red mitten on his stump. He looks so adorable that I laugh out loud. That is, until I notice a girl's mustard-yellow purse resting against Peg's left haunch.

Don't jump to conclusions. It could be his mom's. Not all middle-aged women carry purses that look like knitting totes.

But I don't believe a word I'm telling myself.

I don't want to sound like some insecure nag, so I text him back: *"A purse?"* And tell him that Peg has gender-confusion issues.

Fifteen seconds later, I get a selfie from Liam's cell—of Stephie! (She's obviously holding the phone herself, judging by the position of her shoulder.) She's grinning, her perfect teeth bit together. The message says: *"It's mine."*

I slip into the shower and turn the water on full blast. I'm so upset I can hardly think straight. Sure, maybe we only argued over Stephie that one time, but we would have at least twenty times since then, if I hadn't been trying so hard not to sound like a jealous freak.

I come out to pour myself some orange juice, and find all the glasses dirty—again! I start loading the dishwasher. I'm jamming the last glass into a gap between two others when it shatters. I cuss, then lift the bottom rack to get at the scattered shards. And the whole time I'm picking up glass, I'm wondering how a guy as smart as Liam can be so stupid!

Just friends? How could he not see that Stephie's been finding any excuse she can to spend time with him, and that her mom helps her plot? And what about every time we come across her and Melissa and Misty in the hall, huddled together like a coven of witches—can't he tell they're plotting against me? *Really?*

I go out on the back porch to call Maylee. Abby's with her, but I don't care.

"I can't wait to hear what excuse she had for showing up at Liam's today—and what excuse he'll have for why she was in his room. The conniving bitch! But what I don't get is Liam. Can he really be that blind about her?"

"I want to punch her," Maylee grumbles.

Abby grabs the phone then. He starts explaining to me that, yes, guys *can* be complete idiots when it comes to manipulative girls. I find some solace in what he says. Well, until I remember that his only experience with girls is with his sisters, who are all under the age of ten.

"She's going to have to come on to him before he sees that you're right."

"If she hasn't already," I say.

"No," Abby says. "She won't do that just yet. She knows you don't put out, Blessy. So she's going to play it cool. Innocent. Be sweet. Thinking that's what Liam likes in a girl. Well, until she gets desperate. Then she'll unleash her inner slut."

Maylee takes the phone back. "Did you hear that?"

"Yeah," I say.

"Wait . . . wait . . . he's saying . . ."

I can hear Abby chattering in the background, but can't make out what he's saying. "Okay, okay," Maylee says. "He said that whatever you do, don't go off on Liam while Stephie is there. He said . . . what? Say that again, Abby. Oh, Bless, he said—"

Abby rips the phone from Maylee again. "Think of swimming in shark-infested water—you don't dare bleed. No tantrums while Stephie is there, Blessy. You hear me? Your tears will be like blood in the water."

I know Abby's right—and that he'll make a good shrink someday, which is what he wants to be. So for the next few minutes, I text Liam back as if I'm perfectly okay with that bitch marking her territory in his room. But when I can't do it for even one more text, I tell him I have to go clean. *Call when Ur free.*

He doesn't call until late in the afternoon, and I make him hold until I get my shoes and coat on, and move to the porch again. I stand so close to the screen that I can smell the rust. The last of the ice has melted from the trees, leaving the bark damp and so dark that the trees look singed. The magic of the day is gone, and all that remains is the water slipping from the eaves. I take a deep breath, then ask, "So, what was Stephie doing there *this* time?"

Before he can answer, I jump in again—even if I hate myself as I'm doing it. "Wait, let me guess. She had a nail-polish bottle that wouldn't open so she needed your help. You know, because you have such biiiiig, stroooong hands."

"Actually," Liam says, his voice a little too deep to sound casual, "she came over because she was scared. She was the only one home, and Drake kept circling the house."

"Oh, so she hiked over to your place. Isn't that kind of like seeing a train coming and lying over a railroad track, then shouting for help?"

He ignores my sarcastic analogy. "She was shaking when she got here. Mom told her to stay until her mother got home."

"And your room was the only place to hide, of course."

"She just came in here to listen to my new CD, that's all. She likes Shipwreck on a Desert, too. Man, where's all *this* coming from, Bless?"

I go off big time. "Wise up, Liam! She likes *you*, not your music. She probably had to look up the band on YouTube to even know who they are." *I did.*

I don't tell him how hurt I am that he played the CD for her, when I haven't even heard it yet. Or that I'm upset because Steph's probably been in his room twenty times, while I've never been in it once. Okay, so maybe he would have taken me in there the day we decorated eggs, if Stephie's mom hadn't shown up. But still—

Liam starts defending Stephie, like she's his little sister and I'm bullying her. That's when I *really* lose it. Screaming like a lunatic, even though I know the whole house can hear me. I rant about what a manipulative bitch Stephie is, and how much I hate her. "If Drake is as big of a threat as Stephie claims he is—and I doubt it—then she should have been calling the police department, not your house!"

"Bless, she showed me a couple of the notes he left her. He's nuts."

"Does she show you what she posts online, too? *Went to the store with Liam for Peeps. Liam played his new CD for me. It rocks, just like him! Liam thinks I look better in red than navy.* Or what about the pictures she posts on Instagram? Your heads side by side, both of you with the ends of the *same* Twizzler clamped in your mouths? Has she shown you those?" *What about her boobs?*

"I don't know what Stephie does online. I've never bothered to look. But I'll bet she posts pictures and stuff about all her friends. She came because she was afraid of Drake, that's all. She was even embarrassed about imposing on Mom and me."

My head's going to explode. Seriously, it's going to. "I bet!"

Liam sighs, and I keep ranting.

"Okay, okay, let's pretend that Drake *is* a dangerous nutball— although I think what's more true is that he's just depressed. Probably because everyone treats him like he's a circus freak and makes fun of him right in front of his face, like he doesn't have any feelings. But for the sake of agreement here, let's say it's true that Drake's gone nuts—as you and your mom obviously believe he has—then has it dawned on either one of you that, in protecting Stephie, you might be putting *yourselves* in danger, too? Did you ever think of *that*?"

"We have a pistol here if we need one—not that that's the point. Man, Bless. Can we stop all this drama? Stephie's nothing but a friend. But she *is* my friend. Wouldn't you have done the same for Maylee if she needed a place to hide out for a while?"

I clutch my head as I pace. I'm so steamed I can't control myself. "Get her out of your space, Liam, or stay out of mine! Got it?"

I hang up and shut my phone off.

I come inside, and Trevor and Jud start mocking me. "Lamb.

Lamb. Love me, not her. Boo hoo." Surprisingly, Jeanie tells them to shut up.

Dad is sitting at the table when I yank open the fridge to grab a bottle of flavored water for my rage-parched throat. "Get used to it, Bless," he says. "I'll tell you right now, there's always gonna be somebody out there, ready to stick it to you. Look what happened to me." He flicks another ash onto the plate. *Use the damn ashtrays!* I scream to myself. *Or better yet, go outside so we don't have to choke on your nasty smoke!*

"I tweaked the engine and sandblasted that deck. I had one coat of varnish on it already. Like my labor isn't worth anything."

It's always about you. Always!

I unscrew the water bottle and am taking a long chug when Jeanie comes out of the bathroom, dirty jeans and underwear rolled in her arms. "Bless, what'd you do? Get out of the shower and step right over these clothes without bothering to pick them up? You were heading right to the laundry room."

A pair of boys' underwear drops to the floor.

"Why are you getting on *my* case?" I shout. "I'm the only one besides you who does a damn thing around here!"

She tells Jud to pick up his boxers. He doesn't.

"Those two don't do anything I tell them to do," Jeanie whines— as if this justifies her bitching at me. She bends over to pick up the boxers. "Alls they do is sit around and play those stupid computer games and fight all day."

"Then disconnect the Internet! Take away their laptops! Do *something!*" I shout.

Shaky jumps in then. "It's not Jeanie's fault. They don't listen to her, like she says. You know that."

I'm so mad I'm shaking. "Then *you* step in. Help her *make* them listen!"

Shaky shrugs. "They aren't my kids," he says.

"Would you step in and help, if they were?" I scream at him. "Would you?"

Jeanie slips over closer to Shaky, and I glare at them both. "What's the matter with you two?" I scream, my voice getting so loud it's hurting *my* ears. "You're supposed to be the adults around here! Why don't you freakin' act like it?"

Jud and Trevor are just standing there like avatars on a frozen screen. "And you two little morons! Is it too much to expect you to act like decent human beings? I'm surprised you can blow your own snotty noses for yourselves!"

I stomp to my stupid laundry room/bedroom and slam the door behind me. There's not a sound in the kitchen.

I drop onto my bed, my back against the wall. I grab my pillow and cradle it to me like it's Marbles, and think about how I wish Shaky had never brought me here.

The house pretty much stays quiet for the rest of the afternoon. I keep my phone turned off and stay in my room, reading my essay over, even though I'm not absorbing a word it says. Finally, I hold my pillow to my face and allow myself to cry the tears that I've been holding in since my phone call with Liam. I had to say those things, even if it means losing him. And I had to say those things to Shaky and Jeanie and the boys, even if it means they'll send me packing. Or so I keep telling myself.

Around five, the house fills with the smells of frying hamburger and onions. I hear a rap on my door, and Jeanie pokes her head in. I'm expecting her to tell me it's time for dinner, but instead, she says, "Your boyfriend's here."

I stiffen.

She leans into the door frame. "He looks like a puppy who got caught piddling on the floor," she whispers. "Course, they all put on that face after they've been jerks."

I slip into the bathroom to check my eyes and brush my hair, then go into the living room. I stand with my knees bumping up against an empty chair, my arms crossed.

Liam keeps glancing at me, then at Shaky, who, surprisingly, isn't whining about losing his boat.

"Bless, can we talk?" Liam finally asks.

I grab my coat, and Liam follows me outside. The road's been salted, but there's still ice sitting under a coating of water on the walkway, a closed lid over the bucket of salt on the steps. Liam puts his arm around me and lifts my hood to cover my head. *Don't cave, just because he's being nice. Don't!*

He leads me to his SUV and backs down the empty logging road just far enough to get out of sight from any would-be spies inside the house.

"Bless, please. Let's not fight about Stephie Dillon. She's someone who got tugged into my life because her mom and mine are old friends. That's it. She's not my type, and I've no interest in her in *that* way. I know it, and so does she. Now I just need *you* to know it."

Stephie knows it? REALLY?

He reaches over and tugs my arm out from under my opposite elbow. He works his fingers in between mine. He sighs, then says, "Sometimes, Bless, I think you just don't know how to let things be good. Maybe because you've never had them that way. You're always waiting for the next shoe to drop. The next punch to land."

I yank my hand away from his and recross my arms. I stare at what I can see of the yard, which isn't much more than the broken swing rocking in the breeze. I know Liam's right. And that's what hurts the most.

Suddenly I'm blubbering so hard I can hardly breathe. "I'm

sorry. I'm sorry," I say, even though I don't know that I am; I only know I don't want to lose him.

"It's okay. I just don't want us to fight."

"I don't want to fight anymore, either," I say. "My whole life has been one big fight."

"I know," he says. He helps me up over the console, and onto his lap. I bury my face in the soft hollow of his neck as if it's my cradle, and cry seventeen years' worth of tears.

Liam hands me a napkin from Taco Bell, and I mop my face and blow my nose. Then he lifts my chin and looks at me with haunted eyes. "I dreamt about you last night," he says, kissing my eyelid softly.

"You did?"

Please let it have been a good dream. Please!

"I was on *The Meredith*, pulling up a lobster pot, when I spotted you in the water, your hair wet and black as night, your skin glowing as if it was made of the moon." He makes a deep moan in his throat. The kind you make when something sweet is on your tongue.

"I called to you, but you didn't come. I knew you'd heard me, though, because you turned to look when you heard your name.

"I ripped my boots and jacket off, thinking maybe you were in trouble. Logic said you weren't, since you weren't thrashing, but it was the only explanation I had as to why you wouldn't come. So I went to dive in and rescue you." Liam utters a soft laugh. "You know. Like a big hero."

He gets solemn again. "You held your hand up to stop me before I could jump. Then your tail came up out of the water and you turned and swam away."

"My *tail*?"

He nods. "You were a mermaid. Your bottom half the same color as a blue lobster. You were so beautiful in the water that it broke me up to see you swimming away. So I went up to the helm so I could follow you. And I called and called your name as if it was a prayer."

I get chills when he says this. "Did I stop?"

"I don't know. I woke up then. I was ringing wet—as if I *had* jumped in."

An eagle circles above the trees, then glides off as if it, too, is a mermaid getting lost in a sea of blue. I sit quietly for a moment. "Was I running away from you, or leading you someplace?" I ask, because although I don't know much about mermaid folklore (and nothing about interpreting dreams), what I do know is that while some stories are about mermaids leading ships to safety, most tell of beautiful, malevolent mermaids who lead boats into torturous rocks where the sailors meet their deaths.

"I don't know," Liam says. "But in the dream, what I did know, for sure, was how much I loved you. And when I woke up, that feeling was still with me." He shifts and looks down at me, his eyes intense. Tender. "And it's still with me, Bless. I love you. Do you know that? I love you so much."

I can't hear a thing after the words "I love you." Not a thing. Because although my mom might have said those words to me once, and maybe Grandma Gloria, I don't have the memories, so it's like I'm hearing them from another human being for the first time.

Liam tilts the steering wheel up and out of the way, then scoots his seat back and reclines it. I spread my legs to straddle his lap so I can hug him full-on. I hold on as though I'm drowning and he's the only one who can save me. "I love you, too," I mutter. "So much it hurts."

As we kiss, Liam's hands stroke my head, my back, my butt, my thighs, and no matter how close he pulls me to him, it's not close enough for either of us. I pull away from his mouth and catch my breath. "I'm sorry that I get like this. I really am. I don't mean to. But I'm so scared you'll leave me like everyone else has."

Liam kisses my lips, my eyes, my forehead. And in between each peck, he says, "I'll never leave you. I'm yours forever. Promise."

I fall against him again, my whole body pulsing as if it's made of nothing but heart. There are no soft kisses this time. Only hard ones, with eager tongues and deep, throaty moans. And when I feel his fingers slip up my shirt and fumble with the hooks on my bra, I reach back and unsnap it for him. He touches my nipples with his hands, his tongue, until it seems my whole world is about to explode.

Then he slips his hands into the back pockets of my jeans and pulls me closer. So close that his hard-on is pressed low on my pubic bone. We gasp for breath in between our kisses, our hips rocking like boats riding a single, powerful wave.

Afterward, I collapse against Liam and we wait for our breaths to come back.

He helps lift me so I can pull my right leg in and sit crossways on his lap again. "I hope nobody came out of the house and saw that," I say, embarrassed.

"I doubt they could have seen a thing, even if they'd been standing alongside of us," he says with a laugh, gesturing toward the windows that are so glazed with steam that we can't see out them.

I move over to my side, and Liam drops the wheel down into driving position. "I brought you something," he says.

"What?"

He reaches into the backseat and hands me one of his shirts, rolled into a ball. "Remember when I brought you home the night before last and I asked what you were doing—besides tickling my neck? You said you wished you could rip my shirt off and keep it so you could smell me all night long." He hands me the soft, blue button-down shirt he was wearing over a T-shirt that night. "It's yours. Sniff away." He laughs a little, like he feels kind of stupid for giving it to me.

I bunch it in my hands and hold it to my face. It smells of soap, and fresh air and skin. It smells like him.

Liam pulls his Yukon back into the driveway. I open the car door, but before I can slip out, he takes my free hand. "Bless?" he says.

"Yeah?"

"Don't ever swim away from me, okay?"

My whole inside melts when he says this. And then I grin. "Fat chance of that. I don't even know how to swim."

I slam the door and skip off to the house, knowing he's watching me with a dropped jaw.

Jeanie's on the couch, watching some old blonds in gowns and cleavage snarl at each other. Shaky's stretched out over the cushions, snoring, his head on her lap (bet he promised to go fetch her money in the morning). I can smell his feet from here. "Everything okay?" Jeanie asks. I tell her it is. A commercial comes on while I'm slipping off my shoes, and she looks over, her expression one of concern. Maybe she didn't hear me, so I repeat myself.

Then I realize that her concern isn't only about how the argument ended. She's studying my face. My cheeks, that are probably still flushed, because I can still feel them burning. And my lips, that when I feel them with my tongue, are still puffy.

Jeanie's eyes narrow and she gets serious. "Take it slow, honey. Young love comes with lots of risks."

Gee, thanks for reminding me.

I take a quick shower, put on Liam's shirt and my softest PJ pants. Then I crawl into bed and turn on my cell. It shows eight missed calls—five from Maylee, and three voice mails from Liam. I don't listen to Liam's messages; the fight is over. But I don't delete them, either. Because after he graduates and I'm stuck in school without him, I'll listen to them between classes just to hear the sound of his voice.

I try calling Maylee, but it goes straight to voice mail.

Maylee's mom is taking Maylee's car in for new tires, so we're both forced to ride the school bus on Monday. Different buses, since we're on different routes. Maylee is waiting for me when I get in the lobby. She tugs me to the side. "I tried calling you all yesterday afternoon," she says. Her cheeks are bright pink, her eyes wide, her hair extra chubby.

"I had my phone shut off for most of the day, but I turned it on last night, and yours was shut off."

"I was babysitting for the Nortons. Mrs. Norton doesn't let her babysitters sit on the phone."

"I didn't see any messages from you, either," I say.

Maylee gives me a duh-you look. "You never listen to your messages. You always just call me back. But water under the bridge now—did the two of you make up?" I can tell she wants a quick response because she's got her own news to share.

"We did," I say. "Your turn."

She tucks her head and leans over toward me. "He talked to me, Bless!"

"Who?"

"*Who?* Kenneth, that's who!" Maylee cringes when she realizes that she said it loud enough for the freshman couple in front of us to hear.

Kenneth Dubble. When we were paired for that science lab last month, I came right out and told him that Maylee liked him. The second I said it, he looked like he'd just inhaled a vial of sulfuric acid. I took that to mean he wasn't interested, so I never said anything to Maylee. But obviously, he was just dumbstruck at the thought that a girl liked him. Because really, he probably doesn't get *that* every day.

"Cool. What did he say?"

"He said, 'We're in study hall together on Thursdays, aren't we?' I can't believe he talked to me!" Maylee squeals.

"Who talked to you?" A dark head pops in between us and Abby nudges us apart with his shoulders.

"Abby, we're talking girl talk."

"Oooo, I love girl talk. Fill me in."

"Anyway," she says, looking over Abby's head to address me. "He invited me to the Subway on 3rd Avenue tonight. That's where he works."

"Who?" Abby asks. Maylee rolls her eyes, then cups her hand over the top of Abby's head and moves him like a chess piece to her other side.

"Is he picking you up, or are you meeting him there?"

"Who we talking about?" Abby asks. We ignore him.

"He's working. So I'm driving myself there. He's going to treat me to a sandwich."

"He's working?" What kind of a date is THAT supposed to be? There's something that strikes me so hysterically funny about it, but I don't dare let on. Besides, I'm scouting the halls for Liam.

"Whoever he is," Abby says, "don't cube your food. He'll think you have an eating disorder." Okay, maybe Abby *won't* make a good shrink.

Maylee is punching Abby's arm when my pulse starts beating faster.

We turn the corner, and there Liam is, coming down the hall.

His whole face melts into a smile when he sees me. He stops and spreads his arms wide, a book in one hand, and shouts, "I'm in love with Bless Adler! Hear that, everyone? I'm crazy in love with Bless Adler!"

Maylee giggles an *"Oh my gosh!"* And I know what she's thinking. How she hopes she'll hear those words from Kenneth someday—though probably not shouted in the middle of a crowded hall, because her face is as red as her math book.

"Blessy, look—"

Abby's pointing out Stephie, who's standing by her locker, a notebook poised in midair, her mouth hanging open as if Liam's words have knocked the wind out of her.

Right before Liam reaches me, Misty and Melissa, and another cheerleader I think is named Amber, rush to console Stephie. Game over.

Maylee leans down and whispers, "I hope nobody tries to interfere with Kenneth and me. I couldn't take it as well as you." And okay, that strikes me as funny because they haven't even had a first date, so I laugh. Because really, unless Kenneth has an overbearing mother who wants to be the only woman in his life (which would be just plain creepy), I doubt there's going to be another female trying to foil their romance. But that's not the only reason I'm laughing. I'm laughing because Liam is three steps away from me, his arms spread, his eyes on me only.

Chapter 16
46 Days Ago

Liam drives me home from school. He has another night shift, so he can only stay about an hour. Jeanie's still working, Shaky's who knows where, and the bus isn't here yet. I make us peanut butter and jelly sandwiches. I hand Liam the sandwiches, pour him some milk, and grab a handful of cookies. "Come on," I say.

"Welcome to my laundry room *slash* bedroom." Liam shakes his head, laughing.

We sit on the cot and laugh over next to nothing while we eat.

"I want to show you something," I say after we're finished. I roll onto my knees, and Liam holds on to my belt loop so I don't fall as I lean over and reach under the cot. I sit back beside him and prop my stocking feet on the mattress. Liam does the same. I open the front and back flaps of the penny folder and spread it over our legs.

"You collect pennies?" he says with a little chuckle.

"No. But Susan Marlene Harris did."

"Was that your mom?"

"No. My mom's name was Maura."

"I have an aunt named Maura," Liam says. "My dad's sister. The name means *of the sea*."

I smile.

"So who is Susan?"

"I don't know. The folder was in my bag when Shaky dropped me off at Cactus and George's."

His fingers smooth over the pages, and he points at the only empty space on an otherwise filled board. "So you weren't just making conversation at Angelo's, when you asked if the blue lobster was as rare as a . . . a . . ."

"A 1972 doubled die obverse Lincoln penny."

"I don't even know what that means," Liam says, laughing.

"Well, I looked it up a few years ago. Something goes wrong on the surface of the coin when the die stamps it."

"The *die?*"

"That's what they call the piece of machinery that forms the impression on the coin. Here, look at this one," I say, pointing to the first penny in the folder. "It's a 1955 doubled die. See how the words are overlapped? *Doubled?* The year, too. See? The same thing happened with the '72 penny I'm looking for."

"And obverse? What does that mean?"

"It means the mistake is on the front. *Reverse*, and it's on the back."

"So kind of like a mutation in the penny world," he says with a grin.

"Yeah. A man-made one. Anyway, from the time I was little, I've wanted to fill this space. For her—Susan. Because I think it was important to her. And that makes it feel important to me, if that makes any sense.

"I don't know . . . maybe I'm obsessed with the whole thing, because it's all I've got from the years I was too young to remember. Anyway, I'm as determined to find this penny as I am to find out who Susan was and why I have her collection."

"There's a coin shop right in Logan. Maybe they'd have it. Or, I'll bet we could find it online."

I shake my head. "No." I pause, as I try to think of how to explain this. "Well, think about if you'd only seen a blue lobster in an aquarium . . . or someone had given you that chunk of shell. You might have appreciated both, because a blue lobster is rare, but it wouldn't have been the same. Because it's about more than the lobster itself—it's about what it means to you. The story that goes with it."

Liam nods. He gets it.

"Without a story to go with this folder, it's just a dumb penny collection. But it's the meaning this Susan put into it that made it special to her. I realized this after you told me about your blue lobster. But look. Look how worn the edge is around the space where the penny should be. She must have dwelled on its meaning every time she opened the folder and rubbed her finger around it." I sigh. "But I guess trying to uncover the meaning around this folder would be like somebody looking at your chunk of blue lobster shell long after you're gone and trying to guess why it was special to you."

Liam follows the path Susan's finger took, with his own.

"Have you searched for her online?"

"Yeah. I didn't find anything."

Liam's finger passes slowly over the rows of coins. "Weird. The years aren't lined up in order—they're random. The doubled die ones have to be valuable—all mistakes are—what about the rest of these? Are they special for some reason?"

"No. They're just common pennies."

"Huh," Liam says. "Then maybe these particular years themselves were important to her."

I stare at the folder, feeling foolish that I hadn't thought of that possibility.

"Especially these years," Liam says, tapping the three spaces that are decorated.

"Well, this one is special. At least to me," I say, laughing as I tap the 1997, the last penny in the book. "That's the year I was born."

"Maybe that's not a coincidence," Liam says. "Hey, what year was your mom born?"

"I don't know."

"You don't know?"

"I was only four when she died. I know her birthday was June 9, but I don't know the year."

"What's your grandma's name?"

"Gloria." I'm embarrassed that I don't know her last name.

"Ask your dad what your mom's birth year was," he says. "It would at least be a place to start."

The front door bangs open, and Jud and Trevor barrel into the house, their schoolbags and shoes thumping when they hit the floor. Or the walls.

I take the penny book and fold it shut. "Anyway, I wanted to show it to you."

I slide it under the cot. "You're the first person I've shown it to."

Liam smiles and pulls me beside him. And for the first time, I understand why he appreciated the fact that I listened so carefully when he talked about lobster fishing. Because I can't imagine anyone but him showing this much interest in a dumb penny collection.

Liam brushes my bangs away from my face, and smiles as I'm watching him. "Bless, I'm sorry you lost your mom. And that you don't have anything from your past but a coin book."

"Well, you can't miss what you've never had, right? Or at least what you can't remember."

"Yes, you can," Liam says. "I missed you before I found you."

I shove him playfully. "You did not!"

"I did too. There was always a little piece of me that felt lonely— like something was missing. But it's not there anymore."

He leans in to kiss me.

We're still kissing when Jud bangs the door open. "She is *too* home!" he shouts.

Jeanie bumps her way into the room. Liam and I pull apart. I'm just about to introduce Liam to her when she shouts, "Bless, what are you doing with a boy in here?"

Jud giggles, and Trevor, who's just outside the door, starts panting like a dog.

We get off the bed. Liam looks sheepish, but I'm furious. "What? Like it's a crime to bring a boy into your laundry room? Since when did this family get all proper?"

"I'd better go," Liam says, touching my upper arm like we're just buds. "Sorry, ma'am," he says as he squeezes around Jeanie to leave.

I follow Liam out, and Jeanie watches. After I shut the front door, I spin around and glare at her. "I can't believe you'd embarrass Liam like that! Like what, we were just about to do it, or something?"

"Looked to me like you were about to," Jud says with a smirk.

"You're such a little creep!" I shout.

Jeanie puts up her hand. "I don't want that kind of stuff going on in this house, Bless."

"What a joke! So it's okay to scream and cuss and cut each other down, but it's not okay for people to show that they care about each other? It's what normal people do, you know!"

"I wasn't born yesterday," Jeanie says. "I might not know what *normal* people do, but I sure as hell know what normal *teens* do. That's why I'm making a fuss. Plus, I've got two young boys here, Bless. What kind of example do you think you're setting for them?"

"Yeah," Jud says, grinning, mashed cookie coating his teeth. "What kind of an example do you think you're setting for us?"

I clutch my head at the absurdity of it all and stomp back to my room.

Jeanie calls when dinner is ready, but I don't go out. And when Shaky pops his head in to repeat the message, like maybe I didn't hear her, I tell him I'm not hungry.

Liam and I are texting goodnight when someone raps on my door. I don't answer.

"Bless, can I come in?" Jeanie asks in almost a whisper—like she ever asks before coming in. When I don't answer, she opens the door. "Can we talk?"

She glances back into the living room, where the TV's blaring, and Shaky is snoring, then slips inside and closes the door behind her. "Bless, I know why you're mad at me," she says. She sits down on one end of my cot, and I scoot closer to the wall.

I'm staring at the dryer where stained socks are tumbling. "Just for the record, I'm not a slut," I say. "And Liam's not some creep who's just looking for sex. So if you came in here to give me a lecture, you can save your breath."

Jeanie gets quiet and stays quiet for so long that I glance out of the corner of my eye to see what's up. She's staring at the floor. Finally she says, "I just don't want you making a mistake you'll pay for for the rest of your life."

I turn and stare at the wall again. "I'm not stupid," I say.

"Bless. You don't need to be stupid or a slut to make a mistake. I should know.

"I was a good girl. And my boyfriend was a good boy, too. But we were in love, and thought it was forever. And, well, one thing led to another, and I got pregnant—the first time we did it, too. We were fifteen years old."

I don't mean to stare at Jeanie, but I'm shocked stupid.

"We thought we could handle it, with a little help. We had it all figured out. I'd move in with Tony's family—my dad was a drunk and mean, so Tony's place seemed the best bet. His mom didn't like me, but Tony was sure she would once she got to know me better. He'd get a job after school and . . . well, we were just kids, you know? A little dumb and a little smart at the same time. We didn't know what it took to raise a kid—or that we were only half grown ourselves, for that matter. But Tony's folks said that no little whore was going to ruin their son's life. And, well, I guess my folks felt the same. Because when I told them what Tony's dad said, they said I wasn't gonna ruin their lives, either."

I already raised my kids, I can hear Cactus saying.

Jeanie is forty-one, so obviously she's not talking about getting pregnant with Trevor. I wait, afraid to ask, hoping she won't say that the baby died.

"My folks told me I was giving the baby up for adoption, and that's all there was to it."

Inky black rivulets of mascara start running down Jeanie's cheeks.

It feels awkward putting my arm around her. And I can tell by her flinch of surprise, that it feels awkward to her, too. She starts crying harder, and I struggle for something to say.

She shakes her head. "I can't tell you what it feels like to carry a baby around inside you, feeling it kick, and knowing that when it comes out, somebody's gonna take it. Bad as the pains were when they came, I fought them hard as I could, because I didn't want to let my baby go."

Tears are stinging my eyes now, and my arm tightens around her, the unease gone. "I'm sorry they made you do that," I say.

"My baby girl was born on December third. And on December fourth, they took her. They let me say good-bye to her, at least through the glass, because I wasn't gonna sign the papers until they did.

"I named her Ashley Rose—I don't know what the people who adopted her named her. She'd be twenty-six now, but in my head, she's still a newborn."

"Is Tony Jud and Trevor's dad, too?" Crazy as it seems, I'm hoping she'll say yes. Because it would seem less cruel somehow, if they had made it at least that far, rather than it ending then and

Jeanie having to say good-bye to both her boyfriend and her baby at the same time.

Jeanie shakes her head. "Tony's family moved away before the year was over. I don't know if he tried to get a hold of me and his parents, or mine, stopped him, or if he didn't bother. I never did hear what became of him. I married a mean drunk just like my dad, soon as I got out of high school."

My arm drops onto my lap. "Does my dad know?"

"Yeah. Shaky doesn't fault me for it—he's good that way. And like he said, he made mistakes, too."

Did he say that I'm one of them?

"I ain't telling the boys until they're older."

I think of Jeanie's daughter, and wonder if she wonders about her mother, too. Then, as I look over at Jeanie again, I think of Gloria, who has kept the four-year-old me in her head all these years.

Jeanie exhales. "Anyway, I just want you to be careful. Your dad and I would never force you to give away a baby if you got in trouble. But still, it would be a lot of heartache for a girl your age. I don't want that for you."

Jeanie sniffles and stands up. "I shouldn't have embarrassed you like I did. But I wanted you to know why I did it. We good now?"

"Yeah," I tell her.

Jeanie nods, then says, "Bless?"

I look up.

"I hope you and that boy make it. I really do. I may love your dad, nuts as he makes me sometimes, but still, there's no love like your first love."

Chapter 17
40 Days Ago

It's April 20 and Liam's picking me up early, though what we're going to do on a rainy Saturday at seven o'clock in the morning is beyond me. Get the most out of our three-day weekend, I suppose (we get Monday off for some districtwide Professional Development Day—whatever that is). So groggy or not, I get up and shower, happy because I'm going to be spending the whole day with Liam. And because I won't have to spend the day with Trevor and Jud. Jeanie got summoned to a meeting with two of Trevor's teachers and the guidance counselor on Wednesday, and was told that Trevor will be repeating most of his freshman classes unless he turns in every assignment he missed over the semester. Then Jeanie checked with Jud's teachers and learned that he's failing in two subjects himself (safe to say, Jeanie doesn't do parent-teacher conferences, because she was shocked). So that was it. She had the Internet disconnected on Thursday, and now the boys are in withdrawal and making all of our lives a living hell.

It doesn't take me long to figure out that Jeanie knows exactly where Liam is taking me, even if I don't. Because when he arrives, she's up and dressed. "Bless, could you unload the dishwasher before you leave?" she asks.

Really? I've already got my jacket on.

I know it will take me longer to argue than to just do it—not that I've had the heart to argue with Jeanie after what she told me—so I toss my purse down and head to the kitchen. I can hear some quick whispers in the living room and the front door close. I stick my head in the room, "Where'd Liam go?"

"He'll be right back." *She probably gave him a little job, too!* I go to peek out the bay window and see Liam slamming his SUV's hatch shut.

Shaky shuffles into the kitchen while I'm putting the last of the silverware away. His face is grizzly with stubble and his hair is standing up like an orangutan's. He looks at the coffeepot and says, "Get me a cup, will you, kid?" I roll my eyes—these guys never get up before eleven on Saturdays!

Shaky grunts as he drops onto the couch, and Liam asks him how business is going. "I've gotta work on Peters's brake line today," he says, like that answers everything. "You check your oil like I told you?" Since when does Jeanie check her own oil, I'm wondering—and then I realize that he's talking to Liam!

Before we leave, Jeanie gives me a quick hug, and Shaky says, "Drive safe."

This is getting too weird.

I say bye, and out the door we go.

"Where we going?" I ask Liam once we get on the freeway. He tells me it's a surprise. And two hours later, when we stop so I can pee and I ask him again, he only laughs and says, "You'll see."

We drive for hours—hours!—and cross into Minnesota. "Okay, what's going on?" Only this time when I ask, I'm not laughing. "Jeanie and my old man knew you were taking me a distance, didn't they? That's why Shaky told you to check your oil." I think of Jeanie sending me to do a job she could have easily done. "What did Jeanie give you to put in your trunk?" I ask. "My backpack?"

"Nope," he says. I study his profile and blood starts pumping in my ears. Jeanie gave me a hug, like it was the last time she was going to see me, or something.

"Did my old man ask you to take me back to Wicks?"

Course he did. George's check bounced, so the deal's off.

Liam doesn't answer. Maybe because he's glancing behind his shoulder to pass someone going sixty—or maybe because he doesn't know how to say yes.

I turn around, hoping I can stretch tall enough to see what's in the hatch. But I can't. "Tell me what's going on," I say, my voice ominously low, "or the second you get off this freeway and reach the first set of stoplights, I'm bailing. I'm serious. Because I'm not going back there."

"Whoa—hold on," Liam says. He's actually laughing! "Your dad didn't bribe me to take you back there—I wouldn't if he had. This was *my* idea."

He's lost his freakin' mind! And I tell him so. "What, you think I want some sentimental journey back home? Haven't you heard a thing I said about living with Cactus and George?"

"I'm taking you back to Wicks, Bless. But only for as long as it takes for you to grab Marbles." He looks over at me and grins.

I'm so stunned, I'm speechless. I bring both hands over my mouth.

"Jeanie picked up a litter box and cat food. That's what I put in the back; it's a long haul back to Logan."

I pull my legs up and hook my heels on the seat. I press my hands over my cheeks, my eyes.

"You okay?" Liam asks, his voice soft as kitten fur.

I nod.

It's almost a twelve-hour drive to Wicks. We stop for subs at noon, and grab soda and chips when we stop for gas. And when we break at a wayside because I've had too much soda, Liam stands guard outside the door of the women's restroom. Shaky didn't even do that for me when I was four. And after we get back into the car, I tell him Jeanie's story. Liam finds it just as sad as I do.

By the time we reach Lincoln County, my stomach is in knots at the thought of barging in on George and Cactus—they don't know we're coming. And while I'm freaking out over that, a new terror grips me. "Liam, what if Marbles starved to death? Or George killed her?"

He reaches out and rubs my leg. "That's the difference between you and me, Bless. You always expect the worst, and I always expect the best. Marbles isn't dead."

It's 9:30 p.m. when we reach Wicks. I'm hoping George and Cactus will be sleeping. But when we pull down the drive, the TV is still on, red and blue colors flashing like cop-car lights through the window. The curtains, discolored the same shade as George's fingernails, move. I groan, knowing it's Cactus. "We should have parked on the road and hiked in."

"No," Liam says. "You'll face them."

"And we'll probably end up facing George's .22, too."

Liam laughs, like I'm kidding.

I see movement at the edge of the woods and unhook my seatbelt. I scoot forward, hoping it's Marbles. But the cat is gray, with white paws.

I expect to feel nothing but hatred when I spot Cactus gawking out the window, her hands cupped around her eyes and pressed to the glass. But, surprisingly, that's not what I feel. I feel hurt, mixed in with a little homesickness—*how crazy is that?*

Liam puts the Yukon in park, but leaves it running, the dims on. Cactus opens the door and calls out, "Who's there?"

"You look for Marbles, I'll handle her," Liam says quietly.

Lingering flat patches of ice clot the shaded areas. I avoid them, my feet hurrying over brick-hard mud to get to the pump house. I'm hoping that if I find Marbles there, it won't be with a litter of spring kittens.

"Ma'am," Liam says behind me, without a hint of anxiety in his voice. "My name is Liam Reid. Your granddaughter, Bless, is my girlfriend. We came to get her cat."

I shove the pump-house door open and slip inside. There's one small window on the opposite wall, and dirt-bloated cobwebs are dangling like shredded curtains to keep the lights from the yard light, Liam's car, and the moon from peeping in. I blink fast, willing my eyes to hurry and adjust to the dark.

"Marbles, here Marbles," I call. But only silence replies. I shuffle my feet across the heaved floor and feel for fur inside the drawer. When I find no kittens, I go back outside. Just in time to see George emerging from the house.

Liam greets George as "Sir," and introduces himself, though more quickly this time. Cactus stretches around George's shoulder to gawk.

"Who'd you say you were?" George shouts, his thermal underwear shirt glowing as if it's made of radioactive toxic waste.

Liam repeats himself, while I hurry to circle the dark edges of the yard, calling for Marbles.

"I don't know you from jack shit," George says. "Get off of my property. And get off it now." He turns to Cactus and says something I can't hear. She shakes her head in little jerks and he snaps at her.

I hurry to step out where the yard light can find me. "It's me. Bless. I came back for Marbles."

"Who?" he says.

"Marbles. My cat. Is she still alive?"

George backs up and slips inside. The door only half closes, and I'm terrified that the lunatic is reaching for his rifle. "Here

Marbles, here kitty, kitty," I call. Two cats come, and one peeks out from under George's pickup. But none of them are Marbles.

"You'd better go, Bless," Cactus warns. She's gripping her robe.

I used to sneak the scraps to the back door about this time of night, and I glance at the side of the house hoping Marbles is back there, waiting. That she'll hear me and come. But as soon as I have the thought, I realize that it's probably as ridiculous as my grandma Gloria thinking that I cried for my stuffed skunk every night since I left, when in reality I'd not only forgotten the toy, but her. Marbles has probably forgotten me, too.

Cactus glances at the partially opened door, then calls, her voice faint. "How's Donny?"

I don't have time to answer before George is back, his rifle propped inside his elbow like a bride's arm. "I don't know why you came back, Bless. There's nothing here that belongs to you. Go back to your worthless old man, and leave us be."

His comment makes me furious, and the only fear I have left is for Marbles. I stomp closer to the porch, my eyes on George. "You're the poorest excuse for a father, a grandfather—a human being—that ever walked this earth," I snarl.

He raises his rifle an inch.

"You gave Shaky a check you had no intention of letting him cash, just so he'd get out of your life, and take me with him."

Cactus gasps. "George," she mutters, like this is all a shock to her. It probably is.

"If Shaky believed I was going to cut into my savings for one of his get-rich-quick schemes, then he's even dumber than I thought."

Liam comes up behind me, and I put up my hand to keep him silent. This is my battle.

"No, that's not why he's dumb," I say. "He's dumb because he still holds out hope that he can do something to make you proud.

And that's not going to happen, no matter how much money he makes, or how much respect he earns."

"Money . . . respect . . . that worthless piece of crap ain't gonna ever have either."

"George—" Cactus moans. But George just tilts his head back and spits off the front steps, contempt shooting from his eyes like bullets.

"Maybe not," I say. "But he'll have something you'll never have. People who care about him. But you? You'll wither away in this run-down shack, and nobody will come to your funeral. Not your kids, your grandkids. Not even a stray neighbor. So really, George, who's the bigger loser?"

George just stands there, the frosty night air ruffling the wild fringe of hair above his ears.

Cactus pulls the collar of her robe up to her crumbling face, and slips indoors. But George's face doesn't budge. And neither does he, or his gun.

Liam's hand rubs between my shoulder blades. "Come on, Bless. Let's find your cat." I shoot a look of disdain at George, but I don't move. I don't blink.

George watches us for a bit, then goes inside and slams the door. Through the sheer curtains, I can see him dropping into his chair, and Cactus shuffling off to the kitchen.

"Is that her?" Liam asks. He's pointing to a dark shadow darting across the yard. The cat slips behind the front wheel of the Yukon, and I get on my knees and reach for her. Only to pull her out and realize that, although she's the right color, she's not Marbles. I pat the poor thing and send her scampering.

Liam heads toward the west edge of the yard and calls Marbles's name into the field. But I just stand there, my arms limp at my sides. I don't know where else to look. I think that bastard might have killed her.

I tip my head back and sigh. The stars between the scattering clouds are bright and winking. *Do you see me? Do you see Marbles?*

"Bless—" Liam calls, his voice soft with relief. I look, expecting him to be holding my cat. He isn't. Instead, he's pointing to the side of the house where something is moving, just out of reach of the yard light. It's Cactus, still in her robe, George's unlaced Sorels gaping around her calves. She holds out her arms and the yard light catches the cat dangling from her hands. Even from this distance, I know it's her.

"Marbles!" I cry into my hand. I hurry to the house, my arms reaching.

Marbles feels heavy, so I hold her out, expecting to see her empty like a tube sock, but for a bloated middle with already-formed kittens. But she's plump all over and solid in my hands. She looks into my eyes and meows, and I hug her to me and murmur her name into her fur.

I look at Cactus, confused. "You've been feeding her," I whisper.

Cactus is standing in the shadows, but nonetheless, I can make out the regret on her face, though I'm not sure what it's for.

"Take her and go," she says. Then she turns, and using the house as a brace to help her keep her footing, heads back toward the back door.

I press my face into Marbles again and wet her fur with my tears.

"Come on," Liam says, his voice peaceful.

I tuck Marbles into my coat, and she sniffs my neck, my chest. Liam puts his arm around me and before we even reach his SUV, Marbles is purring against my skin.

Liam pauses to shoo an old cat out from the rear wheel.

"I wish we could take them all," I say. "They're starving."

"It'll be okay," Liam says. "Tomorrow, I'll call the nearest animal protection place and see if they'll rescue them."

I can't explain why I want it this way, but Liam accepts my request for him to drive to the end of the driveway and wait for me there. But he doesn't move more than six feet ahead of me, and veers at times, no doubt because he's watching in his rearview mirror, making sure I'm okay.

I turn when I'm halfway down the driveway, and look back at the house. The window to my old room is nothing but a black hole. More than once while in Logan, I'd wished to be back here. Now I wonder why. Because in reality, this house was never my home.

I turn around and follow the glow of Liam's taillights. To my left is the field, and beyond it, darkness is nestled at the foot of the trees where I played as a child.

I breathe in deeply, my insides swelling with gratitude for everything that surrounds me. For out here, *this* was my home. The trees, my walls; the stars, my ceiling; the animals, my family. And I smile inside at the thought that, after George and Cactus are gone, the house will crumble to ruins and the land will reclaim this place.

Chapter 18
24 Days Ago

Maylee shows up while I'm still in my PJ pants, my hair poking in every direction but down. We're shopping this morning so she can get some flip-flops for summer before they get picked over—she's got ginormous feet. Size ten. Sometimes, eleven. The stores never get more than a couple pairs each in those sizes, she claims, so if she waits she ends up having to buy men's shoes, which are too wide and don't come in pretty colors.

Maylee sits on my bed petting Marbles, as I dig through the laundry basket for something to wear. "Your cat is so sweet. I still can't believe Liam took you all that way to get her."

"I can't, either."

Maylee, like Marbles, has filled out to "normal" weight. The day she met Kenneth at Subway, she ate most of her six-inch sandwich. "How could I not, with him looking over at me the whole time?" she'd said. It filled her up to the point of feeling sick, but she did it. And she's only cubed her food a few times since then. I tell her how good she looks—baggy clothes or not—and she beams. "Life's going good for us, isn't it, Bless?"

"Yeah." We share a smile.

I leave Maylee petting Marbles—Maylee adores her—but by the time I'm showered, Marbles has wandered off into the living room, where the boys are watching a movie. Jud has the upper half of a fishing pole, a chunk of a loofah sponge dangling from the line. Marbles is crouched down, watching it sway. She pounces.

"Look at this goofy bastard," he says while he laughs. There isn't a bit of malice in his tone, in spite of calling her a bastard.

"Wow," Maylee says when I get back to my room. "Trevor and Jud are actually nice to Marbles."

"I know. Shocking, isn't it? And did you see that cat tree in front of the bay window? Jeanie bought it for her."

Shaky promises me that he'll see that the boys don't let Marbles out (this place is still too new to her; plus, she's not fixed yet), and I believe him. Because ever since Liam told Shaky that I'd stood up to George, he's been extra nice to me, even though he has no idea that I stood up to George on *his* behalf; he'd have stayed mad for weeks if he knew what George said about him. Maybe forever. And he's cranky enough as it is these days, because Oiler—though he did return Jeanie's money—wouldn't let him make monthly payments on *The Carol.*

Before I go out the door, Jeanie nods to Shaky, and he pulls two twenties out of his wallet and holds them out. "What's this?" I ask, thinking he wants me to pick something up for him in town.

"Just a little spendin' money for ya."

I'm confused. "I don't need this. Jeanie's been giving me a weekly allowance for keeping the house up since I got here."

Jeanie frowns. "You let your dad do something nice for you, Bless."

"Okay," I say, still confused. "Thanks."

Shaky nods. "And that old green Lumina that was behind the garage?" he says. "I brought it inside the shop this morning. I know it ain't much, but without *The Carol* to bank on it's the best I can do. I'm gonna fix it up for you so you can get a job this summer, like you want."

"Thanks," I say, smiling. Jeanie stands up to dig in her jeans pocket—probably for a different cigarette lighter, since the one she was flicking never sparked—and some change falls from her pocket. She leaves the coins on the floor, then heads for the kitchen, patting me on the arm as she passes. I stare at the two pennies lying on the carpet and ask Dad what year my mom was born.

He gives me a where'd-that-come-from look, then his eyes roll up as he calculates. "Well, lemme see." He ticks time off on his fingers, then says, "1972."

My heart starts beating fast.

"Why?" Dad asked.

"I was just wondering, that's all."

Maylee and I go to the mall. She finds four pairs of flip-flops—one sporting a big plastic flower, one glittered, and all of them in pastels. *To each her own.*

"Hey," Maylee says, as we're sharing a soft pretzel. "You should get something pretty to wear to Liam's graduation with the money your dad gave you."

I refuse to count the days until graduation, but the mood at school alone says it's not far off. The seniors are acting nuts, the guys are rowdy and grinning, the girls soft-eyed and sentimental. Their behavior is a constant reminder that my days of seeing Liam at school are numbered. But I'll see him most every evening. I smile, as I remember him saying that he'll never leave me.

"I should put this money away toward Liam's graduation gift, though," I say. "I've been saving my allowance. Almost every penny of it. But it might not be enough."

"Why, what are you getting him?"

"I'm thinking of a tattoo, but I don't know how much one costs."

"Oh, he doesn't have one, does he?"

"No. But he told me on the phone the other night that he's getting one as soon as he can think of something he'd want to look at the rest of his life. He doesn't want one just to have one."

"Bless," she says. "I've got money. If you run short for his gift, I'll loan you some and you can pay me back this summer when you get a job. Get a dress."

The last dress I had was for my sixth-grade Christmas concert. It was maroon and two years (maybe two decades) out of date. I'm not sure I cared then, but ever since Liam came into my life, I've wanted to look pretty. Sexy, even.

We're passing an outlet store, and I stop and clutch Maylee's arm. "That's it! Right there!" It's short, scoop neck, sleeveless, and has a bubble-shaped skirt. But those features aren't what caught my eye. It's the color. It's lobster blue!

I race inside, mumbling, "Please, please, please come in my size." Maylee and I search the rack and Maylee finds one. "Cool!" she says, "And it's $39.99. How perfect is that? I'll loan you the tax, if you need it."

She makes me try it on and raves about my "cute legs." I feel stupid when other shoppers look over to see if Maylee's claim is true.

For those few moments, as the clerk rings up my dress and we spin the jewelry display, pointing out what we'd wear, and what we wouldn't get caught dead in, it suddenly strikes me that Maylee and I are just like all other teenage girls on a Saturday afternoon. Having fun with our best friend, and picking out things we hope our boyfriends will like. And while maybe that idea would have made me gag once, right now it only makes me happy.

We're laughing as we leave the store. But stop when we find ourselves toe to toe with Misty, Melissa, and a girl with hair the color of red velvet cake, whose name, I think, is Madison. They eye our shopping bags, and Melissa yanks Maylee's open. She snatches the glittery pair of flip-flops and holds them up. Melissa turns to her friends and snickers. "Some ten-foot-tall drag queen must have lost her flip-flops. And look who found them!" I yank them from Melissa and nudge Maylee to skirt around them, since I'm against a glass storefront and have nowhere to go.

But Maylee is frozen like a scared rabbit, and Misty is too quick. She butts up in front of me. "We know that Liam and Stephie were together—sleeping together, even—and that you weaseled your way in and broke them up."

"That's not true!" Maylee blurts out. She looks over at me as if she's asking, *Is it?*

Misty sneers, like she expects me to cower. Fat chance of that. I wasn't afraid of George when he was holding a gun, so I'm certainly not going to be afraid of three girls armed with nothing but spite.

I laugh, mockingly. "You bitches think I'm scared of you? Well, I'm not. So get the hell out of our way before I make you sorry you didn't listen."

"Ooooooo," Melissa and Madison say in unison.

Misty's eyes are hard, her glossy lips pulled taut. "You'll be sorry for what you did to Stephie," she says, a spray of spit spewing out from between her clear braces. "Stephie will see to it that you are."

"And we'll help her," Madison says.

Inside, I may be sighing—I just want things to be good—but I keep my face hard, my feet firmly planted. My voice is snow cold as I say, "Stephie is a desperate, delusional bitch. Now get out of my way, *Lispy.*" My insult slams Misty back a foot, but Madison steps into her spot, ready to take her best shot. "That goes for you, too, clown head," I tell her.

"You'll be sorry, slut!" Melissa hisses as Madison backs off to let us pass.

Maylee hop-runs ahead of me, moving as awkwardly as a newborn fawn. "There's nothing Stephie can do to ruin things for you and Liam, is there?" she calls back to me.

"Of course not," I say, hoping it's the truth.

But I don't need Stephie to ruin things. Liam kind of does that himself when I get to his house.

Cheryl calls, "Come in." She's pulling eggs and milk out of the fridge; a mixing bowl and canisters are on the snack bar. She nods toward Liam's door, where music is playing, and Peg's nose is bumping against the wood, no doubt because he heard my voice.

Peg prances and sniffs when he sees me. I ruffle his ears and push him back so I can get in.

Liam is lying on his back, tossing his basketball toward the ceiling and catching it when it comes down. "Hey," he says with a smile.

"Your mom looks extra happy today."

He lets the ball roll to the floor and sits up. "Yeah. She and dad were on the phone a long time last night, and again this morning. He asked her if she'll come home if he gives up *The Meredith*."

"She'd ask him to do that?"

"No. She'd never ask him to give up fishing. Only to give her more of his time. I think they're going to get back together."

First I'm happy for her—then I panic. But only for a split second. Liam is eighteen. He doesn't have to go back to Maine if his mom decides to.

Liam changes his CD, and in a voice I know he's trying to make sound casual, says, "I called Jib last night. He usually knows what's going on. He said Dad's been preoccupied the last couple of weeks. And Friday, Dad didn't go out. He put Jib in charge, instead. My dad's never done that. Ever. If that boat leaves shore, he's the one steering it and running the crew."

"So what do you make of it?" I ask, my throat tight.

"I think maybe he went to square up the paperwork that turns the boat and the business over to me. I think he's giving them to me for a graduation gift."

My stomach knots. "He'd do that just to win your mom back?"

"No, not just for that reason. But the lobster-fishing business is in hot water. Literally. Water temps are too warm again this spring—forty-eight degrees. The ocean shouldn't see those temps until June. It's been that way the last couple of years. The lobsters are molting too soon and the business is being glutted with soft-shelled lobster. We have to work longer hours, and a hell of a lot faster. Jib said last Tuesday, Dad's daily profit after paying his sternmen and buying bait and fuel was sixty-six cents per pound. A guy can't make it on even two bucks a pound. And he certainly can't afford to fish year-round. Hell, even during the peak season, some guys docked their boats because they couldn't afford to go out.

"The lobster company is feeling it, too. Soft-shells don't pack as well and too many are dying during shipment. Quality means as much to Dad as quantity. It kills him to see things going to hell like this. He says this country will let the world boil and fry before they force corporations to cut down emissions."

"Why would your dad want to give you a business that's headed for disaster?"

"Hey, it's temporary. Dad doesn't think so, but he knows I do. I've got the time and stamina to ride this all out until the weather gets back to normal, or the lobster-fishing industry adjusts. Dad doesn't."

"So if you're right in your guess, then you *are* leaving me, after all."

Liam pulls me down to sit beside him on his bed. "Don't put it like that, Bless."

"But you promised you wouldn't leave me," I say, my voice sounding whiny, even if I don't want it to.

Liam tilts his head sideways. He actually looks perplexed. "I promised you I'd never leave you and I meant it. Wait. You didn't think that meant I wasn't leaving Logan after graduation, did you?"

The look in my eyes must answer for me, because he lifts my hand and gives the back of it little kisses. "Bless, I was going back to Maine to work on *The Meredith*, whether it was Dad's boat, or mine. It's where I belong. It's what gives me my breath."

My throat clogs and my hands start shaking like my old man's. *But I want you to be with me. I want to be what gives you breath.*

"I can't stay here for a year, slinging burritos for minimum wage. I just can't. I've got to make money for our future. But I'm not leaving you, no matter where I go. I love you and I'm yours forever. I'm sorry if I didn't make that clear—I thought you knew that's what I meant."

He leans over to kiss me, but I turn so his lips land on my cheek.

"Look, Bless, you've got one year of school left, and nothing to tie you here after you graduate. You can come to Maine. Enroll in school there, and we'll live together. I'll take you out on my boat now and then. We'll make love on the beach at midnight. I'll take you to Authors Ridge. I'll even be a good sport if you want one of those fancy weddings with me in a penguin suit."

Sadness and happiness wrestle inside me. I stand up, my feet moving in place. Liam stands up too. He takes my shoulders. "Look, Bless. Being apart for a year isn't going to be easy for either of us. I'm smiling right now, but I'm hurting inside at the same time." He pulls me close. "I love you so much, baby. It's going to be hell. But we'll Skype, and text, and talk on the phone until we fall asleep each night, just like now."

He cradles my face in his hands and tips my head back. "Please, Bless. Don't cry. We're forever, you and me.

"I love you, Bless. You know that, don't you?"

I nod.

"Then please be happy for me. Even as you're sad. I've waited my whole life for this."

I wrap my arms around him and squeeze. "I know."

I pull away and fake a smile. "Hey, I need to hike down to the store. I'll be right back, okay?"

"I'll walk with," he says.

I shake my head. "It's girl stuff." Like what? I'm going for tampons and would be too embarrassed to have him know I get periods?

He reaches for his keys on his nightstand. "Then I'll give you a lift and wait in the car."

"No, no, it's only a couple of blocks. And it's nice out. I want to walk, okay?"

I tell him I'll be back as soon as I can, and I get on my tiptoes to give him a quick peck on the lips.

"Bless, you sure you're okay with all of this?"

"Yeah," I say, my voice too high-pitched to sound honest.

I get outside and walk so fast I'm almost running.

Chapter 19
24 Days Ago

I walk past IGA and ditch into Barnes & Noble. I order a chocolate latte, just to justify taking up table space. But my stomach is too full of dread to put anything else in it.

He said he wouldn't leave me!

I sit hunched over the table tucked back alongside the food case, stirring my drink with a straw until it's a soupy mess. I decide it's a good thing I don't have a pen on me, or I'd be maiming the book jackets of every happy cover in the store.

He's just like everyone else who left me behind. He is!

I stew until my drink is completely melted, the paper casing from my straw shredded to bits. Then I fold my arms on the table and lean my forehead against them. I sigh so deeply I shudder. I think of Liam on his knees by the bathtub, fishing for a plastic lobster with his Easter basket, and I feel like a jerk. He's about to get the gift he's waited for since he was a little boy. I should be happy for him. And I am. But I'm upset with him, too. He should have told me he was still leaving.

I lift my head and rest my elbow on the table, my chin in my hand. I have every right to be upset, I tell myself. I even tell myself that Liam is only thinking about himself. But I know that's not true. He's thinking of us. Our future. And if Liam believes our relationship is forever, even if we have to spend a year apart, shouldn't I have the same faith in us?

When I hit the street, I run, wanting nothing more than to

wrap my arms around Liam and tell him that I'm happy for him. And apologize, because an hour ago, I wasn't.

Cheryl's voice is faint when she calls, "Come in." She's slumped in the recliner, her fist propped on her cheek, the cooking stuff untouched on the snack bar.

"Liam's in his room," she says. Her eyes are red, the lids puffy. I want to ask her what's wrong, but I don't.

Liam has music playing, and doesn't hear me knock. So I open his door a crack and call to him. Peg gets to his feet and scoots past me to get out the door.

Liam's sitting on the edge of his futon, elbows pinned to his knees, hands knotted together into one fist.

"Liam?" I know he hears me, but he doesn't look up. And for a second, I wonder if it's because I was such a bitch earlier. But no. That wouldn't explain Cheryl's tears.

I slip inside and quietly close the door. I go to his bed so I can sit directly across from him. He looks even more destroyed than his mother. I reach out and cup my hands over his. "What's the matter?"

I move to the futon to sit beside him when he doesn't answer.

Liam doesn't look at me, but his fists tighten under my fingers, a muscle in his forearm twitches. Then he gets up and leaves the room. Just like that.

I wait, thinking he's gone for water or something. I hear the front door open and slam, and I think it's Cheryl. That is, until she steps into Liam's room.

She has a teacup in her hand and a wadded Kleenex trapped under her fingers. She sits down on the bed. A frizzy curl falls down across her blotched cheek. "Jib called Liam after you left. He thought Frank had told us what he'd done—but he hadn't."

"What he'd done?"

Cheryl gets up. She goes to the window and mindlessly tucks the curtain behind the dresser that's piled with stray CDs, a couple LPs, Liam's wallet, and an electric razor with a coiled cord that's stuck in the haphazardly closed top drawer. She pulls the cord loose and leans against the drawer to close it. Then she pivots to face me. "Liam's father sold everything. *The Meredith.* The lobster company. Everything."

My fingertips come up to press against my lips.

She sits back down and stares into her steamless cup. "Liam's devastated, of course. He never thought in a million years that Frank would do something like this."

My heart feels like it's breaking. "He told Liam it would all be his if he ever lost his sea legs."

"That's what Liam remembers. And who knows, maybe Frank *did* say that to him once. But if he did, either Frank doesn't remember it, or he changed his mind. And as usual, without consulting anyone. That's how Frank is, though. He may need a crew to run a boat, but when it comes to life on shore, he sails solo.

"Frank was wrong to make this decision without talking to us first. And I told him so. But he thinks he's in the right. Things have been hard in the lobster business the last few years and he's bitter about the whole thing. He gave his life to the sea. Now he thinks it was all for nothing."

"But the boat, the business—those were Liam's future," I protest. "Did you ask him why he didn't at least offer them to Liam?"

She nods. "I believe his exact words were: 'Cheryl, he's an eighteen-year-old kid, for chrissake. One with starry eyes for the life. What does he know about running a boat? A business? Working your ass off to barely break even?'

"He pointed out that Liam would be leading men two or more times his age, and that he'd only spent three summers, four

Christmas vacations, and a few weekends on the boat. He claims he would have ended up training Liam for a good couple of years, and believes that by then, he'd be so wrapped up in those ropes that he'd never get himself untangled."

"But Liam had Jib. He would have taught Liam anything he still needed to learn."

"Jib McDowell is seventy years old, Bless, do you realize that? He gave Frank thirty-one years of his life, so Frank's not had the heart to let him go. But the old guy can't keep up anymore. Regardless, Frank didn't want to hand his son a business that's destined to fail. It's a hard enough life during boom years, much less times like these. If not for my paychecks, we'd not have been able to pay our taxes most years."

My insides are ablaze with rage. Because—damn it!—it doesn't seem to matter whether it's about love, or dreams, or whatever, everyone over the age of thirty-five tries to bring you down, telling you why this won't work, and that won't last. Like what? Just because they failed at those things, we're doomed to fail at them, too? Doesn't it ever occur to them that maybe things will be different for us because *we're* different?

"Bless, this doesn't mean that Liam's father doesn't love him. I hope you can help Liam realize this. It's just that, Frank's not only lost his sea legs, he's lost his enthusiasm. To him, he would have been handing Liam a curse."

"But he didn't have to make that decision for Liam," I snap.

My face crumples and I'm bawling. Cheryl's eyes are leaking again, too. But while her tears are radiating understanding, I'm positive mine aren't. How could Liam's dad have so little faith in him? How could he go back on his word like this? Doesn't he know he's Liam's hero?

Cheryl looks up at me, her head tilting to the side. "Bless, I hope you don't take this wrong, but as sad as I am for Liam, and as angry as I am with Frank for not talking to us first, I have to agree with him on one point. Liam *is* too young for such a big responsibility. He doesn't see that now, but when he's older, he will.

More famous words from the over-thirty-five crowd.

"And if I'm honest, I have to admit that a part of me is relieved that Frank made this choice. A lobster fisherman's life is not only a hard one, but a dangerous one. You know how many experienced fishermen get tangled in the gear and fall overboard to drown? We live in a small, close-knit community and the loss of any fisherman that goes down is felt by us all. Some years ago, four, no, I guess more like five now, there was an accident on a boat owned by Frank's lifelong friend, Teddy. His son—Liam's friend—was on the boat, horsing around, I guess, and went overboard. Teddy jumped in to save him, and that was it. They never found either body.

"I've spent well over three decades worrying every time my husband headed out. It about killed me to think of spending the rest of my life worrying like that over my son."

I look down, my jaw so tight it's making my teeth ache.

Cheryl rubs her free hand down her thigh, then gets up. "You can wait for Liam here, if you'd like. Though who knows how long he'll be gone. Even as a boy, when he got upset he'd disappear for hours. Like I said, he's like his father. And like Frank, he'll sort this out alone and stay moody and distant until he does. Try not to take it personally. That's what I had to do after Teddy and his boy died. Frank and Liam barely spoke to me for weeks."

Cheryl leaves the room, but her story stays behind to sit with me. I fidget for a time, then get up and start straightening the room. Not because the mess bothers me, but because I've learned that when life becomes an uncontrollable mess, it helps me to put something in order. And right now, what I'm trying to control is the bit of relief I'm feeling that the boat is gone. And feeling like that makes me feel like I'm betraying Liam.

I pick up the CDs that have fallen on the carpet—a couple of cases trashed, one upended like a teepee—and square them in my hand. And as I do, I think about Cheryl's warning that Liam will shut me out for a time now. It's an unbearable thought. Liam is the half of me I didn't know was missing until he came along.

I set the CDs on the dresser and lift the corner of the LPs to reach under them and remove whatever's keeping them from lying flat, so I can stack the CDs on top of them. I brush at what I think are food crumbs, and tiny bits of blue, smashed like Easter egg shells, scatter over the carpet.

It's his blue lobster shell. He must have smashed it after he heard the news.

I scoop the shattered pieces into my palm, then look for a place to put them, other than the trash basket. I spot a small, slightly lopsided clay pot on the windowsill above his bed. I crawl on my knees across the mattress and grab the pot. I brush the bits inside. A few fragments float to the floor between the bed and wall, and when I reach down to rescue them, I feel foil against my fingers. A candy wrapper, no doubt. I pull it up and stare down at two unopened condoms in glossy wrapping, strung together like packets of dry yeast.

CONDOMS? Behind his BED?

I hear a clunk in the living room and freeze, clutching them to me in case Cheryl comes in. I wait. But when the house quiets again, I study the packages.

I have no idea how many of these things are sold together, but upon closer inspection, I see the perforated edge where at least one was torn away. I glance over at his wallet and wonder if the missing one is tucked inside in anticipation for when the two of us are ready. Or—

I shove the picture of a half-dressed Stephie out of my head, and drop the condoms back where I'd found them.

I stop cleaning and just sit there, waiting. But when Liam doesn't come back by dark, I tell Cheryl good-bye and call Maylee from the steps. I tell her what happened and ask if she'll drive me to the water. "I want to see if he's there."

"Okay," Maylee says slowly, her voice flatlining; the beach at night creeps her out.

"You could bring Kenneth along if you want to."

"He's working on his term paper. I just left."

"Well, you can park under the streetlights then, over by the marina, where it's bright. You can lock the car doors. It will only take a couple of minutes. Promise."

Maylee looks relieved to see the stretch of sand empty, but gets distressed again when I tell her that if he's here, he'll be out by the lighthouse.

When I open the door, Maylee is staring wide-eyed out at the pier. There are no light poles embedded in the concrete, but the anemic sliver moon and lights along the boardwalk over by the marina are working together to cast just enough light onto the water to show the waves crashing high above the boulders at its base. "You're not walking out there, are you? Look at the waves! Uncle Bob says that the concrete gets real slick when it gets wet, and people have been washed over the side."

"I'm not going to fall in."

"What if he's not even there?"

"Then I'll be right back."

I slip out and the door lock clicks before I even slam the car door. I take two, three steps, and Maylee calls to me. I turn. She's got the window rolled down about two inches, her neck stretched, her mouth sucked to the gap. "Let's keep texting, okay?"

"Sure." Maylee texts so slowly, I'll probably be to the lighthouse and back before I get her first one.

I hurry along the pier, walking down the center. I avoid looking to my sides. I don't want to see the water, black as death.

Liam is all the way down by the lighthouse, standing with his hands in his pockets, his head down, staring at the water a good ten, eleven feet below, swirling, reaching.

I call his name, but he doesn't turn around. I squint, questioning for a moment then, if it's really him. Liam would acknowledge my presence. Or would he? He didn't in his room.

But of course it's him. I've seen his hair luminous in night skies before, and I know the curve of his back and the slope of his shoulders, even though I've never seen them this weighted down before.

"Liam?"

I want to move in front of him so he's forced to look at me, but he's standing too close to the ledge and there's no guardrail. So I go up behind him and carefully wrap my arms around his waist. I know what it's like to cling to a promise from your dad, only to realize years later that he never meant it as a vow in the first place—probably didn't even remember saying it. I press the side of my face against his back and whisper, "I can't believe he did this to you."

Liam doesn't respond, and I think that maybe with the wind whipping and the sound of the water roaring, he might not have heard me. But then he says, "I would have thought you'd be happy right about now."

"No, no," I plead, talking to his back. "I was upset at first because I couldn't imagine us being apart for so long. But then I decided that we could make it work—that we *would* make it work. So I came back to give you my support and to be happy for you. Honest."

Liam stares into the water as if my words dropped into the

crashing waves and drowned under the milky foam. That's when my phone alerts me that Maylee wants reassurance that I'm safe. I step back and text her quickly, telling her to hold on. Then look at Liam's back and silently beg, *Turn around. Believe me. Talk to me. Why aren't you moving at all?*

Suddenly, fear whooshes up the hem of my jeans like a biting wind, and up my sleeves to chill my pulse. Because for the first time in months, I recall his words: *"I tried to hang myself once."*

He wasn't serious, I remind myself. He'd read that crazy essay and—but then I stop. Because I'm hearing Cheryl again: *"Four . . . no, five years ago . . . Frank and Liam barely spoke to me for months."*

Liam would have been twelve years old then.

I gulp hard. "Liam, please. You're scaring me."

The wind ripples through his hair as I wait. Wait for some assurance that he still cares about life. Wait for him to turn and hold his arms out and tell me that as long as he has me, he has enough. Instead, he keeps his face lowered and says, "I just want to be alone right now."

I stand there for a minute, feeling rejected and scared, then reach out to at least rub my hand up his back so he knows I care. But my hand falls away before it even reaches his shoulder blades, because he's no more responsive to my touch than the concrete lighthouse wall would be if I stroked it. So I stuff my hands into my pockets and head back toward the beach, where Maylee's headlights are watching like eyes too fearful to blink.

Maylee drops me off at home, asking if I'd like her to come in for a while. I shake my head. All I want is to get inside and curl up with Marbles. But the house is in chaos again, with everybody snipping and shouting at each other. So I tuck Marbles in my coat and hike out to the red pines to hear their reassuring whispers. But all I hear is the long, mournful moans of the wind.

Chapter 20
5th Street

The traffic is thickening the closer I get to the beach.

I hear more sirens. Leaving? Coming? I can't even tell anymore.

My skin feels scorched, my lungs are burning, and my legs feel too heavy to be mine. I'm pushing with all my might, but I'm slowing. I'm on a gradual incline, but the block up ahead is so steep that the street looks to be leading to nowhere but the sky.

I veer around a couple with a baby stroller. The red-faced, wailing toddler with an empty cone in his hand is looking down at the glob of ice cream melting on the sidewalk. "We'll get you another one," the father promises. My skin prickles, wondering if the father will keep his promise. Wondering if any fathers ever keep their promises. Maybe not. But hopefully, boyfriends do.

Last Saturday, while waiting for Maylee to shower so we could hang out until Liam got off of work and Kenneth got home from his aunt's, I started flipping through one of her lame magazines and came across an article about things you should do if you suspect that a friend is contemplating suicide.

I didn't want to read it. But ever since Liam's world came crashing down on him, burying him so deep in depression that I couldn't dig him out, the subject of suicide had been nagging at me. Sure, maybe Liam is ordinarily a positive person, but as Shaky said after he saw Liam so down, "Every man's got his breaking point." And after the way Liam had been hurt and betrayed, I feared he'd reached it. So I read the article. Just in case.

I skimmed the list of signs quickly, my eyes snagging on lines here and there: dramatic mood swings, loss of interest in day-to-day activities, major changes in sleeping and eating habits. They were all symptoms I recognized from those cheesy commercials for antidepressants, where they list them, as well as the scary side effects, in tones as soothing as a slow-flowing stream; they were all symptoms I recognized in Liam. So I skipped to tips for how to help.

The suggestions were things I'd heard before, also. Except for one. It suggested you ask the depressed person to say out loud, "I will not kill myself by accident, or on purpose." The article claimed that the promise itself, if said to someone they care about, might be enough to make them pause and think twice when they're teetering on the edge.

So when I got to Liam's, and he said he didn't feel like doing much of anything, I dragged him down to the lake and made him place his hand on the water (because having him recite the words alone didn't seem like enough, and I didn't know whose grave to have him swear on) and begged him to say those words to me. Liam wrinkled his nose, like he thought my request was crazy. But when I got upset, he did it.

A boyfriend who claims to love you would keep his promise, wouldn't he?

But not if he didn't mean it in the first place.

What a hellish week that was, after Liam's dad sunk his dream. I know I shouldn't be thinking about it now, just running, but I can't help it.

Liam was out of school that whole week. On Monday, he was absent because he was heartsick. But by Tuesday, he was just plain sick. It took his mom and me until that Thursday to talk him into letting her take him to the doctor. It was strep throat, and he had to be on antibiotics for twenty-four hours before he could return to school. He texted me a few times while he was sick, but said his throat hurt too much to talk. All week long, I had trouble sleeping and shuffled through the halls in a fog.

But maybe it was better that way. Stephie's friends were out for my blood. Circling and stalking, while Stephie held back, making herself look small and wounded. They cooked up rumors in their drama caldrons and passed them out to anyone with a thirst for gossip, and I was met with stares and whispers in every classroom I entered, every hall I turned down. But in my state of exhaustion and worry, I couldn't have cared less.

"They've got everyone believing that you broke Stephie and Liam up, Blessy," Abby said when he stopped me in the hall that Wednesday. "And they're saying that the reason Liam's absent is because Drake heard that he was sleeping with Stephie and beat him up with a baseball bat, breaking two of his ribs and his nose."

"That's absurd," I said, and Abby agreed.

"As absurd," he said, "as the rumor Katie Springer, that big girl from the Chub Club table next to the cheerleaders, is spreading. She said she'd heard that you'd gotten Liam drunk so he'd sleep with you."

I snapped at Abby to stop referring to those girls as The Chub Club, and told him that I didn't care about the rumors. And I meant it. He said, "I hate gossip too, Blessy." To which I snapped, "Then stop spreading it. Even to me. And stop calling me Blessy while you're at it!"

I don't know how far I might have sunk had Maylee not come to pick me up on Mother's Day to take me to Verna Johnson's. I'd forgotten we agreed to go, until she came. I followed her and her stupid idea out the door like a zombie, but came back feeling better. At least, that first time.

I force myself to stop right there, for fear that if I don't, I'll be remembering that second trip to Verna's. And I can't go there again. Especially not now. The hill is still ahead of me, and already I can hardly breathe.

It's like my lungs are filled to capacity with heavy, musty air, and no matter how hard I try to empty them so I can take a breath, I can't. I'm light-headed, and my vision is messed up. I see dark fog moving in from the sides, no matter where I look or how hard I blink. Maylee passed out once, and she told me this is just what happened first; she started seeing through a narrow tunnel. I bend over and brace my hands on my knees and try to calm down. But the fog won't lift, and the sounds of the city start to muffle.

I feel my body slumping and put one hand down to catch myself before I topple over. In front of me, a hedge shudders.

I struggle back to my feet, trembling as I back away from the bush.

It's just exhaustion. Fear. Just breathe. Breathe.

I stay bent over while my vision clears and I try to steady my breath. Then I turn and will my legs to move. I remind myself that all I have to do is keep running for water and sky.

Chapter 21
15 Days Ago

Liam calls me early in the morning, before I'm even out of bed to get ready for school, Marbles still curled near my neck.

"I'm sorry, Bless," he begins, his voice so hoarse that he sounds like his strep is back.

I go so stiff that Marbles opens her eyes and lifts her head.

He's going to tell me that he's sorry, but that he just can't do a relationship right now. "Don't say it, Liam. Please."

"Don't apologize for being an ass?"

"I, I thought you were going to say something else."

There's a painful silence, but for the hum of either my phone or his. Not that I have to have constant yapping, but there's a difference between silent closeness and what a lull in our conversation feels like now—empty distance.

"Liam, don't shut me out. Talk to me, please."

"Talking won't change anything," he says.

It will between us.

I glance at the time. "You could have waited until we got to school, you know."

"No I couldn't. I've been lying here half the night, thinking about what a jerk I've been to you."

"Do you work tonight?" (Two weeks ago, I wouldn't have needed to ask.)

"Yeah. Until nine."

"Do you want to come over afterward?" Liam hesitates.

Probably because the last thing he wants right now is to listen to Shaky whine about losing *his* boat, when he's mourning the loss of his own. (Weird, that both my dad and boyfriend had dreams of owning their own boats, and that both of their dreams have capsized; proof that truth is stranger than fiction.)

"Or I could come over," I suggest.

"How about you come over tomorrow night," he says. "I didn't sleep. I'm gonna be beat by the time I get home."

"You work tomorrow?"

"Yeah. Until nine again."

"Okay. I'll come then."

"We'll take a ride or something. Not like I want to sit around here."

"Liam?"

"Yeah?" He sounds impatient, distant.

"Never mind," I say. "Another time." Or maybe never. Because really, do I want to know the truth about what I found in his room? Or if he was serious about ending his life, after his friend's life was ended? Probably not.

We say good-bye, and I toss my phone on the bed, even though there are other things I wish we had talked about. For three days now, I've been bursting to tell Liam about Maylee and my visit to Verna's. To share with him what she said so he can help me figure out what the message means, and how Susan's penny folder might play into it all. To ask him what he thinks about me calling Gloria to try and get some answers.

But the time hasn't seemed right to talk to Liam about anything. Not with him so devastated over what his dad did. Yeah, I've talked with Maylee about the penny folder (but not the condoms). Even showed her the penny folder. And while it felt good to share that with her, it isn't like she'll be of any help in solving the riddle—even though every time she gets a penny for change, she closes her eyes like she's trying to make magic happen, then drops it in my hand and waits until I check it to see if it's *the* penny. Over and over—in between fretting about Liam—I roll Verna's message over in my head. Someone will give me the penny, and then I'll drop it. And when that happens, I'll understand fear? I don't get it. And as hard as I try to tell myself that it means something good, the cryptic message only sounds ominous.

Marbles inches up to curl over my chest and starts butting the top of her head against my chin. Her gesture warms me, and for the millionth time, I'm grateful that I have her. But I fear that in the end, she will be all I'll have. Until I lose her, too.

I force myself to get up and shower. I don't want to go to school today, but if I don't, Stephie and her witches will think they've scared me off.

Liam is busy most of the day—all the seniors are—and I'm almost glad. We can't hold hands in the hall anymore (new school ordinance, or an old one now enforced), and since we don't talk anymore, we end up walking side by side like strangers whose strides just happen to be in sync for a moment. And that hurts.

As I'm darting to English class, one of the junior boys' PE classes is letting out. The athletic boys are coming at me like an unorganized army, their hair damp from either showers or sweat. And behind them, Abby and Kenneth are walking side by side, their faces stained with exertion. Suddenly, I'm smelling lilacs again. I know the scent isn't coming from the boys, so I smile. At least inside. I've been smelling them on and off since Maylee dragged me to Verna's on Mother's Day. And every time the scent comes, I feel a quick ripple of warmth.

But the smell and warm feeling doesn't last long, and I'm back to feeling sad and worried.

I turn the corner. Drake Collins is headed to Mr. Johnson's room, his bad leg scuffing the floor with a *clump, swish. Clump, swish*. When I get right up alongside of him, he veers over and our sides collide.

Drake's algebra book hits the floor. I jump over it, turn and pick it up, grab the folded assignment that slipped out of it, and hold them out. I've never really looked in Drake's eyes before, and now that I am, I don't want to be. His eyes weren't injured in the crash, but something in them looks wounded all the same. I look down at the book and wait for him to take it.

"Sorry," he says, his face flushing where there are no scars.

"That's okay. I wasn't paying attention, either," I tell him. I force myself not to turn away too soon, and Drake, he actually seems confused by this. Maybe because people stopped looking at him almost a year ago. "Well, bye," I say, smiling. He gives me a cautious smile, then turns away.

I watch as Drake heads into the classroom, and think of how, if I lose Liam for good, I'll become a ghostly figure like Drake. Floating the halls of Logan High in my own hellish little bubble; ignored, shunned, a dropout of the human race.

"Everything's going to be okay, Bless," Liam says right before he heads out after school to go to work. I smile like I believe him, and he tells me that he'll see me later.

When I pull into the driveway, Shaky is standing on the front steps, squinting at the Lumina. "How long's that thing been squealin'?" I shrug. I didn't notice that it was. He holds out his hand for the keys so he can bring the car into the garage and check the belts. "Okay, but I'm driving it to town tonight, fixed or not," I tell him.

I go inside and straight to bed. And that's where I intend to stay until it's time to head to Liam's.

That is, until Trevor screams from the kitchen, "Fire!"

I jet out of my room, Marbles in my arms.

I expect to see a grease fire roaring up from the stove, but instead, Trevor is leaning out the back door on tiptoes, Jud behind him like a jumping bean, trying to get a peek. "Oh, man! Mom, MOM!" Jud calls.

I shove them out of the way to look. Smoke is pushing out from under the eaves on Shaky's shop and seeping out from the edges of the window.

Jeanie shuffles into the kitchen in her work clothes and bedroom slippers. "What are you two yelling about now?"

"It's the garage! It's on fire!" Trevor darts toward the living room, and Jeanie hurries to the porch. She utters a string of curses, then reaches for the phone to call 911.

"Where's Shaky?" she shouts.

"In the garage," Jud yells from the porch.

I close Marbles in my room, then rush back to the kitchen. Trevor and I almost collide. He's got an armload of shoes—surprisingly, mine included—and shouts at me to hurry and grab them so he can get outside to "catch the action."

By the time I've punched my feet into my shoes, the boys are leaping off the steps, laces flapping, whooping like they're about to see Fourth of July fireworks. Considering the gas cans, drain oil, and grease rags in that wreck of a building, maybe they are.

I follow them out, Jeanie right behind me.

I dart around the boys, shouting to Shaky, who's coming out the side door of the garage, hacking and dragging a garden hose across the muddy yard. He runs it halfway to the house and tosses it at Trevor like a lasso. "Hook this up!"

Trevor just stands there—he probably doesn't even know where the outside faucet is, much less how to hook it up—so I grab the hose and run to the spigot. While I'm screwing the hose on, Jeanie is screaming at the boys to stay back.

I crank the valve and run the hose back to Shaky. There's no spray nozzle, so the water comes out in a thin arch that goes no more than five feet before it peters to the ground. My old man splits the water with his thumb to lengthen the spray. Now it's going a whole six feet. Trevor starts snickering. "He might as well piss on that fire, for all the good that hose's gonna do."

It does look futile. Flames whooshing out from under the roof, a mushroom of smoke swelling in the sky.

The fumes and smoke are burning my eyes and throat, so I step back from the inferno.

"What are you doing, Shaky?" Jeanie screams. "Spray the house!"

"The house isn't on fire," he snaps back, "the garage is!"

His comeback sends the boys into fits of giggles.

I'm embarrassed for Shaky. Seriously, I'm embarrassed.

"The garage is gone, Shaky," Jeanie shouts. "Spray the house, before that goes, too!" Trevor and Jud glance at the house, like it never dawned on them, until Jeanie said it, that the house and everything they own could burn up, too.

Shaky drops the hose and runs to the garage door, yanking up on the metal handle to open it.

"What's he doing?" Jeanie bellows, as she unkinks the garden hose. "Shut that, Shaky! You give it more air and the whole damn thing's gonna blow!" She starts spraying the side of the roof and the house that are facing the garage.

"Mom, that crazy bastard went back in there!" Trevor shouts.

Jeanie drops the hose, and we both edge closer to the billowing building, screaming at Shaky to come out.

And he does—in the Lumina!

He all but falls out of the car once he's got it backed into the driveway, choking until he pukes. A red burn is sliced across his palm. When Jeanie and I get him to his feet, he tries to go back inside to get his welder. But Jeanie gets a hold of his belt to keep him back. "Are you nuts? Everything's gone!" Jeanie lights him a cigarette and pops it into his mouth like a pacifier.

By the time the fire trucks are screaming up the road, the shed is gone, the metal sides blackened and buckled, the guts a charred mess. Cars are parked along the road now, a couple of men shouting out offers to help, as if it's not too late.

With the fire department here, any fear Trevor and Jud had is gone and now they're awed to hysterics by the power of the firemen's hoses. Jeanie and Shaky are in the driveway, Jeanie pointing here and there, like she's trying to find a place to put the blame. But Shaky, he just stands there, his head wagging, his shoulders slumped with defeat. He coughs some more and folds over. I go to him and ask if he's okay. He nods and straightens up. "At least I got your car out," he says.

Liam calls me an hour after the danger passes. "You answered," he says with a sigh of relief. "Someone said your place burnt to the ground. Thank God you're okay. Everybody else, too? And Marbles?"

I hear thumping, then Liam snaps, "I'll be right there!"

"You at home, or at work?"

"Taco Bell. Where I'll obviously be for the rest of my stinking life. I just had to make sure you were okay."

"It was the garage, not the house. Thanks for caring enough to call."

He sounds almost annoyed when he says, "Of course, I care. It might not seem like it right now, but I do. Look, I've gotta go."

There's no time to ask him if we're still on for later.

CHAPTER 22
15 DAYS AGO

Maylee calls as I'm going out the door to head to Liam's. "Oh man, Bless. I'm so glad you guys are all okay! What's your dad going to do now?"

Maylee's actually naive enough to believe that the garage was making Shaky a living.

Probably the same thing he's always done. Find a new dream he'll never realize.

"I don't know," I say, as I slide into my car. Covered in blistered paint, squealing, and ugly as sin as it is, I'm glad I still have it. "I'm heading to Liam's now."

"I'm in the car, too. I'm going to the library to meet Kenneth. He's got some research to do, and I'm going to look at magazines. I hope they've got good magazines there."

I know if I wasn't so on edge, I'd be laughing, at least inside. Because really—*Subway*, while he works? *The library*, while he does research? What next, *Walmart*, while he picks out socks?

"Bless, do you think maybe Kenneth thinks of me as only a friend? He hasn't even tried to kiss me yet."

"Do you want him to?"

"Yeah. But only because I've seen his tongue—he licked a bubble of blood off his hand when he nicked his finger at Subway. It's not bumpy. Not fat, either. I don't think I'd puke. Do you think I'd puke?"

"No, I don't think you'll puke." *Though I would, if I saw him sucking his own blood.*

Cheryl's car is gone, so I text Liam, and he tells me to just come in. I step inside and I swear I can smell depression in the air.

Liam is slumped on his futon, his legs propped on his bed, ankles crossed, his chin covered with blond stubble. He has a tennis ball, gnarled from Peg's teeth, in his fist and is absentmindedly squeezing it. I step inside and partially close the door behind me.

He doesn't look at me (almost like he's too ashamed to) but his left arm rises, inviting me to sit down beside him.

I tuck myself close to him and drape my arm across his belly. It feels good to be beside him again, but I don't know what to say that I haven't said already. That I'm shocked. Sorry. So very sad for him.

He lets the ball roll under his bed without notice. I'm jittery. I want to comfort him, but if truth be known, I don't know how to comfort anybody. Not even myself, really. And for the first time in my life, I couldn't be sorrier for my ignorance.

I ask him if he wants to go down to the beach. He doesn't. To the park? No. So I stop asking and just nuzzle my face to his neck and drink in the scent of him—at least that hasn't changed.

His arm tightens around me, and he turns to kiss me. His kiss isn't lethargic, as I would have guessed it would be, but intense. His hand sifts through my hair as he turns his body toward mine, his mouth still pressed to mine. His groan sounds sad, which only makes me hold him tighter.

We slip sideways until he's lying down and I'm on top of him. I can feel his abs heaving against me as if he's sobbing. His hands stroke my back, my butt, as though he's blind and that's the only way he can see me. I feel dizzy with wanting him. Wanting to make him feel better. I feel him hard against me, and our hips begin moving together.

I lift my body so I can get my hand between us. I reach for the button of his jeans. Liam pauses for only a second, then fumbles to help me.

I don't know how far I intend to go. I'm not thinking, only feeling. "I love you so much," I whisper as I fumble to tug his zipper down all the way.

My hair is brushing his forehead, curling over his eyebrows, his lids. But he doesn't blink. He just stares up at me as if I'm the mermaid that will keep him from crashing into the rocks. That is, until I wrap my hand around him. Then his lids come down over his eyes like a soft blanket.

He moans.

I moan.

And then the front door groans, and Peg bumbles into the house.

"Li-am!" Cheryl calls.

Oh! My! God!

I scramble to my feet, and Liam quickly zips and buttons his jeans. He bolts up and tugs his T-shirt down over his hard-on.

There's a rustle of paper bags. "Liam!" Cheryl calls again. "Could you give me a hand here? There's a gallon of milk and a jug of orange juice in the trunk. I couldn't get it all."

Liam's door swings open, and Peg rushes in, panting as hard as we are. He's dragging his leash.

"Liam?" his mom calls again.

"I'm getting my shoes on."

He isn't. He's behind the door, waiting to wilt.

I tuck my hair behind my ears and blow air up over my burning cheeks. Through the gap in the doorway that Peg left, I see Cheryl in the kitchen lifting two heavy grocery bags onto the snack bar. "Oh hi, Bless," she calls when she turns.

"Hi," I call back.

"Liam, take Peg out when you go, will you? It's been awhile."

I leap up to go with him—I could use the cool air!—but Liam just picks up the handle of Peg's leash and goes out the front door, shutting it behind them.

Cheryl gives me an apologetic look.

I ask if she needs any help putting groceries away, but she tells me to sit and relax (as if that's possible).

Finally the door opens, and Peg runs in. He pauses by me, his fur smelling like spring, then scuttles to his water bowl. Liam plunks the milk and juice jugs on the counter without looking at his mom.

"I'm making lasagna from scratch," she tells me. "We'd love for you to stay, wouldn't we, Liam?"

Liam doesn't respond. He heads to his room and slams the door behind him, leaving me standing there. Just like I stood in the yard watching Shaky drive away when I was four. Just like I stood at Shaky and Jeanie's, waiting for someone to tell me where I'd sleep.

I stare at his door.

"Bless," Cheryl says, her voice hushed. "That slam wasn't for you. It was for me. He feels so betrayed right now. He doesn't understand how his father could have done this, and he thinks I knew. But in time, a penny will drop."

I'm so stunned that I can only stand there, staring at her.

"What did you say?"

She glances up. "I said he's just angry right now . . . he feels—"

"No. About a penny—"

"Oh." Cheryl flicks her wrist. "It's just an old English expression. My grandma used to say it."

"What does it mean?"

"Well, it's a belated understanding that comes in a flash, after you've been confused for a long time. In Victorian times, slot machines were common, and they jammed a lot. So people would put penny after penny into them, but only when a penny dropped did they get what they wanted. So we use it to mean that moment in time, that instant, when you suddenly understand something you've been trying to figure out for a long time.

"Right now, Liam doesn't understand how his father could have done what he did. But a penny will drop, and he'll at least understand that it wasn't because his father doesn't love him or doesn't believe in him. Have patience, Bless. And go in there. I'm sure he's waiting for you."

But I'm hardly listening to Cheryl anymore. Instead, I'm listening to my mom through Verna: *And when the penny drops, you'll understand the nature of fear.*

I snatch my purse and jacket from the couch and leave, Cheryl sighing behind me.

I drive back home in a fog. Everything feels so surreal. So confusing.

Liam texts after I'm back home, asking why I'd left. I don't answer. I just curl on my bed, Marbles under my arm, the coin folder under my bed.

When I don't reply to Liam's fifth text, he calls to ask why I left. I don't have the energy to raise my voice. "You left with Peg without asking me to come along," I say, my voice flat, "then stomped off to your room without inviting me in. What was I supposed to do? Stand outside your door and beg like a dog?"

"Look, Bless—"

"No, *you* look," I say, my voice firm, but still quiet. "Ever since your dad sold the boat, the company, I've been doing everything I can to be here for you. But it doesn't matter what I do, it's either not good enough, or not the right thing. I get it that you're upset, but *I'm* not the enemy here. And I have stuff going on, too, you know."

"Bless—"

I start crying. "You want to break up with me, then just do it and get it over with."

"Bless, I don't want to break up with you. Though I'm wondering why *you* haven't broken up with *me* yet."

"What are you talking about?" If I wasn't so drained, I'd get up and pace. But you can't pace in an eight-by-eight room cramped with a washer and dryer, overflowing laundry baskets, and a litter box anyway, so good thing I don't have the energy to do more than sit up.

"Well, I don't know why you'd still want me," he says. "I'm graduating in less than two weeks. I have a minimum-wage job. I didn't apply to any schools. What in the hell do I have to offer you?"

"You," I murmur.

Liam goes quiet, and I have to strain to hear his breath to know he's still on the line.

"Bless," he finally says. His voice soft with emotion, maybe even tears. "I don't deserve you."

"*You* don't deserve *me*? Considering that I'm neurotic, jealous, clingy, and negative, I'd say *I'm* the one who doesn't deserve *you*."

"You deserve someone better than me. Someone with a future."

"What is it with guys?" I ask. "You act like all girls care about is what you have or can give us in the way of money and things. Maybe some girls are like that, but not all of us. I wouldn't care if you didn't have anything but the shirt on your back, because it's *you* I want." My voice trembles with tired tears. "You're the best thing that's ever happened to me."

Our argument is over, but one is starting up in the living room between Jeanie and Shaky. My old man's been sulking and drinking even more than usual since the garage burnt, because of course now that it's gone he's sure *that* would have made him a fortune.

I flick the light off and curl on my cot. I have the phone to one ear, and wrap my pillow around to cover the other. Marbles curls in the nest my bent legs make, and purrs against my belly.

I tell Liam how I wish I hadn't left the way I did, and he tells me he's sorry he slammed the door. We spend the next hour talking about nothing but how much we love each other. Then, I tell him about going to Verna's, and the words I'm supposed to remember.

"Your mom's the one who filled me in about what a penny dropping means. I just don't know what it is that's going to become clear to me when it happens."

"Whatever you've been confused about, I'd imagine."

I half laugh. "What am I *not* confused about?"

"How you feel about me," he says, in a cute little-boy's voice.

"Okay, so I'm sure about one thing."

"Bless, I don't know about psychics, or how anything's going to go. But what I do know is that we're going to be all right."

"You mean that?" Because I'm thinking of Jeanie's words, *There's no love like your first love. It doesn't work out, and you never get over them.*

"Yeah."

I don't want to ask him, yet for my peace of mind, I have to. "Liam, you're not so depressed that you're going to do something stupid, are you?"

"Stupid?" he repeats, like he's clueless.

My mouth goes dry. "Yeah. You know, like you tried after your . . ." I won't say it. Not now. "When you were twelve? The shoelace? The stool? You wouldn't try that again, would you?"

Liam laughs, but in a subdued, dark, sardonic way. "Well, I wouldn't use a shoelace again, that's for sure."

I prop up on one elbow, and Marbles's head rises, alert. "That's not funny, Liam."

His laughter drifts off. "Sorry. I thought we could both use a little humor about now. Stop being such worrier, Bless."

I hang up smiling, because in spite of everything that's wrong, *we* at least feel right again.

I go into the kitchen, and Jeanie's at the table with the boys. The vase of flowers I picked up for her, along with a birthday card that I made the boys sign, sits between them. All three have their heads resting on their hands, and are staring into schoolbooks, blank sheets of paper pinned under the grubby arm of each boy. Jeanie looks distraught. "I told you boys, I didn't have this kinda math in school." So I sit down at the table to help the boys with their makeup work.

Chapter 23
14 Days Ago

After school, Maylee and I wait under the awning with huddles of other girls because it's pouring, and Maylee doesn't want her hair to flatten (Kenneth likes it poufy). We have two hours to kill, then Maylee is dropping me off at Liam's on her way to meet Kenneth. My car's out of commission again, because Dad picked up a new serpen-something-or-other belt to cure the squealing, but after he cut the frayed one away, he realized he'd picked up the wrong length. Liam's bringing me home, since Maylee's mom won't let her out after ten o'clock on a school night.

I tap my foot. "Maylee, it's been pouring all day. What are we going to do, stand here until a high-pressure system moves in?"

We might have, had Stephie and her friends not shoved their way through the knot of girls, and stopped right alongside of us. "Look at how hard it's raining!" Stephie whines.

Melissa peers at the pavement beyond the eave, where drops are splashing haphazardly in a half-inch of water. "I don't think it's raining that hard anymore." She gawks over at us, and I turn away.

I'm watching girls screaming their way to their cars, hoods or backpacks covering their heads. And then I notice him: Drake Collins, slumped behind his steering wheel, directly across from us. He's watching the building through rivulets of rain and a peephole he cleared on the steamed-up glass. I see his eyes, two dark holes burning from the back of his hood. I'm creeped out, because they don't look like the eyes I looked at in the hall. Not at all. And I wonder if he believes that Liam is the reason Stephie won't come back to him.

"It is too!" Stephie shouts—I'd almost forgotten why.

Misty says, "We should send somebody out there to test how hard it's raining. Someone who looks like a drowned rat, anyway."

Stephie and her pack cackle; the misfits flinch. Misty's attention lands on Maylee, and Maylee wilts like the rest of the wallflowers. The truth is, my hard edge isn't as hard as it used to be, and what came spontaneously to me a few months ago doesn't feel natural anymore. But when Stephie cues Misty, I don't have a choice but to sharpen my edge quickly.

In one quick step, I'm between Misty and Maylee, but staring at the lead witch. "Hey, Stephie," I say. "Why you worried? You don't have far to go. Your ride's right there." I nod toward Drake's car, just slightly, because I don't want him to know I'm talking about him.

Stephie scowls, and I laugh for her sake. I feel bad using Drake to get to her. But hey, I'm not going to stand still and let them humiliate Maylee.

I tug Maylee's arm. "Let's go." She tosses her backpack on top of her head, and we sprint to the car.

"You okay?" I ask once we get inside.

"Yeah," she says, humiliation burning her cheeks.

"They're just jealous, you know."

"Come on, Bless. Why would they be jealous of me?"

"Because you have something they don't have."

"Yeah, right."

"You do. You have a boyfriend. One who happens to be about the smartest boy in school."

Maylee cocks her head, ponders for a second, then grins.

I'm actually looking forward to spending some time at the Bradleys. After the hellish days at home since the fire, Shaky's drinking beer for breakfast again, and he and Jeanie are fighting practically nonstop. And at school, I'm getting threatening notes squeezed through the slats on my locker (during fourth hour, I found my gym clothes slashed by either a knife or scissors). Little wonder then, why the Bradleys' sunflower wallpaper, a plate of meatloaf and homemade mac and cheese, and an hour in Maylee's bubblegum bedroom actually sounds good to me. Besides, I want to find out what's behind the giddy smile Maylee wore all day.

We eat until we're stuffed (for Maylee, that happens sooner than for me, though she didn't cube), then we go upstairs. "Okay, spit it out," I say.

"Spit out what?"

"The secret that's got your cheeks so flushed that your mom asked three times during dinner if you're coming down with something."

A grin peeks out between Maylee's fingers, but she makes her face serious before pulling her hand away from her mouth. "It can wait, Bless. You're having a rough time right now."

"That's exactly why I could use your good news. Cough it up, Maylee."

She flops on her bed and crosses her legs. "You sure?"

"If I didn't want to hear it, I wouldn't have asked."

"I would have," she confesses.

"Okay. Well, last night, Kenneth and I went to Computer World, so he could check out some new software, like I told you today. Then we stopped for Chinese takeout. You should see Kenneth eat with chopsticks. He's so good at it! We ate in the car, even though it was dark, which is probably a good thing because I was dropping food all over the place and at least I had an excuse. Anyway, afterward . . ." She clamps her hands over her cheeks as if to keep them from bursting. She takes a big gulp of air and squeals, "He kissed me!"

I laugh. "Did he hold the pickle?"

She looks confused, but just for a second, then she squeals, "He did! And I didn't puke. I didn't even gag!"

"Way to go!"

"It was funny at first, because we whacked noses. You know, because he tilted his head to one side, and I turned mine in the same direction. But then, man Bless, it got sexy!"

The thought of anything about Kenneth—including his kisses—being sexy cracks me up, and I roll back on the bed because I'm laughing too hard to sit up. Maylee laughs right with me. "He's SOOOOOO hot, Bless!" That only makes me laugh harder.

There's no laughing, though, when we pull up in front of the Reids' house and there's a white Volvo parked out front.

"Geez Louise. Do you know whose car that is? It's Mrs. Dillon's!"

"Does Stephie drive it sometimes?"

"I don't think so. You still want to go in?"

I'm about to say no, when Mrs. Dillon comes out, stomping and swaying like Cruella de Vil in search of puppies to kick.

"My hair's not as big as that, is it?" Maylee asks, pointing at Mrs. Dillon's fat platinum-blond hair.

I shake my head. "Nobody's is. Nobody's lips are that fat, either. She must have had to swallow a whole cow to get that much Botox."

Maylee giggles.

Mrs. Dillon tosses her giant purse inside the Volvo, slips in behind the wheel, then peels out without checking behind her. Unfortunately, nothing's coming.

I knock on the door when nobody answers the bell. I can hear Liam's mom inside, ranting. Her words are too muffled to make out. Well, except for the phrase, "The gall!"

I stop knocking and text Liam. *I'm @ the door. Bad timing?*

I wait a few more seconds, wondering what's going on, and if I should text Maylee and tell her to turn around and grab me. Drop me off at the mall, or something.

There's a thump from a slamming door, then Liam steps outside. His fists are jammed so deep into his pockets that the seams along the shoulders of his hoodie could easily rip. He walks right by me as if I'm not here. As if our makeup conversation last night never happened.

"Liam, where do you think you're going?" Cheryl shouts from inside. She appears in the doorway. "Damn it, Liam. We have to talk!"

"I told you, there's nothing to talk about!" he shouts over his shoulder. He continues down the sidewalk, his steps long and stiff.

I turn to Cheryl. She props her hands on her hips and calls to him to stop. When he doesn't, she slaps her hands against her thighs and shouts down the street, "You hate the way your father is, do you? Well, you're just like him! Running away from the messes you don't want to face! Leaving me home alone to deal with them!"

Isn't there a normal family anywhere?

She stands there, huffing, watching Liam disappear, then looks at me. She blows out some steam, then says, "Come in, Bless." It's more like a command than an invitation.

Once I'm inside, she starts rubbing her fingertips over her forehead so hard that she's leaving red slash marks.

"I shouldn't have lost my temper like I did, but I was just so upset after Regina left—and she calls herself my friend?" She spins in a circle, scraping her frizzy hair out of her face. "I'm so upset that he stormed off like that. I need some answers."

She juts out her bottom lip, then blows air up to cool her face. She asks me to please sit down.

She remains standing as she explains. "Bless, Regina Dillon is claiming that Stephie and Liam were having sex. That everybody knew about it."

I gasp. "Those are just rumors that Stephie and her friends are spreading."

Cheryl paces. "Well, that's not what Regina alleges. She claims even *she* knew that something was going on between them. That she'd warned Stephie more than once that guys will always try to get something from her because she's beautiful, but that sex before marriage is a sin.

"Regina insisted Liam come out of his room and face her. He did, and she started screaming at him for taking advantage of her baby, then dumping her. Leaving her hurt and publicly humiliated. He denied it, and wasn't about to be drilled. You know Liam."

I'm hoping I do.

"She's filing statutory rape charges."

Blood immediately hammers my eardrums, and my stomach starts swirling. "She's saying Liam raped Stephie? That's insane!"

"No. Statutory rape is different. It's an adult having sex with someone not old enough to give legal consent. Liam is eighteen. Stephie doesn't turn seventeen for another month—she started kindergarten early, being so brilliant and all, you know." *No, I didn't know.*

"I guess here in Wisconsin, the age of consent is eighteen."

I leap to my feet. I want to scream. To run. "You don't believe it's true, do you?" *Please, don't say you have reason to believe it's true. Please!*

Cheryl sighs and drops into a chair, pulling a decorative pillow to hold against her stomach. "I have no reason to believe it's true. But I'm not one of those ignorant mothers who thinks her kid's incapable of making a mistake, either. They did spend a lot of time together. Especially before you came into the picture. Stephie is a beautiful girl—and every bit as pushy as her mother."

My God, if his own mom has suspicions, what then?

I think of the condoms I found in his room, conveniently tucked behind his bed. Did he buy them in the anticipation of having sex with me, or—

And if his own girlfriend can be made to be suspicious?

Cheryl sets the pillow aside and leans forward, her voice soft and sorry. "Bless, honey, ordinarily this wouldn't be any of my business. But under the circumstances, I have to ask. Did you ever accuse Liam of cheating on you with Stephie?"

I shake my head, protesting like someone on a witness stand after the prosecution twists the truth to make them look guilty. "No!"

"You never accused him of sleeping with Stephie? Regina claims you did. That you knew about it."

God, how did Stephie find out that we fought over her? I grit my teeth. *Abby!*

I don't want to say any more—it feels like a betrayal to Liam to be talking about this with his mom, after he refused to. But how can I keep my mouth shut?

"I was suspicious of Stephie, not him. Not of *them*. She had the hots for him and was being wickedly manipulative. But Liam couldn't see either fact, and it ticked me off. I didn't like her hanging around here so often, I admit it. Or him running to do favors for her. But it was my lack of trust in *her*, not in him."

Cheryl slumps back in her chair and drops her arms over the armrests. "I just wish that kid would have stayed so we could have talked this out."

Me, too.

A phone rings in the kitchen, and Cheryl leaps to her feet. "That might be our lawyer back home," she says.

I sit dazed, but snap out of it when Cheryl grabs her phone and announces, "It's Frank."

I don't want to hear what Liam's dad has to say, so I get up and leave. I text Maylee from the front step, telling her to pick me up at the Starbucks on Washington Street when she's done.

I get to the sidewalk, hoping to see Liam coming, his eyes filled with gratitude that I'm still here for him. Hurrying toward me as if I'm the mermaid who will lead him back to calm waters. But the street is empty, and ominously still.

Chapter 24
4th Street

A few short yards from the top of the hill, two old guys to my left are talking over a white picket fence. One of them is yapping, pointing in the direction of the lake, while the other one shakes his head in that the-world-is-going-to-hell way. I edge into the street to run along the curb, fearful that I'll hear one of them use the word "dead."

A woman one yard up, who no doubt was tipped off by the gossiper, is facing the lake, her arms folded, her left arm rubbing the right. She's dressed in bright red. Two little girls in cotton sundresses are chasing each other in circles behind her. The older girl orbits her sister to reach their mom. I don't need to hear her to know that she's begging to leave for Spring Up, nor to guess that the mother's hesitation is about what their innocent eyes might see.

Thwack! Thwack! It's the jangle of dropping coins.

The two little girls look into the street and squeal. The mother stares dumbly at the sky, then looks up and down the street for a person or a car that might have tossed the handful of gleaming pennies. The littlest girl darts into the street. A car is coming up over the top of the hill. The mother's voice is too slow, too warped to sound like a scream—yet I know it is one.

I veer into the street and nab the little girl.

I dodge the braking car, the kid's dangling legs thumping against my shins. I race to plunk the girl down on the grassy patch between the sidewalk and the street. The mother is rushing toward us. The little girl watches as two pennies leave her unfurling hand and roll onto the grass. She looks up at me, her face making ready to wail. And in the pudgy palm she's holding up is the source of her anguish; two pink circles the size of pennies, scorched into her baby skin.

I start running again, the mother's gratitude nothing but gibberish behind me.

I hadn't imagined the pennies a couple blocks back! I hadn't imagined these!

They had dropped from nowhere. The mother had seen them. The little girls had seen them. The pennies had burnt the little girl's skin.

Instantly, I see Verna like the Wicked Witch, watching me in her crystal ball as if I'm Dorothy trying to get to Oz, and she's the one determined to foil me.

And then I'm smelling lilacs again and my thoughts jumble. Mom might have sent the scent to me, but the fear I felt as the pennies fell, both times, is still with me and makes me fear where they've come from, what their dropping means.

And then, as clear as day, I hear—no, I remember—Verna calling to me as I was fleeing her house on that second visit. But I couldn't listen to her anymore, so I cut her sentence in half with the front door.

When I got to the car and realized that Maylee was still in Verna's house, I'd banged on the horn repeatedly, then rocked myself as though a thousand kittens' heads were getting smashed, telling myself that if Maylee didn't come out in an instant—no, sooner—I'd leave without her.

Maylee was shaking just like me when she got in the car. "Bless, what did that—"

"Don't talk about it," I'd screamed. "Not now, not ever! Do you hear me? Don't even think about it. She's nuts. A fake. A malicious two-bit act that fell off a circus train!"

Maylee had to stab the ignition at least ten times before she got the key inside. And the whole time, I screamed for her to hurry.

Stop it! Stop the memory. Fast-forward. Go past the blood-curdling part. Do it!

As we left, the wiper blades thumping, me still rocking, I knew I'd forget most of Verna's words—that was the easy part. But her premonition, the image, that was harder to reject. So I tucked that image into a dark recess in my mind and worked hard to forget it was there. Even if it meant looking at Maylee as Cactus used to look at me, my eyes veering off to the side of her face so I wouldn't have to look into her eyes and see the image burned into them. Even if it meant lying to Liam and telling him that the reason I freaked out when he fell asleep while watching a movie was because the movie scared me, rather than that the sight of him with his head lolled to the side, his eyes closed, his mouth slack, made me think he was dead.

But more and more over the last two weeks, as Liam's life continued to crumble and I watched him sink further into the dark pit of depression, I'd feel that premonition behind the door where I'd shoved it, bumping, rattling the knob. And in those moments, the thought that Verna had proved herself authentic on that first visit would roll out like smoke seeping out from under the door of a burning building.

"Excuse me, miss? Miss?"

The voice calls three times before I realize it's coming from a car rolling alongside of me.

It's an old man in a Hawaiian shirt. "Could you tell us where—"

But I can't tell him where anything is—I'm not even sure where I am anymore.

CHAPTER 25
13 DAYS AGO

We're on our way to Verna's for the second time. Maylee's driving because I'm too rattled. She keeps glancing at me as we leave town, worry gripping her eyebrows. She's been looking at me like this ever since things went from bad to worse for Liam.

"I don't know why I'm doing this," I confess to Maylee. "What did that first visit accomplish, anyway? I'm more confused now than before I went."

"That's only because you haven't figured out what all the stuff she said before means. But she knew about the penny collection, Bless. And about how you wipe your feet when you come out of bad houses. She said enough to make you know she's for real, so that when she tells you that Liam will be okay . . . that the two of you are forever, you'll know you can trust that."

I hope for my sake, *and* for Maylee's, that she's right. Everything is going great for Maylee and Kenneth, and I feel bad that my anxiety is bringing her down.

"Yeah," I say, even though the nagging fear sitting in the pit of my stomach says that's not going to be the case. Liam didn't answer my texts last night, so I called his mom early this morning. She told me that he got in around 3:00 a.m., soaked to the skin and silent. He was still sleeping. Cheryl said Frank intends to hire the best lawyer money can buy, and that Liam will be okay. Her words didn't comfort me, and I have my doubts that anything Verna might say will make me feel any better.

"Oh, cripes!" Maylee says, when we get on the highway and the sky splits open again, dropping fat raindrops. The road is already pooled with water, and she's afraid of hydroplaning.

A flash of lightning veins the sky and the rain starts coming down harder, the wind scooping it sideways, taking a few stray leaves and skinny twigs across the road with it.

"Oh man," Maylee says, as she leans closer to the wheel. "Help me watch for Treeline Road. I can barely see."

Maylee's relieved when we reach it. There's less traffic here, and she won't need to clutch the wheel and drive blindly every time we pass a semi and get hit with a tsunami.

I try to help Maylee watch for Verna's driveway, but over and over I catch myself staring mindlessly at the bloated ditches.

We're only a few yards down Verna's driveway when Maylee asks, "Did we turn down the wrong drive?"

"No," I tell her. I remembered us curving around Verna's mailbox, the rain sliding down the glass making the Halloween-black lettering appear to be melting.

"But everything looks so different."

Feels different, too.

Menacing.

Dark.

Another crack of lightning slices the sky and a low rumble of thunder vibrates the car windows—and my insides. Maylee lets out a yelp. "This is creepy," she says.

I understand why Maylee is creeped out being so deep in the woods on such a stormy day. Maylee is a town girl. Her getting into nature means spending an hour at Fountain Park on a landscaped lawn, with its transplanted trees strategically placed for aesthetics. But me? Any forest with a floor tangled with roots and leaves, moss and needles, has always felt as homey as carpet to me. Granted, the Wisconsin woods are thicker, but so far, that's only made me feel safer.

But I don't feel safe now. The rain beating on the roof is too loud, the dense foliage smothering. I crack my window, even if it means letting raindrops pelt the leg of my jeans.

The opened window doesn't help, so I fix my gaze on the soupy road ahead and avoid looking at the trees crouched close to the road, like pumas ready to pounce.

My unease doesn't leave me when Verna answers the door. In fact, it mushrooms when I see her. She's shrunken with fatigue, her eyes brooding.

"Come in, girls," she says. She leads us slowly through the kitchen.

The house might have smelled musty when we were here before, but this time, it's as if the dampness from the storms has seeped through the walls like vaporous ghosts and rubbed mildew over everything inside. Maylee cranks her head around and clamps her nose shut with her fingers. She puffs out her cheeks and crosses her eyes. But then her expression abruptly turns to one of horror. Probably, because it dawned on her that a psychic might know that she's horsing around behind her back.

Verna moves slowly to her chair. She braces her hands on the armrests, and her arms bow and quiver as she lowers herself onto the cushion. "Are you all right?" I ask, because her skin is pallid, her eyes blood red.

She waves her hand as if to say, *it's nothing*, then pauses to rest her head against the chair back. She just sits there like that, quietly, leaving us to wonder if she's fallen asleep. And with her eyes still closed, she says, "I never asked for this, you know."

"For what?" Maylee asks.

"To see things nobody wants to see. Things I can't stop from happening." She doesn't lift her head, but she opens her eyes and stares up at the ceiling. "The tidal wave in Japan . . . 9/11. Martin Luther King Junior's assassination . . . Katrina. I saw them all before they happened. But what could I do?"

I flinch, and Maylee stares up at the window behind Verna as if the pelting rain might sweep the whole house away, us with it.

"I got this blessing from my grandmother. That's what my family called it, you know. A blessing. But some days, it feels only like a curse."

Maylee and I exchange looks. I knew we shouldn't have come.

Verna lifts her head and manages a weak smile. "So let me guess. You girls came by today to ask if the boys in your lives will love you forever."

I squirm, because in light of what Verna just said, our worries seem childish.

"You're good," Maylee says.

"Oh, the spirits didn't tell me that. Experience did. Young people always want to know about love. But it's fear that brings them here, more than hope." She pinches her eyes at Maylee and gives a weak smile. "Your young man will always look back on these days with fondness."

Maylee giggles like that's good news.

Verna watches me as she pulls the TV tray around to meet her knees, her eyes narrowing and going hazy again. "The spirits are restless today," she tells me.

My shoulders stiffen.

She raises her bony, bent finger and it wobbles like it's caught in a small whirlwind. "So I do need to ask again, but answer me carefully this time—do you want to know *everything* the spirits show me today?"

Fear scours my throat as I say, "Everything."

Verna closes her eyes for a second, and everything in the room goes still.

We wait until she opens them again. She leans forward. "One thing you must remember, dear, is that what I see is what's on your path, and the paths of those around you. Where one is headed and will end up unless they choose to change their course. We all have free will and can change our minds in a single heartbeat, and thus, change the route to our destiny. It's true for every one of us. But remember, while we can choose what we will do, we have no power to choose what others will do."

Why is she telling me these things? So I won't blame myself if Liam decides to take his life?

Maylee interrupts. "Yeah, but we can help other people decide to make different choices, can't we?"

Verna's attention sways to Maylee. "Oh, everything we say and do affects others, have no doubt of that. But while we are our brother's keeper, we don't own the key."

She turns back to me, her words almost a whisper. "That's why, when your heart is breaking for someone who's broken, but your words can't seem to reach them, and your love can't save them, you ask the spirits that watch over them and whisper into their hearts what they can't hear with their ears: 'We will not give up on you. So don't give up on yourself.'"

"That's beautiful," Maylee whispers.

Maylee glances over at me, then back to Verna. "Will that help then? Will they come around and feel happy again?"

"Maybe. Maybe not," Verna says. "But it's all one can do. As I said, we are our brother's keeper, but we don't own the key."

I cross my legs, and then my ankles, making it harder to bolt—which is what I want to do right about now.

Verna bends over her crystal, and within seconds, the room goes cold, and the rank odor strengthens as if it's been stirred by the spirits.

"I see a dark-haired man. Older. Middle age. He's staggering."

"Must be your dad," Maylee whispers.

"Hmmm," Verna says. "Such a troubled man . . . foolish as a child."

Now I know she's seeing my old man.

Verna looks up, her watery eyes peeking from under her brow bone. "But he loves you. That much your spirits want you to know."

I feel my mouth, lip pressed to lip.

Verna looks back down, and color returns to her cheeks. "I see children."

Trevor? Jud?

Verna laughs softly. "Their laughter is so sweet."

Not Jud. Not Trevor.

"Oh—and ice cream cones." Verna chuckles, as though she's with those kids, chocolate soft-serve on her tongue.

But then, it's as if something, or someone, chases the children away. Her skin goes sallow again, her voice lowers. "I'm seeing a blond-haired boy," she says.

Liam!

I reach for Maylee's hand.

"He believes that life has betrayed him," she says, her cadence quickening. "Bitterness rushes in his blood . . . muddles his mind." Her body quivers, like it's being plunged into ice water. Maylee squeezes my hand so tightly that my knuckles hurt. *Life has betrayed him*, I want to shout.

Verna watches. Waits. Her torso weaves ever so slightly. "He's hiding something," she says, her voice as cold as the room. She peers closer to her crystal. "I don't know what he's hiding."

Please. Please don't let it be a secret. The secret that he WAS with Stephie!

"I see water. People milling about. But the boy, he only sees two."

I'm terrified and wish she'd stop. Yet I'm too scared to even breathe, much less speak out loud and ask her to.

"He has something . . . what is it?" she asks, her bony finger tapping the armrest.

She sighs deeply then. "It's a gun. The spirits are saying it's a gun."

A piercing crack of thunder sounds, and Verna lurches as if she's been shot. Maylee yelps. Maybe I do, too.

"It's lying next to him," she says, her voice so breathless it's barely audible.

And then I'm the one seeing images. Liam's head against concrete. His life, his blood, seeping out through the wound. The tips of his hair, glossy, red paintbrushes dipped in animosity.

I spring from the chair and bolt for the door. Verna calls behind me, "Wait! Wait! Tell your young man—"

The door bangs behind me, cutting her sentence in half.

I run for the car through pelting rain, choking on my sobs.

CHAPTER 26
13 DAYS AGO

After we leave Verna's, Maylee takes me to her house to spend the night. It's where I want to be. Neither of us wants to be alone. We're going to make cheese popcorn and watch old episodes of *Friends*.

Liam texts me about seven o'clock to tell me that it's not true, about Stephie. *"U know that right?"*

I reply, *"Yes."*

"Everything's gone insane, Bless."

"I know."

"Pls be patient. I'm trying to sort things out."

He texts me a heart, and I text him one back.

And then he's gone.

Two hours later, Liam shows up at Maylee's. "Sorry, I had to come. I'll only keep her a minute," he tells Maylee. He leads me to his SUV, but doesn't start it.

Liam looks deflated. Defeated.

I avoid looking at him for fear I'll imagine blood seeping from his head.

"Bless, you were right about Stephie," he says. "She hit on me the day of the ice storm. I was going to tell you then, but I didn't want to upset you more. But if these charges go anywhere—well, I didn't want you to find out through gossip."

I try to keep my sigh invisible. Inaudible.

"That day, she kept hinting that maybe there could be an *us*, so I told her outright that I'm in love with you. Then she hit on me, and I, well, I put her in her place. She bawled. Pleaded. Screamed. And in the end, told me I'd pay for humiliating her."

"She threatened you? Your mom didn't hear this?"

"She was out shopping."

"But if she threatened you—"

"It's my word against hers, Bless," he says, obviously knowing where I was headed. "And Regina Dillon has connections in high places. But that's beside the point. Right now, the only person I want to know believes me is you."

"And all I want to know is that you still love me."

"I love you more than ever. I know I'm not acting like it, but I do."

He tells me his head is pounding, and he's beat. He says he's sorry he interrupted my evening, but that he wanted to tell me these things in person.

He holds my hand as he walks me to Maylee's door. The streetlight is illuminating his eyes like water under a bright moon. "I love you so, so much, Bless. I'm not sure why you love me—seems your life would be a lot simpler if I wasn't in it."

My insides clench, and I reach up to take his face in my hands. "Don't say that, Liam. Don't ever say that. You're the best thing that's ever happened to me."

He doesn't say anything more. He gives me a soft kiss, and squeezes my hands gently before heading down the steps.

"Thanks for telling me," I call to him. "But you didn't need to. I knew it wasn't true." I hope I sound convincing.

He looks back and pats his hand over his chest.

"See you tomorrow," I say. "Right?"

Maybe he didn't hear me.

"I said, see you tomorrow—right?"

He nods.

"Promise?"

"I'll see you tomorrow."

Maylee and I just can't get into TV, and it's far too early to fall asleep. So we turn off the TV, thinking we'll just talk. But our trip to Verna's sits like a canyon between us and any frivolous, safe topic. Surprisingly, Maylee finds a topic for us: the penny folder.

"I keep thinking about Susan. . . . I bet your grandma in Nebraska knows who she is. She has to. She's the one who put the folder in your bag."

"I've been thinking about calling her," I say.

"Do it!" Maylee grabs my phone off the nightstand and tosses it on the bed.

"I didn't mean right now."

"Why not?"

I don't know how Maylee does it—probably by hinting that maybe we're safer messing with the past than with the future—but however it happened, five minutes later I'm dialing the number I've memorized.

Maylee keeps her hand on my back to give me courage, and when Gloria answers and starts crying again when she hears my voice, I need it.

"Maybe this isn't a good time," I say. I don't want to hear her cry.

"No, no. It's perfect! I'm just so happy to hear from you, honey."

I know I should probably do some small talk, but I can't think of anything. So I just blurt out, "Do you know who Susan Marlene Harris is?"

Maylee has her head against mine so she can hear better; I don't want to put Gloria on speaker. It might make her less apt to talk openly.

"Ah, the penny book," she says. "Do you still have it?"

"Yes."

"I'm glad. Your mom wanted you to have it."

"I was wondering if you could tell me who Susan Marlene Harris is."

"I'm not sure," she says, "but I've got my suspicions.

"Honey," she says while my mind is racing, "I don't know if your dad told you this, but I didn't give birth to Maura. I adopted her. But from the moment I first held her, she became my true daughter.

"Maura found out about her birth mother when she was about your age. It caused a rift between us that didn't heal until she got sick and came home. To this day, I'm sorry I didn't tell her sooner—but there never seems to be a good time to say something like that. No offense to your dad, Bless, but I can't help but feel that it was her anger toward me for the secret I'd kept that pushed her into your dad's arms.

"It was a closed adoption. They all were back then. But somehow, Maura found her birth mother. I think that's who Susan Marlene Harris is, and that Maura met her after she'd left home. I think it was her birth mother who gave her the penny book. But I can't prove any of that. She never talked to me about it. I think she was afraid of hurting me, even after I hurt her. That's how Maura was."

I feel a catch inside.

But now *I* need proof. Proof that Verna had told the truth. "Did Mom hand you the penny folder while she was in a hospice?"

"Yes. I didn't open the bag at the time. The fact that she was handing me something to keep for you told me she knew she wasn't going to make it, and I couldn't get beyond that."

Grandma Gloria is crying, and now Maylee and I are both snif-fling. I thank Gloria for answering my questions and apologize for upsetting her.

"No, no," she protests. "We all have a right to know where we came from. I see that now. I only wish I could tell you more."

Grandma Gloria asks me if I'll send her a picture of me, and I tell her I will. And that I'll call her again soon, but have to go now. She tells me she loves me before I hang up.

Maylee and I turn out the lights and lie awake without talking.

CHAPTER 27

11 DAYS AGO

It's the morning of Spring Up, and I wake with an idea for the perfect graduation gift for Liam: a tattoo of me as a mermaid! No, I know it won't make everything that's wrong in his life better. But it might cheer him up some. He's been so quiet. So lost in his own thoughts. I'm trying to give him time. Space. Be patient, like he asked me to be. But I want to see him smile like he used to before his dad and Stephie Dillon betrayed him.

I lie there for almost an hour visualizing how the tattoo should look. Now it's 10:10—I'm meeting Liam at the beach at noon. Kenneth's great-aunt died and her funeral is today (funny he didn't invite Maylee as his date). Maylee said she'd feel dumb hanging out with Liam and me all day, so I think she's almost glad that her cousin Aubrey is in town.

I wake up and pee, brush my teeth, change Marbles's litter box, and fill her dishes.

Shaky's at the table drinking a breakfast beer. He's got the entertainment section of the *Logan Daily Herald* spread out next to an ashtray, trying to find out for Jeanie what time the live music starts.

Jeanie shuffles around me to get to the coffeepot. I ask her for the name of a good tattoo artist, and how much a tattoo costs. I've got $216 saved. Jeanie tells me Tula's, on 15th Street, then starts pulling her pajamas out here and there to expose her tats, putting a price tag on each. She's about to show me the one on her hip, when Shaky flips the page and flips out. "That low-down, slimy—!"

Jeanie stops. "Who?"

Shaky gets up and paces in circles. Jeanie hurries to the table.

"Right there!" Shaky says, jabbing the newspaper with his finger. Jeanie scoops up the paper, and I go to peek. It's an ad for Rupert's business, Big Catch Charters.

Jud appears out of nowhere, his head blocking my vision before I can read the ad or look at the picture. "Hey, Gilligan. Ain't that your boat?"

I push Jud's grubby head out of the way, and there it is, *The Carol* painted on the side. Rupert is standing on the dock beside it, holding up a stuffed king salmon. "Hey, he's giving free boat rides today. I'm gonna get one!" Jud shouts.

Jeanie biffs him in the head, while Shaky pounds his fist into his hand and rages, "I should kill that thieving son-of-a-bitch."

I roll my eyes, and turn to Jud to ask him if I can use his laptop for a minute. He's been decent to me. Trevor, too, since I helped them get their makeup work done, which earned them back their Internet privileges.

I spend too long looking for mermaid pictures, and by the time I find a good one, I realize I'm never going to make it to the beach by noon. I text Liam to tell him I'll be about a half an hour late. I text Maylee the same. Both say they'll just hang out at the beach until I get there.

I drive straight to Tula's, the pictures for Liam's tattoo tucked in the same envelope as the photo of me. I park the car on the corner of Mactaw and 15th. A bell sounds when I step inside. A few minutes later, I'm explaining the tattoo to Tula when my phone starts vibrating in my pocket. I glance down to see that it's Maylee. Again! I know if I don't answer it, she'll only keep calling.

"Let me guess, Maylee. You . . ."

I stop when I hear how she's breathing. Hard. Moaning almost, like her soul's being torn from her chest. In the background there's the droning of music, the thumping of drums.

When Maylee's just being a drama queen, her voice gets quiet, no matter how exaggerated her facial expressions are. But now, Maylee's seriously freaking out.

I stiffen. "Maylee, what is it?"

She bursts into a series of *Oh my Gods*, and I picture her eyes crazed, strings of spit the only thing keeping her lower and upper jaws hinged together. I hear the rumble of a crowd in chaos. A couple deep voices are shouting orders I can't make out.

"Maylee? What's going on?"

There's rapid clicking now. Maybe the tapping of her teeth, like what happens when someone's blood goes cold. The sound makes me shiver. I'm about to scream at her to spit it out, when she cries, "It's happening! Just like she said it would!"

"What's happening? Like who said?" I ask, even though a part of me already knows.

"Verna Johnson!" she says. "The psychic! Just like she said—"

Chapter 28
11 Days Ago

My past.

The present.

They collide.

I feel the impact, then feel for my face, my arms, my solar plexus. My skin, hot and slicked with fear, the sound of my labored breaths, and the rapid thudding under my breastbone assure me that although my past just flashed before my eyes, I'm still here. Still whole.

I'm at Lakefront Drive. And although I know it couldn't have taken me more than thirteen minutes to get here, a lifetime has passed in that time. Mine.

The north end of the beach is near empty, but the sidewalk is busy with people coming and going from cars parked bumper to bumper on both sides of the street.

I don't wait for the traffic light to tell me I can cross Lakefront Drive, like the families clotting both sides of the crosswalk do. Nor do I wait for a slight break and dart across like the other teens, the girls screaming giggles, the boys trying to look like they're not hurrying, even though they are. I just run, ignoring the screeching brakes and honking horns. Let a car run me over. Splatter me like a bug against a windshield. Crush me like a worm under a tire. What difference will it make if Liam doesn't make it? He's my everything.

That thought, though true, makes me cringe. I've always

despised girls whose whole identity relied on some guy loving them. But that's how I feel. And maybe, I tell myself, it's a good sign.

Last year, back in Wicks Rural High, the psychology teacher handed out copies of some lame test she probably tore out of a teen magazine (Maylee no doubt took the same one). It was supposed to tell us if we were socially well-adjusted. According to my score, I wasn't. Miss Palmer looked concerned. Some kids snickered. So I defended myself by pointing out that just because I was a loner and wasn't talkative didn't mean I was more of a social freak than anybody else. Didn't the class clown stack his jokes up like a fortress so nobody could see the sad him behind it? And what about the sluts? Just because they let everybody between their legs, that didn't mean they let anybody into their hearts, did it? The teacher blinked, the kids looked down, and the bell rang. I'd won my right to normalcy in that moment. Yet I knew I hadn't won anything. Not really. I knew something about me was out of whack, the way I didn't trust anybody and shrugged off anyone who tried to befriend me. Hell, I even knew I was lonely. I just didn't know how to care about those things. Or, how to change them.

But then Liam came into my life: the *Beauty and the Beast* story revisited, only reversed, because I, the girl, was the beast. But when his hands touched my skin and I felt them, when I curled on my bed at night with my phone and whispered him secrets, when I laughed without effort and cried without control, I realized I'd passed the test. Not the bogus one given by some thirtysomething teacher in braces, but the real test. The one that life gives you. The one that, when you pass it, proves to you that you really *are* worthy of love. And capable of letting it in when it comes.

But what good are lessons learned too late?

The middle of the beach is filled with people wandering the sand in summer brights and winter-pale skin, chasing toddlers, and examining crafts spread on card tables. Guys with potbellies and balding heads are huddled at the beer tents, while their flush-faced women dance old school on the wooden platform in front of the band.

I take the sidewalk, zigzagging around people moving so slowly they might as well be standing still. It seems crazy to me that the crowd should be oblivious to the fact that only about two football field lengths away, a gun was fired and someone is down. But apparently, while the speed of sound might move at eleven hundred feet per second, and gossip maybe even faster, neither move as quickly on a crowded beach with music blaring. Sure, they would have heard or seen the cop cars and rescue trucks when they pulled in, but as I learned when I first moved here, after a time those sounds and sights become so commonplace that you don't even register them anymore.

The mood of the crowd on the other side of the makeshift stage is different, though. People are standing in small huddles, hands gesturing.

The sidewalk that diverges to the pier, marking the end of the beach, is about three hundred feet in front of me. It's crammed with people, so I decide to take a shortcut across the sand to get to the pier. Liam would be there. On the pier where he stood staring down at black water.

The beach is like a sandbox that's seen too many shovels and has never been refilled. The drop from the sidewalk into the sand gives me some momentum. Hot sand spills into my sandals. I wait until the beach levels, then kick them off and use my toes to scoop the sand and build speed.

There are three sets of steps that will take me up to the

walkway that leads to the pier. I dart for them, while searching down the concrete pathway to the lighthouse for the sight of paramedics carrying medical bags or pushing a gurney. But all I see are couples and families strolling, tiny as dolls at this distance. They couldn't have taken him already, I reason. I'd heard them racing here; I'd have heard them leaving, too.

Not if there was no longer a reason to rush or sound a siren because Liam is already dead.

No! I'm not going to imagine the worst. I'm not. Liam is here. Somewhere. He has to be. I feel him here!

The awkward moment when I realize I'm tripping is followed by a jolt to my kneecaps cracking against the concrete. I hear a yelp, then wracking sobs that logic tells me are mine. And then gasps that reason says aren't mine.

"Is that Bless Adler?"

I roll myself into a sitting position. I lift my hands, turning my palms up. Dots of blood are appearing on grated skin. I look at my knees. A string of skin is dangling from one, and I bloody my fingertips trying to pat it back in place.

I cup my hands over both knees when the stinging sets in.

Flip-flops underneath puffy ankles and pastel toenails salted with sand appear before me. I look up into faces I recognize, but can't quite place. Their eyes are hidden behind sunglasses, but for one pair—brown, outlined in black, the lids decorated with shades of sparkly green. "Bless?"

It's Katie. Katie Springer. The rest are the same three girls that always hurry behind her to grab a lunchroom table next to the popular girls.

"Em, give me a hand," Katie says.

Two pairs of thick arms reach down to lift me to my feet. The skin on my knees stings when I stand, and blood trickles down one shin.

There's a gasp. "She's bleeding. . . ."

A strand of Katie's blond hair, steel blue at the hem, waves across her mouth as she says, "I almost fell, too, when we heard the gunshots and had to run. Oh, Bless, isn't it awful? We came up here, hoping to get a better look. I hope it's nobody from our school."

"Katie, look!"

"Oh my God—even the windows are shot out."

"Didn't I tell you that sound was breaking glass?"

I don't know who's talking.

Katie still has my arm. But the other girl has left to join a couple of other girls, who are standing across the width of the pier, pointing down by the marina.

I shake Katie's hand off and join her friends, the concrete rough against my bare feet.

Maybe I get too close to the ledge, I don't know, but Katie's friend, one with cleavage that starts at the base of her neck, thrusts her arm out to stop me, and it butts against my belly.

I blink against the wind, trying to make sense of what I'm seeing. The boats in the marina are bobbing on the water. And beyond them, along the boardwalk that runs along Lake Michigan and lies between the water's edge and the line of shops, cops are stringing police tape. There's a huddle of people in white coats, a few crouched low to the weathered boards. A couple of gurneys are being pushed toward the huddle, across a bed of iridescent shards of glass.

Two? Why two?

I'm shaking like it's January and willing my stomach to stop swirling.

"That could be us. We'd just left there," the girl who'd pointed says.

"I hope it's no one we know," Katie says, her voice nasally

with tears now, and the girls start listing the kids who were outside of Lola's when they left, using first names only, as if they are all their personal friends. "I wonder if it's one of them," Katie says.

I clutch the sides of my head—it feels like it might explode.

"It's Liam," I cry. "It's Liam who's down, bleeding."

There's a chorus of *Oh my Gods*. They pull me back from the edge and form a huddle around me.

"No wonder she's shaking like this."

They all have a hand on me now. On my arm. My shoulder. My back. I don't shrug them off; their hands are like the ropes that keep a hot air balloon from lifting into the sky to be tossed and lost in the wind.

"I think she's in shock, Katie."

"We should find her some shade."

"She needs water."

A bottle of water is thrust at me.

But I don't need water. And I don't need shade. I need to get to Liam. But first, I need to find Maylee. I can't do this alone.

Down the pier, toward Lakefront Drive, there's a crowd inching its way across the grass to get closer to the parking lot. They are subdued, straining to see. Some with hands pressed over their mouths, or arms crossed. Others texting or holding their phones high, trying to capture video. All of them swaying like snakes mesmerized by the song of death.

I have to call Maylee. I reach for my pocket, then remember.

"C-can I use somebody's phone?"

Katie hands me hers, and I stammer as I thank her. It's an iPhone, tucked in a purple OtterBox. I can't figure out how to unlock it, so Katie reaches in with a glittery fingernail to hit the power button and swipe the screen.

My hands are shaking so hard, I can't make my finger work. So Katie takes the phone to dial for me. I recite Maylee's number, but have to start over four times to get the digits right.

While it rings, I'm bouncing on legs that are threatening to give. *Pick up, Maylee. Please, pick up!*

My chin quivers when I hear her voice; the phone is set to speaker.

"Oh God, Bless, I've been trying to call you. I dialed at least twenty times."

"Where are you?" I scream.

"Behind Lola's—where are you?" she shouts back.

"On the pier."

I hear her recite my whereabouts—as if Aubrey needs to know.

"Maylee, meet me by the parking lot . . . the beach end . . . I'll be there in a few seconds. Come find me."

"Bless—?"

"Just find me," I shriek. "Hurry!"

"Okay. Okay. We're coming!"

I hand Katie back her phone and swallow the bile rising in my throat. I want to run, yet I can't. Not with the sun glinting off the water almost blinding me, and my head so dizzy with fear that I'm wobbling.

Katie and Emma take my arms to steady me. "Come on. We'll help you find Maylee."

They bump people out of the way with quick apologies until we reach the parking lot curb. Flashes of lights are reverberating like silent screams at the far end of the lot. Lights red, the color of blood. And blue, the color of bruises.

My God!

Yellow caution tape is strung between trees, and cops are posted at all three entrances to keep vehicles from pulling in. There are more cops in the parking lot itself, holding clip-boards, talking to the dozens of people inside the marked-off square. Reporters are edging the tape, cameras running.

Cops are patrolling the perimeter of the roped-off area, and one reaches over to clamp his hand over my arm when I lift the tape to slip under it. "Miss, you can't go in there."

"It's her boyfriend who got shot on the boardwalk," Katie pleads.

And then I hear it. "Bless! Bless!"

I wail, my head falling back, the sky so blurry through my tears that no comforting can seep through. Because it's Liam's voice that's calling my name. And unless it's the cry of his soul as it leaves, that can't be.

"Bless! Right here!"

I look up. I cup my hand over my mouth, afraid to trust that the boy who's running across the parking lot close to the bumpers of parked cars, his hair gleaming in the sun, his arms scissoring above his head, is Liam. Maylee is trailing behind, her arms flailing, Aubrey lagging in the distance.

He gets closer. So close I can see the anguish in his sea-filled eyes. And all I can do is step in place, my whole body rattling as I beg God to not let him be a mirage.

Liam picks me up, and I wrap my legs around him. I breathe the scent of him in, as if I can't trust my eyes, my limbs, and need my nose to confirm that it's really him.

"Oh, baby. Shhh, shhh," he moans, as he sways me side to side, his breath brushing my hair. "Everything's going to be okay." He kisses my hair, then sets me down.

I'm sobbing, mouth open, soaking his shirt, cotton fabric sucking into my mouth with each inhale.

"Oh, Bless," I hear Maylee utter. Her hand comes up to cup the back of my head, and I sob all the harder and draw her close so I can hug them both. "I tried calling you the minute I knew that Liam was okay. I called at least twenty times, but you didn't pick up. And just a bit ago, when you called me, I tried telling—"

"Fifty times is more like it," Aubrey says, her voice mocking.

So it *was* a mistake. A horrible, cruel prank. My God! I turn to glare at Aubrey who's standing a yard back. "You miserable bitch!" I scream. "You made us believe Liam was shot!"

Aubrey steps back, a *what-the-hell?* look on her stupid face.

But even Maylee and Liam look confused.

Maylee moves to step between me and Aubrey. She leans down so her face is directly in front of mine. "Bless, we had it wrong."

I blink at her. I don't know what she's saying.

The glaze of sweat on my skin feels like it's turning to ice now that I've stopped running, and I start shivering in spite of the hot sun. Liam rubs his hands up and down my arms to warm me. I'm looking at Maylee, waiting for an explanation when I feel Liam's shirt, sticky under my hand. I look. "You're bleeding."

"No, no," he says. "It's not my blood."

I grab the hem of his shirt to yank it up to see for myself, but he stops my hands. "It's not mine, Bless. It's not."

"Liam," I utter. He bends over, and I give him a flurry of kisses, then nuzzle my face into the hollow of his neck. "I thought you'd shot yourself," I whimper.

"Jesus, Bless," he says.

"That's what I thought, too, when I heard the gunshots," Maylee says.

"Maylee and I went to see this psychic. Verna Johnson. She said you were going to shoot yourself! Didn't she Maylee? She said—"

Katie and her friends budge closer.

"No, Bless." I turn my head toward Maylee, who's looking at me through bloodshot eyes. "That's not what Verna said."

"She *did* say it!" I argue. "You heard her. She told us she saw Liam bleeding from a gunshot he'd given himself. She saw the gun lying beside him. How could she lie about something so awful? How?"

Maylee shakes her head. "No. No. We added that part, Bless. Don't you see? I thought about it. She said she saw a boy with blond hair, down and bloody. A gun lying beside him. She wasn't lying about anything, Bless. It happened. Just how she saw it. But we're the ones who decided that the boy she saw was Liam. And that he'd shot himself."

Car doors are slamming, and more reporters are racing toward the tape, their suit jackets flapping. I'm so confused that all I can do is press my temples. "But she said . . ."

"Everything she said was true, Bless," Maylee says. "It's just the parts we added that weren't."

Liam turns me to him. "The blond-haired kid with the gun, the one who's down and bleeding—it's Drake Collins."

"Drake Collins?"

Liam glances up when Katie and her friends gasp, then echo Drake's name. He looks at Maylee. "Let's find a place where we can talk," he says.

Liam shoves a path through the girls, then the spectators, and finds a small clearing. He sits on the grass, drawing me down in the nest his legs make. Against my shoulder I can feel his heart, beating fast. Too fast. Maylee sits facing us, while Aubrey—well, who knows where she is.

"I was on the beach, talking to your dad," Liam says. "Drake walked past. He turned around and looked right at me. He made his hand into a gun, and pulled the imaginary trigger. I should have known something was up. Drake's never acknowledged me before."

"It wasn't your fault, Liam," Maylee says.

Liam continues, "Drake must have had his eye on me, and when he saw me heading to Sweet Lola's, he must have thought I was heading there to meet Stephie. I don't know, I guess she was there."

"Yeah," Maylee adds. "That's why when you were running out of Verna's house, she told you to tell Liam to be careful."

"I didn't hear that," I say. "Why didn't you tell me?"

"You wouldn't let me."

"Anyway," Liam says. "I got inside Lola's and saw Shaky out on the boardwalk.

Maylee inserts, "Aubrey and I were inside, ordering ice cream."

Liam continues, "I thought I'd go out there and talk to your dad some more, while I waited for you.

"Jud came out on the boardwalk to beg some money off Shaky, and when he was heading inside, he saw Drake coming down from the north end, just this side of the marina. Jud saw him pull a pistol and yelled."

I cup my hand over my mouth.

"Drake started firing then. Round after round. People were screaming, shoving, stumbling to get inside or between the buildings."

"It was so scary, Bless!" Maylee adds, her eyes leaking again. "We were inside Lola's when the gunshots started. Max, Lola's husband, locked the door to the boardwalk and told us all to get under the tables. We couldn't tell exactly where the shooter was, so he told us to stay inside."

"My God," I utter.

There's a pause in the story. Maylee looks at Liam. I do, too.

But Liam is only looking down, plucking at blades of grass with bloodstained fingers. Drake's blood. "Wash your hands," I insist. "Go wash your hands."

"It's okay," he mutters.

I pinch the bridge of my nose. Everything feels surreal. My thoughts are so muddled.

"Wait," I say. "My dad . . . Jud. They were there, on the boardwalk? Are they okay?"

"Jud's fine," Liam says. "That's the thing. Drake could have taken Jud out—pretty much all of us on that boardwalk. But instead, he blew out the upper corners of the windows, and shot off to the side. Bullets were punching the water."

"So are you saying he didn't *really* want to shoot anybody?" Maylee asks. "Just himself? Maybe in front of Stephie, so she'd be sorry?"

Liam shakes his head. "You give him too much credit, Maylee. I think he planned to take us all out. But he didn't want to blow up Stephie, me, and whoever else he had a vendetta against before we knew what hit us. He wanted to see our fear."

"So he shot, then turned the gun on himself, instead?" I ask, trying so hard to get the story straight.

Maylee shakes her head. "No, Verna didn't say that the blond-haired boy had shot himself. She only said the gun was lying beside him."

I grab my head. I want this to stop. All of it. I want the three of us to go get Marbles, then sit at the feet of the red pines until I can breathe again. Or better yet, set sail on a boat and be surrounded by nothing but sunshine and peaceful water.

Fresh tears start dripping down Maylee's face. She goes to put her hand on my knee, must see the coagulated blood, then touches my thigh instead. "Bless? You remember that Verna first saw a crowd. Water. An older guy, drunk and wobbling?"

"Yeah. My dad." The second I say it, I realize that Liam had said that *Jud* was all right, but he hadn't answered about Shaky.

Liam takes over. "Your dad had a concealed weapon on him, Bless. And when Jud yelled, *'Gun!'* Shaky, who was standing to my right, facing the northeast, saw Drake coming down the boardwalk with his Glock raised, and he turned. Your dad was pretty drunk, but when Drake started shooting, he managed to get a shot off to bring Drake down."

"He's a hero, Bless," Maylee says, smiling through her tears.

Liam nods. "If he hadn't shot, Drake probably would have killed us all."

I still have my hand over my mouth, but now I'm laughing. The kind of laugh made from relief and gratitude. I crank myself to see around Liam and peer between legs to find Shaky behind the tape.

"Bless?" Liam says. His voice somber. "Look at me."

I do.

"Your dad took one of Drake's bullets."

I shake my head. "No. Nooooo."

Two gurneys. There were two.

"Is he dead?" I ask. *Please say he's not dead.*

Liam bites his lower lip. "I don't know. He was bleeding heavily when they made us all clear the area." Liam rubs his hands against the grass, as if he doesn't want me to link whose blood is on them.

"They're taking one of them now," Aubrey shouts.

I leap to my feet, as paramedics are slipping a stretcher into the back of the ambulance that's parked behind Lola's. I can't see who it is, only a mound, strapped under a white sheet.

I try to see if the sheet is covering the person's face—in the movies, they cover the face if the person's already dead.

"Dad!" I scream out. "Dad!"

All around me, I hear murmurs peppered with the words: Hero. Hero's daughter. Must be. I hear Katie Springer say, "That's the gunman's daughter, right there. The dark-haired one."

Liam holds me in place, as I struggle to go to Dad.

Sirens scream. A microphone appears. Liam uses his arm like warning tape and cusses at the reporter to get it out of my face.

"There's Jeanie!" Maylee shouts.

Liam pulls me along, parting people. Jeanie's leaning over the tape. Two officers are holding her. "That's my man they're taking!" she screams. "And my kid is in there! Goddamn it, let me through!" Trevor is standing behind her, his face ashen, but for ruddy patches of red over his cheeks.

"Jeanie!" I call. I reach for her, and one officer drops his arm so she can reach for me. She smells like armpits and hair product. "Your dad," she says, her voice hoarse and cracking, "some crazy bastard shot him!"

"I know. I know," I cry. "Is he alive?"

"I don't know." She glares up at the policewoman still holding on to her. "They won't tell me a goddamn thing."

"We will as soon as we know something, ma'am. Please, calm down. Let everyone do their job. That's the best way you can be helpful to your partner right now."

Maylee shouts, "There's my uncle Bob. He's bringing Jud over."

Odd, I think, how I never noticed before just how young Jud really is. He spots Jeanie and starts running toward her as awkwardly as a toddler, his pale face crumbling into a bawl.

The policewoman lets go of Jeanie, and she hugs Jud, then checks him for holes.

Maylee's uncle squeezes her shoulder and asks if she's okay, then turns to Jeanie, to me. "Donald's going to be just fine. He took the bullet in the shoulder. No vital organs were hit. I talked to him myself. They're taking him over to Logan General to remove the bullet, but the paramedics said the prognosis should be good."

We sigh together.

"You should have seen Shaky, Mom!" Jud says. "Drunk as he was, there shouldn'ta been no way he could hit the broad side of a barn. But he got Drake in one shot." Jeanie clamps her hand over Jud's mouth—probably because he just told police officers that Shaky was drunk.

I look up at Maylee's uncle. "Did he kill Drake?" I ask.

He shakes his head. "Drake's alive. At least for now. They're going to airlift him to a trauma center in Milwaukee, soon as they get him stable here."

Jeanie gathers me and the boys to her and huddle-hugs us. Trevor starts crying—maybe for the first time ever—and I realize that as dysfunctional as we are, we *are* family.

Chapter 29
4 Days Ago

I wake up trembling and clammy from another nightmare. I've had bad dreams every night since the "Spring Up scare," which is what a lot of locals are calling it, now that we've all had time to think about how much worse it could have been. I haven't told anyone I've been having nightmares. That is, except Jud, who's having them too. Jeanie heard him yelling in his sleep that first night and called the guidance counselor in the morning. Then over the next three days, Jud had to be excused from his last class to go see her. That might have been a good thing, except that the teacher told the kids he was being excused from class because he was "having personal problems," which to Jud was as good as her saying that he had to be excused because he had a bad case of diarrhea, head lice, *and* jock itch.

So Jud claimed that the nightmares had stopped. Obviously not, though, since when I got up to pee a couple of hours ago, I found him on the couch, swaddled in a blanket, the lights on, cartoons flashing on the TV. "Bad dream?" I'd asked. He made me promise not to tell Jeanie. I told him I was having them too, so he wouldn't feel like such a freak. Then we ate Oreos and watched SpongeBob SquarePants until he fell back to sleep, Marbles on his chest. I shuffled back to bed then, but three hours later, I'm still lying here, unable to sleep.

I smear my hand up the wall, searching for the light switch.

That is until I remember that I'm not in the laundry room any-more. I'm in Jud's room. The room he gave up the night after Spring Up because he was too afraid to be alone at night. Trevor cooperated. Who knows why. Maybe he's afraid to be alone now, too.

It's 2:46, too late to call or text Liam. But I want to hear his voice so I can say to my nerves, *See? See? It was only a bad dream. He's still alive.*

Liam's last day of school was yesterday, and he had to take off immediately with his mom to pick up his dad at General Mitchell Airport in Milwaukee. And today, they had to meet with the attorney who will be defending Liam in the statu-tory rape charge. He wanted to come see me afterward, but Cheryl insisted that he was not leaving the house until he and his dad talked.

I flick on my lamp. *If I could only hear his voice.*

And then it hits me. I have Liam's voice mails from the day we fought about Stephie, still in my phone. Okay, he'll sound desperate, maybe even pissed, but it will still be his voice.

I open the first message: *"Bless, pick up. PLEASE! It was nothing. Drake Collins was . . ."*

I press nine to save the message. I won't delete Liam's voice, but I can't hear Drake's name right now.

The second message starts. Liam's voice softer in this one. Desperately boyish, even: *"Bless, come on. Pick up. Stephie's gone. Sorry I was so stupid. I told—"*

Peg starts barking then, the sound muffled, like he's bark-ing from the next room. *"I'll call you right back,"* Liam mumbles.

There's a beep from his keypad, then Liam's voice, con-crete hard, saying, *"So, you just let yourself back in?"*

There's a dull thud. His phone hitting the mattress? A crumpled pair of jeans, left on the floor?

Stephie's words are muffled, but Liam's are clearer when he answers her because he's shouting. *"Are you nuts, what are you doing? Put your shirt back on!"*

I sit straight up, straining to hear.

There are a couple dull thuds—Liam's footsteps?

When Stephie speaks, her voice is clearer. Louder. Like maybe Liam kicked the phone onto its back, exposing the mic. "Why? Everyone thinks we were doing it, anyway. Even Bless. You afraid that after trying me, you'll have to break her crooked little heart?"

My teeth are clenched—what a sleazebag!

Liam says something, his voice only a deep rumble. Then Stephie starts screeching. "You'll be sorry you just said that, Reid. Trust me. I'll see to it that you are! Nobody humiliates me and gets away with it! You hear me? Nobody!"

There's shuffling, then a bang. Liam mumbles, "Crazy bitch." Then the first cut on his Shipwreck on a Desert CD starts playing. The song plays until the voice mail times out.

I listen to the message four times, hit nine to save it each time, then check to make sure it's still there.

Liam must have gone for the *End* key without looking, hit another key by mistake, then tossed the phone, thinking it was off. Obviously, he didn't realize the conversation was recorded or he would have known that on my phone is his ticket out of this bogus statutory rape charge. Because for sure, when Regina Dillon hears this tape, she'll drop the charge like a chunk of cheap jewelry.

Chapter 30
2 Days Ago

I get to the kitchen and Dad is sitting at the table having his morning coffee and cigarette. His right arm is in a sling.

Marbles leaps onto Dad's lap, and he looks down at her. Marbles is the Florence Nightingale of cats. She hovers around anyone who's emotionally or physically having a hard time, and she's had her work cut out for her since Spring Up. Marbles divides her time between Jud and me in the evenings, but since Dad got home from the hospital last week, most of her daytime hours have been devoted to him.

Jeanie's at the counter, pouring herself coffee while I fill a cereal bowl. She nudges me with an elbow and says, "Look how that cat loves your dad."

"She's a little pest," Dad says, but he's stroking her back affectionately as he says it.

"Hey you guys, you've gotta see this," Trevor shouts as he comes barreling down the hall. He bursts into the kitchen with his laptop, Jud right behind him.

Jeanie giggles. "You boys find something new online, about Shaky?"

Ever since that day, it's been like this. First, there was the local news coverage. In the first couple of hours, they couldn't identify "the hero that prevented a tragedy of massive proportions," and turned the search for Dad's identity into a treasure hunt. Jeanie, determined that Dad was finally going to get the respect he deserves, called the station to identify him. And by the six o'clock newscast, there was Jeanie on TV, singing Dad's praises and giving an update on his condition. Jeanie got Jud into the action, too, prompting him to tell how he was the one who spotted Drake's gun first, and that it was his warning shout that prompted Dad to pull his gun. She mentioned, also, that it was Liam who staunched Dad's blood until help got there.

And of course, the reporter with the plastic hair and artificial empathy had nabbed plenty of eyewitnesses at the scene. People scared enough to stammer or cry while she asked them brilliant questions like, "How frightened were you, when you realized there was a gunman on the boardwalk?"

Had the story stayed confined to Logan, the hype would have died down by now. But turns out, someone sitting inside The Landing was taking video of a sailboat when Drake first pulled his gun, and posted the clip on YouTube. The video was only seconds long, but it had the drama of a Tarantino movie. You could see the blur of people as they scrambled for safety, and hear their screams. Then a frozen waterfall of window glass, the echo of a gunshot, and Drake dropping in slow motion.

The video went viral, with 214,000 hits in the first two days. And Dad had a new name: The Marina Marksman.

The hospital had to post a guard at Dad's door to keep reporters out so he could get the rest he needed after his surgery. Many said that Dad should have killed Drake, while others claimed Drake was just a troubled kid in a troubled world. But what wasn't argued was that Dad was a hero.

Of course there were the reports that focused on Drake, as everyone tried to uncover his motive. Each segment posted Drake's last school picture, showing him looking even more like a psycho than he looked in person, alongside a photo of him when he was the local football hero.

Stephie had her fifteen minutes of fame, too. The police had confiscated the notes Drake had written her, but surprise, surprise, scanned copies showed up on the web. Stephie's touting herself as an innocent victim of Drake's obsessive love (as if she knows nothing about obsessive love, herself), claiming she "hardly knew him."

The eye of the national news blinked quickly, but the local news station is still sucking the story for what it's worth. Last night's newscast had interviews with the mayor and a couple of local aldermen to get their opinions on the issue of Spring Up security.

"Look at this, Shaky," Trevor says, plunking his laptop on the table.

Dad puts up his hand. "I told you boys, I don't want to see any more of that crap. I don't wanna hear about it, either."

For a second, the boys and Jeanie just stand there, looking stunned and hurt. Then Jeanie goes ape. "We're just proud of you, Shaky. The whole country is! What's wrong with you? You won't do interviews. You won't see your neighbors, who just want to come by to tell you they're proud of you."

Actually, I want to know what's wrong with Dad, too. Because frankly, I expected him to be strutting like a cowboy, proud to be called a hero.

Dad gets up, holding his shoulder, and heads for the couch.

With a frustrated sigh, Jeanie rounds up the boys to take them to town to get their hair cut, so they won't look like "hooligans" for Liam's graduation, like Jud did on the news clips. "Soon as you're better, you're getting that mop cut, too," Jeanie yells to Dad as they're heading out the door. "And you boys, you're cleaning this yard this weekend, you—"

I refresh Dad's coffee cup and take it in to him. He sits up with a groan and thanks me.

His hair is grubby, the bags under his eyes fat and purple. I sit down on the couch beside him and carefully ask, "Dad, what's wrong?"

He lights a cigarette and stares out the window. "I ain't no hero, Bless."

I blink. "Of course you are. You saved the lives of everybody on the boardwalk, including Liam's—for which I'll be eternally grateful."

He turns his head toward me. "Liam didn't tell you, did he?"

"Tell me what?"

"Why I had my .38 on me."

I wait.

"I was plannin' on shooting holes in *The Carol.* Sink the son-of-a-bitch to the bottom of the lake. Oiler was out there with Rupert, and well, if I took them both out with the boat, I didn't care about that, either. Because when I was finished with the boat, I was gonna blow my head off."

"Don't say that, Dad."

He rubs his thumb and finger across his eyes and pinches the bridge of his nose. "It's the damn ugly truth, Bless. Ask Liam, he'll tell you. I pretty much told him so on the beach. That's why he followed me over to the boardwalk. To talk me down, so I wouldn't do something stupid."

"Not that his words were mattering. You know me when I'm drunk. But at least he made me hesitate. And good thing Jud came out to beg me for money when he did, too, because that made me pause even longer. If they hadn't come along, the damage would have been done before Collins even had the chance to pull his Glock."

"No," I protest.

"It's true. Soon as I gave Jud what I had in my pocket—not like I'd be needing it—I pulled my pistol. I was gonna use it, too. Right then and there."

"But you didn't. Jud cried, *'Gun!'* and you turned it on Drake instead."

Dad's red eyes are glassy with tears that don't drop. He shakes his head slowly. "I got more of my old man in me than I care to admit, Bless. Always pissed off at the world. Worrying about who's gonna take what I got—like I got anything worth stealin' in the first place. I'm a drunk, just like he used to be. A bitter, nasty drunk."

My eyes start watering. "No, Dad, you're *not* like George. You're not mean. You'd never punch Trevor or Jud, or cuff me. And you're good to Jeanie."

Marbles prances across the living room to stretch herself across Dad's leg. She looks up at me with squinty eyes that seem to say, "I love you, but he needs me now. Sorry." I rub the top of her head to let her know I approve.

"Well, I'm gonna do things differently now," Dad says. "I'm gonna get some help for my drinkin', for starters. Look into AA. And I'm gonna do right by Jeanie and marry her. Help her raise these two punks so they don't turn into a couple of Drakes. And I'm gonna be the kind of dad to you I shoulda been from the start."

Now I'm outright bawling.

"I'm gonna get a job, too. Because let's face it, Bless, I ain't cut out to be my own boss." He nods his head slowly. "Yep, that's what I'm gonna do. I'm gonna make you guys proud."

"We're already proud of you, Dad."

Dad only grunts and stares back out the window.

We sit so quietly we can hear Marbles's purring, then Dad says, "If I've learned anything from all this, it's that there's only a split second between comin' up a hero, or going down a madman."

"Dad," I say, "it's not what you *thought* of doing that counts. It's what you actually did."

He mutters, "Maybe. Maybe not."

After a long pause, I say, "I'm glad you told me these things . . . but you don't need to tell them to Jeanie or the boys. Let them be proud of you. You might not believe this, but I do: drunk or not, there's no way you would have shot Rupert and Oiler. The boat, maybe. Maybe even yourself. But not Oiler and Rupert. You're a good person and wouldn't have hurt anybody else. Proof of that is in the fact that you feel bad about having shot Drake, even if you had no choice."

We sit quietly for a moment before I say what I'm thinking. "You know what, Dad? I'm a lot more like you than I care to admit, too. I'm always pissed. Defensive. Afraid."

"Must be George's bad blood in us," he says.

"No. It's that we learned from George that life is a fight, so we have to keep our gloves up."

Dad doesn't say anything. He grabs the remote and flicks on Animal Planet.

I don't move. What I'm waiting for, I'm not sure.

"Bless?" he says. "You know that front page of the *Logan Daily Press* that Jeanie has hanging on the fridge? The one with my picture on it, calling me The Marina Marksman?"

"Yeah?"

"A couple days ago I was gonna send it to Pa. Had it folded in an envelope and everything. But then I asked myself, 'What you trying to prove, Shaky?' So I hung it back up. Because even that story wouldn't have changed the way the old man feels about me."

"You're right about that, Dad. It wouldn't have earned you

an ounce of respect from George. But what it would have done is sucker punched him. Because the last thing George wants is for you to be anybody's hero. That's why I sent him a copy of it myself."

"You did?"

"Yeah. I'll bet Carol hung it on the fridge, too. And every time George steps into the kitchen it's like a squirt of lemon juice to his eyes."

Dad reaches over and pats my knee. He chuckles softly.

I'm heading out of the room when Dad calls me. I turn.

"Hey, Jeanie told me that Liam came by to get your cell phone yesterday. What did that fancy lawyer the Dillons hired have to say about that voice message you found on it?"

"I doubt their lawyer heard it," I tell him. "Liam and his parents took it over to the Dillons' place themselves—after their lawyer made a copy of it. Mrs. Dillon went ballistic when she heard it, and actually comforted Stephie when she got hysterical. Within an hour after Liam and his parents left, the Reids' lawyer got word that Stephie had recanted her story. The charges were dropped."

Dad laughs. "Good. Good," he says.

"Jeanie's picking up a graduation card for Liam today, and we're gonna put something nice in it. I'm gonna sign it, but I don't think I can go to graduation tomorrow, Bless. I don't want people pattin' my back. So if I don't see Liam before then, you apologize to him for me, will you?"

"Sure. He'll understand."

Dad nods. "He's a keeper, that one," Dad says.

I grin. "I know it."

CHAPTER 31
2 DAYS AGO

Around dusk, I'm in the kitchen wiping down the cupboard doors. I'm so filled with questions I can't answer, and nerves I can't calm, that I know if I don't keep moving I'm going to jump out of my skin. Maybe I've always been like this, but since Spring Up, it's been worse. It doesn't help that Liam's helping his parents pack up Cheryl's things; I dread what that means.

I look up and Dad's standing in the doorway, watching me. He shuffles over to sit at the table and then asks me to sit, too.

He holds up my phone. "Bless, Jeanie grabbed this off the counter by mistake. She saw Gloria's name in the contact list—that's how she knew she had the wrong phone. Now that the Reids are packin' up, she's thinking you'll have no reason to stay here. Are you talking to Gloria about going to stay with her?"

I pick at a speck of crusty food I missed when wiping the table. "No. I just called her to get some information from her about Mom. That's all. I wanted to ask her about Susan Marlene Harris. Who she was."

Dad cocks his head, like he's busy trying to place the name.

"Dad, why didn't you tell me that Mom was adopted?"

He looks back at me. "What, I told you."

"No, you didn't."

"Course, I did. I must've said it the night I brought you here . . . when we called Gloria."

I don't see any reason to argue about it now, so I don't.

"She was your mom's birth mother. She gave your mom a penny book," Dad says, like he's proud to be adding a detail.

"Susan did?"

"Yeah."

So it WAS Susan's folder then.

"I guess one of those pennies in that book was worth a little chunk of change. I had my sights set on this Harley at the time. I tried to talk your mom into unloading that penny to help me pay for it." Dad's eyes cloud over. Like maybe he's thinking about another pipe dream. "She wouldn't give it up, though," he says with a chuckle. "She said something about that penny being a '55, the year Susan was born, and she wasn't sellin' it." Dad chuckles. "That woman was tight with her money, I'll tell you that much. I never saw the penny book after that. She probably hid it on me."

So the decorations around three spaces were for the pennies representing the years of our birth: mine, Mom's, and my birth grandmother's.

I lean over, my arms folded on the table. "Dad, do you know why finding a 1972 doubled die penny was so important to Mom? I mean, now I know that it represented the year of *her* birth, but I wonder why she wouldn't use just any penny from that year. Why did it have to be the doubled die one?" I don't elaborate, keeping the riddle I'm trying to solve to myself.

"I don't know anything about that, Bless. I never heard her talk about searching for a certain penny. She was always checkin' the dates of 'em, though. She'd dig in my pockets when I'd come home loaded. I never minded though. I wasn't stingy with my money."

I put my head down so Dad can't read my face. I don't want him to see the pity I'm feeling for Mom. Maybe Dad will do better from now on—for Jeanie's sake, I hope that's true—but for my mom, it's too late. She lived and died not knowing what it was like to have a guy who really cared. Really listened.

There's a clunk that sounds like it came from Dad and Jeanie's bedroom. "You okay?" Dad bellows. Jeanie yells back, "Yeah."

"Why don't you go in there, Bless? Reassure Jeanie."

"That I'm not mad because she looked in my phone?"

"No. That you're not leavin' us. She'll be relieved to hear it. Just like me."

I blink at Dad.

"What?" he says. "You don't think we'd miss you if you left? You're a part of this family now, Bless." He scoots his chair back to get up, and grins. "Whether you like it, or not."

Jeanie's standing next to the bed that's covered with clothes. "I'm looking for something to wear to graduation," she says, turned away so I won't see that she's been crying.

I glance at the bed. "I could help you put something together."

While we're mixing and matching clothes, I tell her it's okay that she used my phone. And, that I'm not going to go live with Gloria. She stops. "Really?"

I nod.

"I'm glad to hear that. This place was a real wreck when your dad brought you here—and I'm not just talking about the house, either. You've been good for us, Bless. And it sure is nice having another girl in the house to talk to. I didn't realize how lonely I was, living here with these three buffoons, until you moved in."

Buffoons. That cracks me up, and I laugh out loud. Jeanie

laughs with me, then adds, "Well, it's true," which only makes me laugh harder.

We pick out dress pants, a cami, and jacket, and while she tries the pants on to make sure they still fit, she asks if I'll get her good shoes from the top shelf of her closet. I bring in a stool from the kitchen and climb onto it.

"You little stinker, when did you sneak in here?"

I look down, and Marbles is on the vanity. Jeanie takes her and plunks her to the floor.

I use a hanger to move the shoe boxes closer. I have them within reaching distance when Jeanie says, "How about these?" I look over to see her holding a giant, gaudy earring to one ear. "Maybe something simpler."

Marbles leaps back onto the vanity and sticks her nose to a small porcelain bowl filled with trinkets. Jeanie nudges Marbles away and plucks a gold hoop from her jewelry box.

"Get down, Marbles," I call, because Jeanie's busy trying on the hoop, and Marbles is batting at the bowl, scooting it across the shiny surface.

I grab the boxes, and as I'm stepping down, Marbles sends Jeanie's bowl careening off the vanity.

"Marbles!" Jeanie screeches.

She bends down to pick up the mess, and I set the shoe boxes on the bed. When I look over, Jeanie's frozen in place, her face still and colorless as a corpse.

"What's the matter?" I ask.

Jeanie's got her fingers closed around something. She just stands there. Then she opens her hand and peers down.

"Bless, remember when I told you about Ashley Rose?"

I nod.

She curls her fingers back around whatever it is she has,

and gulps. "When I was carrying Trevor, I started dwelling on my baby all over again. Worrying about where she was. If she was happy and being taken care of. I just needed to know that I did the right thing.

"My friend Ann, from work, told me about this fortune-teller—"

I hear myself inhale. "Here in Logan?"

Jeanie nods.

I'm getting chills. "Was her name Verna Johnson?"

"I don't remember. She lived out on Treeline Road."

I wait.

"She told me my baby was beautiful and happy and loved, and that I'd meet her someday. I was so relieved, I can't tell you."

Jeanie looks down at her hand. "Before I left, she gave this to me. She told me it was for a special girl—that I was to save it for her. I thought she meant Ashley Rose, but she said no. That my baby would be all grown up with babies of her own before I'd meet her. So I asked her who it was for, and all she said was, 'You'll know when the time comes.'

"Well, when I picked it up a bit ago, I just got the weirdest feeling."

"What did she give you?" I ask, every nerve in my body tingling.

Jeanie comes to me. "I think I'm supposed to give this to you." She reaches out and takes my hand, then drops something warm into my palm.

And there it is, Mom's 1972 doubled die penny.

CHAPTER 32
2 DAYS AGO

I stumble out of the house and head across the field to reach the pines.

"Bless, you okay?" Liam asks when he answers his phone and hears that I'm crying.

"I have it—the penny! Jeanie just gave it to me!"

"I'll be right there," Liam says. "Literally. I'm on your road. I missed you, so I ditched out for a bit."

"Hurry," I tell him. "I'm in the pines."

I sit at the edge of the trees and stare at the penny that's still warm. I use the light from my phone to double check that I didn't only imagine that it was a doubled die.

Above me, the stars are pinpoints of winking lights, and I lift my fist and tell Mom, "I have it! I have your penny!"

I stand up, bouncing, smiling, and crying as Liam runs across the field shouting, "Let me see, let me see!" I hand him the penny, and we both use our phones for spotlights. "This is so cool," he says.

I tell him how Jeanie came across it, then add, "I still don't have the riddle solved, but at least I have the penny."

"What exactly did the psychic say again?" he asks as he examines it.

"She said, 'The doubled die will come to you unexpectedly. Someone will place it in your hand. And when a penny drops, you'll understand the nature of fear.'"

"The nature of fear," Liam repeats.

And then in a rush, images come: George, ranting at the TV, at imaginary four-wheelers in his field; Cactus, giving me what was supposed to be a hug; Dad, standing before George, his fingers twitching; Maylee, crying as she told me what Todd did to her; Stephie Dillon's face as Liam shouted out his love for me; and Drake, shuffling down the hall like a gray ghost, his dead eyes staring through the peephole he made on his windshield.

And then I'm seeing four-year-old me, watching Dad drive away. Five-year-old me, running to the pump house to check on the kittens after George had been there. I see myself at the age I am now: leaving Wicks, sitting with my head dipped as Liam hands me his phone number, steaming over Stephie, staring at Liam's back at the lighthouse. And just eleven days ago, running to the beach, hardly able to breathe.

And then I see Mom in the visions Verna saw. Her crying into my stuffed skunk and swirling her finger around the space where this very penny should be. Mom sick, near death, yet at the same time, peaceful, as she handed the penny folder over to Gloria.

And then, like magic, A PENNY DROPS!

Liam takes my arm. "Bless, you okay?"

"I know what it means!" I shout.

"We were all afraid. Every one of us. And we let our fears tell us crazy stories about how things were, and how they were going to be. And look what happened, because of it. George chased his whole family away, out of fear that they'd take what he had. And Cactus couldn't even hug, because she was so scared to feel anything. Maylee, she was starving herself because she was petrified that she'd puke again if someone kissed her. And Stephie turned into a liar, out of the fear of looking like a loser. And my dad? He was so afraid that he'd never get respect or get ahead in life, that he almost killed himself.

"And me. Look at me, Liam. I'm always afraid. Afraid of getting close to people. Afraid of trusting. Afraid of being left behind."

I'm talking so fast that I have to force myself to slow down so Liam can follow me.

"I think that's it, Liam. What my mom wanted me to see— how fear works."

"Well, fear's not all bad, though. A fisherman with none is as good as dead," Liam says, going right where my mind is.

"Right. When Dad's whole garage was in flames, he went in there. He would have gone back in for a second time, too, if Jeanie hadn't stopped him. You can't tell me he didn't feel any fear—even animals know to be afraid of fire. Why didn't he listen to his fear? And Stephie, what about her? When Drake was stalking her, she should have been scared. But instead, she turned it into a game to try to win you over. Both of them could have been killed."

"You're right about that," Liam says.

"To ignore fear that's trying to point out real danger, that's stupid. But when we imagine danger that isn't there, that's equally foolish. Look at me. I was so afraid of losing you that I let my fears mutate into make-believe. First, I told myself that Stephie would steal you. Then, that you'd head back to Maine as if we never happened. Even after you reassured me that those things weren't going to happen, I was *still* so sure I'd lose you in the end, that I spun a story in my head about how you were going to kill yourself, and I'd lose you *that* way."

Liam squeezes my hand.

"I was so scared that I went to see a psychic—a fortune-teller with a crystal ball. And even then, I twisted everything she said to fit the story I was already telling myself.

"I think that's what my mom meant by the nature of fear. How it's good when there's a real danger. But how, when there's no concrete threat, and you let fear set up shop in your head, it can create a monster with enough power to destroy you."

"And others," Liam says.

"You're thinking of Drake now, too, aren't you?"

"Yeah. His fear that his life was over because his football career was must have been what made him withdraw so far away from others that he forgot they were human beings— that he was human."

"And it had to be fear that made him stalk Stephie," I add. "He was probably convinced that he'd never find another girl who would care about him, because of what the accident had done to him. That's the only explanation I can think of for why he'd want Stephie back."

Liam shakes his head. "Wow," he says, to all of it.

We sit down, slowly. Both of us a little dazed.

I take Liam's hand and press it over my heart. "Do I feel lighter inside?" I ask.

He smiles. "I think you do."

Liam puts the penny back into my hand, and my whole body sighs. "Now I get why it was so important to Mom that I understand the nature of fear. Because if I keep being afraid, I'll make it so that nothing in my life will be good."

I look at Liam. So levelheaded. More grown-up than my dad in many ways. "I can't believe that I thought you'd commit suicide."

"Yeah, that *was* pretty extreme, Bless. I was just off licking my wounds. It hurt me to have my dad go back on his word like he did. But it didn't make me think I had nothing to live for. I have you. And the boat I hope to own someday."

"But you tried to hang yourself once," I said. "And it wasn't just because you read that essay, either, was it?"

"I was pretty messed up at the time. I had a friend drown. He was the first kid I knew who'd died. I never thought about how it could happen to a kid—to me—until then. It started feeling like death was chasing me. I had no clue why I tried it. Didn't think about it, really, until you asked me. Maybe I wanted to see if I could defy it. Outsmart it. Because I was scared. I don't know. But it's not like I'd try it again. Things may suck, but that's life, isn't it? It gets good. Then it sucks. Then it gets good again . . . an ebb and flow, just like the tide."

He wraps his arm around me, and I rest my head against his shoulder. We sit for a while, holding each other quietly, listening to the breeze sing through the trees.

Finally, I say, "Mom told Verna that she knows what it's like to be born in the year of the doubled die. I wish I knew what that meant."

Liam bites his lip. Thinking, as I am.

"The penny in Mom's birth year was a mistake," I say. "So was the one Susan was born under. The clue has to be there."

"A mistake," Liam repeats. "Sort of like one of life's mutations. An alteration. We have to think about how Susan's and your mom's lives were the same. How your life was like your mom's."

"Well, one thing Mom and Susan had in common, besides their blood, was that neither of them were able to raise their daughters."

"Let me see the penny again," Liam says, interrupting my thoughts.

We use our phones for flashlights once more, and he says,

"But the image is doubled. Okay. Okay. I don't know how to explain this, but when your mom found Susan and got the penny folder, do you suppose she saw the doubling on the penny representing Susan's birth year as—"

"—As a bad omen, that she, too, wouldn't get to raise her kid?"

"Maybe," Liam says. "In the vision Verna saw—the first one—your mom was scared, right?"

"Uh-huh."

"Okay, but wait. In the second vision, she wasn't, right?"

I nod.

"Do you suppose that by then, she started looking at the penny as a promise, instead of a bad omen? As some kind of assurance that, if she found her penny with the same doubling, it would mean that another mother would come forth for you, just as one had for her? You know, a doubled die sort of thing. Two mothers. One stamped over the other."

I get chills when he says this. "Maybe."

We quiet for a little while again. The ground beneath us is cold, so we cuddle to keep warm.

I look up at Liam, his hair lit by the moon. His eyes made bright by the light that shines inside him. I stare at him for a bit, then say, "I'm really going to work at not being so afraid. On learning how to let life be good."

He pulls me closer and kisses the top of my head.

"The doubled die thing," I say. "It's weird, isn't it, how so many things were doubled? You and my dad both losing your boats . . . Jeanie and Susan both having to give their babies away. I don't know what, if anything, that means in regards to the penny, but it's weird. Anyway, like I said, I'm going to work on learning to trust."

Liam unfurls my hand and casts light from his phone on the

penny again, marveling over it all over again, just as I am. "If you backslide, just get out this penny to remind yourself. Look. Look where the doubling is." He points to the words, IN GOD WE TRUST. Then to the word, LIBERTY.

I walk Liam to his Yukon. "I'm staying in Logan until you graduate, Bless. I told Mom and Dad tonight. I'll get a utility apartment and pick up an extra job. I'm not going to leave you. You need me." I hug him, the penny tight in my hand.

After Liam leaves, I go straight to my room and get out the penny folder. I'm putting the penny in its rightful place when Jeanie peeks her head in. "You okay, Bless?" I nod, then I show her the folder and tell her the story.

Chapter 33
Yesterday

I wake early, shower, and put on my lobster-blue dress. When I step out of the bathroom, Jeanie makes a big deal over how pretty I look, then takes my hand and leads me into the kitchen so Dad can make a fuss over me, too. And he does.

I say bye, then head out for Maylee's. Why she needs to see me *before* graduation is beyond me, but she sounded rattled when she called and asked me to stop by. So rattled, that I didn't tell her about the penny; my news will keep.

Kenneth is sitting at the snack bar when I get there, drinking a bottle of root beer. In his sunflower-yellow-colored shirt, he blends right into the wallpaper. Mrs. Bradley tells me that Maylee is upstairs, waiting for me. Her eyes plead with me to hurry Maylee along.

When I open Maylee's bedroom door, she's sitting on her bed wringing her hands. She jumps up and the hem of a sundress drops to her ankles. "Maylee!" I squeal. "When did you get that?"

"Last night. It was Mom's idea. Do I look dumb in it?" She rubs her bare shoulders and flinches. "I feel naked."

"You look great," I say. And she does.

I have to reassure her at least one hundred times that the dress doesn't make her boobs look too big (even if it kind of does), then tug her all the way down the stairs.

Kenneth is taking a swig of his drink when I push Maylee

into the kitchen. He glances over, his eyes bugging out of his head. He starts choking, sputtering root beer across the snack bar. Mrs. Bradley hurries to grab him a napkin. And Maylee, who's looking right at him, seeing root beer foam bubble out of his nostrils, blushes and giggles like she thinks even *that's* hot.

I hug Maylee, tell her I love her, and head out. Liam texts me to tell me that he just got home, and that Peters, Jenkins, and Spats are there with glass chalk and they're decorating their cars; he'll head over to the beach as soon as they're done.

I drive past Erie, because although the boardwalk has been scrubbed clean, the windows replaced, the shops reopened, I'm not ready to go there yet.

I reach Mactaw and look over at Tula's. I should stop, I know. Thank her for seeing that my purse and car keys got returned so promptly, and for doing such an amazing job on Liam's tattoo. Liam got it last week. Tula placed it in a band around his bicep, just above his elbow. She put me lying sideways in a small black boat, floating on blue-green water. My right arm is bent and propped on the side of the boat, my head resting on my arm. My bare left shoulder is pale as the moon, and the wind has my hair swept from the left side of my face, but for a few dark, wayward strands. She inked a depth into my eyes that I hope is really there. My hip that is raised above the top of the railing is lobster blue and the edge of my tail is peeking out of the boat. Liam claims the mermaid looks just like me and that it's the coolest gift ever.

I *should* stop and thank Tula, but another time. I'll bring her a little thank-you card, like I gave to Katie and each of her friends.

I turn and head down the numbered streets. And as I pass—where my phone went dead, where the pennies had dropped, where I could hardly breathe—I wonder how I could have let my fear blow up the way I did.

When I reach the lake, I grab my sunglasses and phone, and put my purse and new sandals in the trunk. The day is balmy, the water bright. Gulls swirl above me, making their noisy calls as I head toward the pier. I squint out to where the sky and water meet.

I'm on the pier, halfway to the lighthouse, when I feel Liam. I turn, and there he is, coming across the beach. The sun in his hair, the wind ruffling his blue tie. His feet are bare, the bottoms of his black pants rolled up to keep sand off of the hems. *God, he's SO gorgeous!* When he sees me, he waves his arm and starts jogging.

When he reaches the pier, he picks me up and says with a laugh, "Oh, Bless. You are one wicked, cunnin' girl!" He takes my hands and steps back to get a full view of me in my blue-lobster dress. Then he showers my face with quick kisses and picks me up to twirl me in circles.

He tells me again how much he loves his tattoo, loves me, and snaps about a dozen pictures of me with his phone.

"Your mom called me early this morning to invite me to go eat with you guys after graduation," I tell him, as we walk hand in hand toward the lighthouse.

"Why? I told her I'd invite you."

"Liam," I say, carefully. "She told me about Jib's phone call. How a friend of your dad's is looking for a replacement on his crew, because his nephew is leaving. That the job is yours if you want it."

Liam looks down at the water. "I don't know why she'd tell you about that. She knows I told Jib that I'm staying here for another year."

"She said it's not easy to find a spot on a crew—that most

boats have family working them and keep the same guys for years."

Liam doesn't say anything.

I look out on the horizon, where the waterline blends into the sky. "Liam, remember when you told me that everybody has a place where they belong?"

"Ayah," he says, slipping back to Maine in two syllables.

I stop, take his face in my hands, and force him to look at me. "I've been thinking about it all day. Take the job. You need to go back home."

"Bless, we talked about this. You need me here."

I shake my head. "I want you here, yes. But what you *need* is to go back to Maine. To work toward owning your own boat. Liam, you don't belong here. The sea is your home."

"But—"

I put my fingertips over his lips. "Remember when you said that some people aren't born in the place where they belong, so they have to go find it? Well, I haven't found that place yet, but I have a feeling that in one year's time when I join you, I'll have found it. In the meantime, I've got my family, and Maylee, and thanks to you, I've got Marbles, too."

Liam looks confused, troubled even. But he forces a grin. "What, you go see that psychic again, and she told you that everything will be okay if I leave?"

I laugh a little. "No. *I'm* telling myself those things. But I won't rule out going to see Verna again. Not to ask about the future—we'll let time take care of that—but to ask her to show me how she communicates with wild animals. Because I've decided that what I want to do with my life—besides be your wife and have your kids when the time is right—is to go to school for veterinary medicine, work with wild animals who've been injured, help them heal so they can go live where they belong. I looked online and the University of Maine offers that as a major and it's less than two hours from Stonington. In the meantime, I'm going to the animal shelter for an interview tomorrow. I'm hoping the job will carry over part-time during the school year. The year will go faster if I'm busy."

Liam gets quiet and stares out over the water. I'm tempted to tell him the rest—how I know that if he's stuck where he doesn't want to be . . . if he misses this opportunity . . . he'll only get dragged down, and that'll drag *us* down. But I don't say it. He'd only deny it, even if he knows it's true.

"It'll be okay," I tell him. "*We'll* be okay. I'm going to trust that. Hard as it will be, I'm going to trust myself. You. Us. Like you said, we'll be together no matter where we are."

He turns and smiles, even if it's a sad one, then lifts me off the pier. I think so he can look directly into my eyes to see if what's in them matches my words.

"It'll be okay," I whisper, our mouths so close that his breath is a soft breeze against my lips.

He whispers *Bless* as if my name itself is the answer to his prayers, and kisses me before he sets me down.

"I know it will be hard," I tell him. "And no doubt there will be times when I beg you to come back. But don't you do it, you hear me? Not until next year. Same time. Same place."

His phone rings, and he reaches into his back pocket. His wallet slips out at the same time, and lands, spread open, on the sand. He hurries to pick it up, even though he knows I've already seen the edge of the condom wrapper, stuffed in the slot above his debit card. He gives me a *just-in-case, you-know?* look and a sheepish grin.

Liam answers his call. "Yeah, Mom. I know. We're on our way. Be there in ten."

I'm sitting on the other side of Cheryl, who's sniffling into a Kleenex and smiling as Liam walks across the stage to accept his diploma. Maylee, who's sitting on the other side of me, Kenneth on the other side of her, tips her head over to touch mine. "Oh, Bless," she murmurs, "I can't believe he's leaving."

She'd sniffled when I told her in the restroom right before the ceremony, but now she's outright blubbering.

Kenneth has another of his stellar dates planned for them—volunteering in the kitchen at his church, for a lock-in party for the graduates (where they'll no doubt play Twister and eat Rice Krispies treats)—so Maylee says her good-bye to Liam as soon as the ceremony's over. She hands him a graduation card, the envelope decorated with a hand-drawn pink heart with "Bless & Liam" written inside with puffy letters. "Take good care of Bless when I'm gone," Liam tells her, and she nods and turns toward me, squeezing my arm like she's at a funeral and doesn't know what to say.

Liam and I go to dinner with his parents. Everyone orders lobster, but me, and Cheryl does her best to keep the conversation going while we wait for our plates. Ending every comment with, "Isn't that so, Frank?" or, "Isn't that what you said, Liam?" until Mr. Reid reaches out and cups his hand over hers and says, "Cheryl, it's okay."

"Liam's going back to Maine with you guys," I say bluntly. "To work on the boat Jib told him about." They both stare down at their empty plates, and Mr. Reid nods.

"No drinking and driving," Cheryl warns when we stand up to leave.

"Yeah, yeah, I know," Liam says.

Mr. Reid stands up. "Nice meeting you, Bless," he says.

"And don't stay out too late. Your dad wants to pull out around nine thirty." Cheryl smiles sadly, then squeezes my hand, like she knows I'm hurting.

We're meeting Liam's friends at Richard Peters' house, and going to move in a pack from one graduation party to another.

Each party is pretty much the same: streamers and balloons in our school colors, old relatives bunched around card tables or picnic tables, with little kids zipping around them, platters of food, cans of beer and soda floating in tubs of ice water, and endless sheet cakes with names drawn in gel icing.

By midnight, we're all at Jenkins's house, partying next to his pool. Music speakers are turned up so loud you can feel the drumbeats pounding in your chest, and the only adult around is the housekeeper, who comes around now and then to pick paper plates and plastic cups off the grass. Jenkins and Spats have been swiping bottles of booze from their parents' stashes for months now, and have the punch so spiked that if someone lit a match around the bowls, the whole place would probably blow.

Liam and I aren't drinking, so what starts out funny—the joking and horsing around—soon becomes obnoxious. About the time Peters is bent over, barfing on the grass, and some graduate named Rhonda is stripping down to her thong to jump in the pool, Liam leans over and asks me if I want to leave. I nod.

We go down to the beach and walk along the water's edge, holding each other with one arm, our shoes dangling from our free hands. The water is shimmering like a mirror to show the moon its face, and the only sound besides our breaths is the lapping water.

A few single silhouettes dot the pier, and a few couples

are combing the south end of the beach. So we head north, where the trees hug the waterline, and we can be alone.

Liam talks about how weird it is to graduate. "You wait and wait, and it feels like the day will never come. Then there it is. It's weird."

I stop him, though, when he brings up what lies ahead. "Shhh," I tell him. "I don't want to think about tomorrow. For tonight, let's pretend that we're going to be together every single day, for the rest of our lives. Okay?"

Liam's hands are strong, but his touch is soft when he cups the sides of my face. His eyes are shining like the water, and when his kiss comes, there's a desperation in it that tells me he has no idea how to pretend.

He takes my hand and leads me to where the shoreline is so narrow that we're up to our ankles in lapping water. He parts the branches and tells me to step carefully. The moss is damp and spongy on our feet.

We find a small clearing between the trees with just enough room to lie down. He tosses his jacket down, sits, and holds out his hands. I sit on his lap, straddling him, and he groans as he runs his hands up my bare thighs, not stopping until he's holding my hips. "You're so beautiful," he tells me.

"Promise me you'll tell me that even after it's no longer true."

"It will always be true to me," he says.

He scoots me down a bit so his hand can fit between us, and moves the crotch of my damp panties aside so he can touch me. For just one second, I wonder if he's ever done this to a girl before; I hope not. When Liam reaches for his wallet, I stop wondering about anything.

Liam's hands are trembling like the rest of him when he moves me off of him, gets out his condom, and fumbles to put it on. He spreads my legs and kneels between them. His arms come down as he braces himself above me, one arm on each side of me, like tree limbs bent into a haven. He looks down, his eyes asking, *You sure?* I don't answer him with my voice, but with my hips.

I knew there'd be pain, so it doesn't shock me when it comes. But what does surprise me is what's happening inside of me, in a place far deeper than where his body can reach. A swelling of emotions every bit as big as the sky. Every bit as soothing as water. And in that single moment, I know that it doesn't matter that there were times when I wasn't loved. Now, I am blessed.

Chapter 34
TODAY

"Oh, God. There's the U-Haul," I say into my phone when I turn onto Liam's street.

"Bless, you sure you're going to be okay?" Maylee asks.

Last night, Liam asked me the same question as he hurried me to my car because the sun was brightening the water in the east, giving us our first clue that we'd stayed at the beach all night. I told him the same thing I'm telling Maylee now, "I'll be okay." Even though at the moment, I don't know if that's true.

The doors on the U-Haul are hanging open, the ramp still down. The front door of the house is open, too, and Peg is outside, sniffing at something in the grass. He looks up and sees me, then hops over to get his pats. "Are you supposed to be out here by yourself?" I ask, as I ruffle his neck fur. "Come on," I say, slapping my thigh so he'll follow.

"Peg," Cheryl scolds when I bring him in.

She gives me a quick hug and a sympathetic smile. "Accepting that someone you love needs to follow their dream isn't easy, is it?" I bite my lip and shake my head.

"Mom? Does this stuff in the bathroom go in the U-Haul?" Liam shouts, his voice echoing in the emptiness.

"The bag of towels and the soap things do," Cheryl says, "but that plastic case goes in my car."

Liam comes out with his arms full. He's wearing a crumpled

T-shirt, and his uncombed hair is still damp from a shower. His dad is behind him, carrying a stack of boxes as if there's nothing inside them but air.

Liam doesn't give me more than a quick glance, and for a single moment I wonder if it's because we went all the way, and he's over me now.

But I stop myself.

No. He feels awkward, just like I do, to be experiencing this kind of pain in front of his parents. Maybe even wondering if his mother can tell what we did, as I am.

"After you get those things out, go ahead and take a few minutes with Bless. There are only odds and ends left."

Mr. Reid doesn't say anything, but he looks annoyed. Like Liam's ten, and Cheryl just told him he can "go play" when he's got homework to do.

"We're pulling out in ten minutes," Mr. Reid says as he goes out the door.

Liam takes my hand, and we go into his room. I stare down at the dents in the carpet where the legs of his bed frame and futon used to sit. There's nothing left in the room, but a small, lavender-colored gift bag that's sitting on the windowsill. Liam gets it and holds it out to me.

"What's this?" I ask as I take it.

"A present. Mom put it in that thing," he says.

He gently rubs his hand over his tattoo as he waits for me to dig through the layers of tissue paper—the mermaid *does* look like me. And there's a depth to her eyes, as deep as the sea.

I pull out a silver necklace, and moan when I see what's hanging from the fine chain. A tiny glass box, with a chunk of blue lobster shell tucked inside. "A lady who was at one of the booths at Spring Up makes them," he tells me. "She calls them Forever Boxes. I had to run home and grab her a piece of the shell, because she solders the box shut for good."

I want him to know that I'll wear it and treasure it forever. But my heart is breaking, and no words come. So I reach for him instead.

He picks me up and rocks me side to side, rubbing my back. "I don't know how I'm going to do it; a year's a long time," he says.

I bury my face in the soft hollow of his neck. Already, I'm crying.

There's a rap on the door, and Cheryl peeks in. "Your dad's got Peg in the U-Haul, and the key's in the mailbox. Just turn the lock when you come out, okay? Don't be long. You know your father." She looks at me, tilts her head, and smiles sadly, then steps inside to hug me good-bye.

I ask Liam to put my necklace on after Cheryl goes out. I hold the box against my skin as he fumbles with the tiny clasp. When he gets it on, he spins me around. "Beautiful," he says. But he's not looking at the necklace. He's looking at my eyes. He steps back, leaning against the wall, and pulls me to him.

"You won't forget me, will you?" I ask in a whisper.

The back of Liam's head clunks against the wall when he tosses it back to laugh. "You're really funny sometimes, you know that? Forget you—I couldn't if I tried. But why would I want to? Especially after last night."

"And you'll come back for me?"

"You know I will."

He leans down, his mouth close to mine. "I was thinking. Maybe I can take two weeks off during Christmas and come. It would help make the year not seem so long. What do you think?"

I nod.

Three quick honks sound, and Liam sighs. "I'd better go."

He's holding both my hands, but drops them to hold my face. We kiss, our hands rubbing each other's hair, back, our bodies pressed tight.

There are three more honks, longer this time. We pull away from each other. "Awww, Bless. It kills me to see you cry like this." He wipes under my eyes with his thumbs. "It's going to be okay, baby."

I sniffle and force a smile for him. "I put a penny in my folder this morning. This year's, to mark the year my life got good."

Liam smiles. His eyes are misty and getting pink. "When I come back to get you, I'll bring you a shiny new penny. One to mark the year your life got even better."

He clicks the lock and leads me down the steps. I follow like a sleepwalker, wondering how on earth I can feel so sad and so numb at the same time.

Mr. Reid is at the wheel in the Yukon, Peg panting out the passenger window. Cheryl is waiting in her car, parked behind the U-Haul.

"Hey, isn't that Maylee's car?" Liam says, pointing across the road, down half a block.

I smile, even as I'm crying. Somehow, I knew she'd come.

I walk Liam to Cheryl's car—she'll drive the first stretch, while he sleeps.

"Let's not say good-bye," I tell him, my voice cracking. "Good-bye always sounds permanent."

He gives one nod and pulls me to him. I feel his heart against me, hammering like mine. I feel the catch in his breaths. "I love you," he says, and I tell him the same.

I can't watch him drive away, so I ask him to wait before getting into the car. My arm stretches behind me, our hands slipping until even his fingertips are gone. I clamp my hand over the Forever Box and dart across the street.

Maylee leans over and opens the passenger door before I even clear the front of her car. "Just drive," I tell her as I slip in.

"Where?" she asks.

"Anywhere. Just drive."

The U-Haul is already pulling out, but Liam is still standing outside, the sunlight bright on his hair. He touches his hand over his heart, then slips inside the car.

I'm crying so hard I can hardly breathe, and Maylee rolls the side window down, as if that might help. And we drive and drive as I cry, and rock, and hold my middle.

Until, finally, the car fills with the scent of lilacs.

Acknowledgments

My heartfelt thanks to the following people who helped me bring this story to life:

My daughters Natalie and Shannon, who helped with editing, and my son Neil, who supplied me with info and ideas. My partner, Kerry, who was quick to offer suggestions, some brilliant, some absurd. My supportive brothers, Jerry, Dennis, and Jeff. Together, you keep my backbone strong and my enthusiasm high.

My friends, too many to mention—some writers, some not—who are such an integral part of my life. I only hope I tell you often enough how much I appreciate your time, your trust. Thank you for sharing your lives with me.

My friends from Backspace: The Writers Place, whose generosity lifted me up when I needed it most.

Author Keith Cronin, who, upon hearing that I was struggling to find a title for this book, offered to read it to see if he could find a title lurking in its pages. I love the title he found, and thank him for his act of kindness.

Vicki Schoenwald, who gave me information on Nebraska, and Todd Jahnke, who showed me the photos from Maine that inspired Liam's story.

The incredibly hardworking team at BookSparks, who made publishing this book such a joy. My unending appreciation to Crystal Patriarche, CEO and President of SparkPress, who championed this book from the beginning, and placed me in the hands of the best team a writer could possibly hope for: Brooke Warner, my publisher, who kept me on course; Lauren Wise, my project manager, who oversaw this project and answered every question I had, any hour, any day; Megan Conner and Taylor Vargecko, my publicists, who taught me more about marketing than I'd picked up in the past twelve years; Julie Metz, who gave me a cover Bless would have loved; proofreader Chris Dumas, who surely got a workout lifting out unnecessary commas; and internal designer Leah Lococo, who made the inside of this book as gorgeous as the outside.

Thanks to my agent Catherine Fowler, who has been with me from the start.

Last but not least, the many booksellers who hand-sell my titles, the bloggers who review them, and my readers, who remind me often that the joy of writing doesn't end when the story does, but rather when what I've written is shared. Thank you for sharing my work with your patrons, your readers, your friends, your book clubs. You are all an invaluable piece of my writing journey, and I will always be indebted to you. Stay in touch; I love hearing from you.

About the Author

© Patrick Peckham, City Pages of Wausau, Wis.

Sandra Kring is the author of five novels, including bestseller *The Book of Bright Ideas*, which was named to the New York Public Library's Books for the Teen Age list in 2007. Her novel *Carry Me Home* was a Book Sense Notable Pick and Midwest Bookseller's Choice Award nominee. She lives in Northern Wisconsin with her high school sweetheart; they have three grown children. Writing is her greatest passion, but she also loves reading, music, and movies. *Running for Water and Sky* is her first YA novel.

SELECTED TITLES FROM SPARKPRESS

SparkPress is an independent boutique publisher
delivering high-quality, entertaining, and
engaging content that enhances readers' lives.
Visit us at www.gosparkpress.com

Within Reach, by Jessica Stevens
$17, 978-1-940716-69-5
Seventeen-year-old Xander Hemlock has found himself trapped in a realm of darkness with thirty days to convince his soul mate, Lila, he's not actually dead. With her anorexic tendencies stronger than ever, Lila must decide which is the lesser of two evils: letting go, or holding on to the unreasonable, yet overpowering, feeling that Xan is trying to tell her something.

Serenade, by Emily Kiebel
$15, 978-1-94071-604-6
After moving to Cape Cod after her father's death, Lorelei discovers her great-aunt and nieces are sirens, terrifying mythical creatures responsible for singing doomed sailors to their deaths. When she rescues a handsome sailor who was supposed to die at sea, the sirens vow that she must finish the job or faced grave consequences.

Bear Witness, by Melissa Clark
$15, 978-1-94071-675-6
What if you witnessed the kidnapping of your best friend? This is when life changed for 12-year-old Paige Bellen. This book explores the aftermath of a crime in a small community, and what it means when tragedy colors the experience of being a young adult.

About SparkPress

SparkPress is an independent, hybrid imprint focused on merging the best of the traditional publishing model with new and innovative strategies. We deliver high-quality, entertaining, and engaging content that enhances readers' lives. We are proud to bring to market a list of New York Times bestselling, award-winning, and debut authors who represent a wide array of genres, as well as our established, industry-wide reputation for innovative, creative, results-driven success in working with authors. SparkPress, a BookSparks imprint, is a division o f SparkPoint Studio, LLC.

Learn more at GoSparkPress.com